Acclaim for Richard Bausch's
Rare & Endangered Species

"So funny and so heartbreaking that it should be read rapidly in one sitting, and savored over and over for its shifting tones and voices." —*The New York Times Book Review*

"This third collection by Richard Bausch will surely solidify his position as one of the best short-story writers working today." —*Los Angeles Times*

"Wonderful . . . luminous. . . . Effortlessly spinning off complications and surprise . . . Bausch shows in this collection that he can indeed, and very well, tell a story from the inside out." —*Washington Post*

"Richard Bausch has a tender comprehensive knowledge of the human heart's landscape and an almost uncanny ability to chart its shifting terrain in dialogue." —*Philadelphia Inquirer*

"Few writers evoke the complexities of daily life as well as Bausch does, and few capture the rhythms of ordinary conversation and the poignancy of sudden insight as well as he. Nothing is contrived in these short stories, where surprising events are grounded in fine character portrayals." —*Publishers Weekly*

Richard Bausch

Rare & Endangered Species

Richard Bausch is the author of six novels, including *Rebel Powers* and *Violence*, and two other volumes of short stories. His stories have appeared in *The Atlantic Monthly, Esquire, Harper's, The New Yorker, The Southern Review, Prize Stories: The O. Henry Awards, New Stories from the South, The Granta Book of the American Short Story,* and *The Best American Short Stories.* Bausch is a recipient of the Lila Wallace-Reader's Digest Writers' Award and the Award in Literature from the American Academy of Arts and Letters. He lives with his wife, Karen, and their five children in Virginia.

Rare & Endangered Species

Rare &
Endangered
Species

a novella and stories by

Richard Bausch

Vintage Contemporaries

Vintage Books   A Division of Random House, Inc.   New York

FIRST VINTAGE CONTEMPORARIES EDITION, AUGUST 1995

Some of these stories have appeared in the following magazines
and anthologies: "Aren't You Happy for Me?" in *Harper's*;
"High-Heeled Shoe," under a different title and in slightly different
form, in *Redbook*; "The Natural Effects of Divorce" and "Weather"
in *Glimmer Train*; "Evening" and "The Person I Have Mostly Become"
in *The Southern Review*; "Billboard," in substantially different form,
in *The Texas Review*; "Tandolfo the Great" in *The Wedding Cake
in the Middle of the Road: Twenty-three Variations on a Theme* (Norton), George
Garrett and Susan Stamberg, editors. "Billboard" also appeared
in *That's What I Like About the South* (University of Texas Press),
George Garrett and Paul Ruffian, editors. "Evening" also appeared in
New Stories from the South: The Year's Best, 1993, Shannon
Ravenel, editor. "Aren't You Happy for Me?" also appeared in
New Stories from the South: The Year's Best,
1994, Shannon Ravenel, editor.

Library of Congress Cataloging-in Publication Data
Bausch, Richard, 1945–
[Rare & endangered species]
Rare and endangered species : a novella
and stories / Richard Bausch. — 1st Vintage contemporaries ed.
p. cm.
Contents : Aren't you happy for me? — Weather — High-heeled shoe —
Tandolfo the Great — Evening — Billboard — The person I have mostly
become — The natural effects of divorce — Rare & endangered species.
ISBN 0-679-76310-4
1. United States—Social life and customs—20th century—Fiction.
I. Title.
PS3552.A846R37 1995
813'.54—dc20
95-6781
CIP

Manufactured in the United States of America
10 9 8 7 6 5 4 3 2 1

There has been a tendency on the part of certain schools of so-called critical theory to make sociological and political constructs out of fictional characters. I wish to say here that concerning the characters in these stories, any resemblance to such constructs is entirely coincidental, and all resemblances to actual persons — that is, to recognizable, complicated human beings caught in their time and place — are exactly, wholly, and lovingly intended, even though I have imagined them all.

To Karen,
for the laughs and
the happy house we love in,
and for the children

*   *   *

and in memory of
Seymour Lawrence,
publisher and friend

CONTENTS

Aren't You Happy for Me?

"WILLIAM COOMBS, with two *o*'s," Melanie Ballinger told her father over long distance. "Pronounced just like the thing you comb your hair with. Say it."

Ballinger repeated the name.

"Say the whole name."

"I've got it, sweetheart. Why am I saying it?"

"Dad, I'm bringing him home with me. We're getting *married*."

For a moment, he couldn't speak.

"Dad? Did you hear me?"

"I'm here," he said.

"Well?"

Again, he couldn't say anything.

"Dad?"

"Yes," he said. "That's — that's some news."

"That's all you can say?"

"Well, I mean — Melanie — this is sort of quick, isn't it?" he said.

"Not that quick. How long did you and Mom wait?"

"I don't remember. Are you measuring yourself by that?"

"You waited six months, and you do too remember. And this is five months. And we're not measuring anything. William and I have known each other longer than five months, but we've been together — you know, as a couple — five months. And I'm almost twenty-three, which is two years older than Mom was. And don't tell me it was different when *you* guys did it."

"No," he heard himself say. "It's pretty much the same, I imagine."

"Well?" she said.

"Well," Ballinger said. "I'm — I'm very happy for you."

"You don't sound happy."

"I'm happy. I can't wait to meet him."

"Really? Promise? You're not just saying that?"

"It's good news, darling. I mean I'm surprised, of course. It'll take a little getting used to. The — the suddenness of it and everything. I mean, your mother and I didn't even know you were seeing anyone. But no, I'm — I'm glad. I can't wait to meet the young man."

"Well, and now there's something *else* you have to know."

"I'm ready," John Ballinger said. He was standing in the kitchen of the house she hadn't seen yet, and outside the window his wife, Mary, was weeding in the garden, wearing a red scarf and a white muslin blouse and jeans, looking young — looking, even, happy, though for a long while there had been between them, in fact, very little happiness.

"Well, this one's kind of hard," his daughter said over the thousand miles of wire. "Maybe we should talk about it later."

"No, I'm sure I can take whatever it is," he said.

The truth was that he had news of his own to tell. Almost a week ago, he and Mary had agreed on a separation. Some time for them both to sort things out. They had decided not to say anything about it to Melanie until she arrived. But now Melanie had said that she was bringing someone with her.

She was hemming and hawing on the other end of the line: "I don't know, see, Daddy, I — God. I can't find the way to say it, really."

He waited. She was in Chicago, where they had sent her to school more than four years ago, and where after her graduation she had stayed, having landed a job with an independent newspaper in the city. In March, Ballinger and Mary had moved to this small house in the middle of Charlottesville, hoping that a change of scene might help things. It hadn't; they were falling apart after all these years.

"Dad," Melanie said, sounding helpless.

"Honey, I'm listening."

"Okay, look," she said. "Will you promise you won't react?"

"How can I promise a thing like that, Melanie?"

"You're going to react, then. I wish you could just promise me you wouldn't."

"Darling," he said, "I've got something to tell you, too. Promise me *you* won't react."

She said "Promise" in that way the young have of being absolutely certain what their feelings will be in some future circumstance.

"So," he said. "Now, tell me whatever it is." And a thought struck through him like a shock. "Melanie, you're not — you're not pregnant, are you?"

She said, "How did you *know?*"

He felt something sharp move under his heart. "Oh, Lord. Seriously?"

"Jeez," she said. "Wow. That's really amazing."

"You're — *pregnant.*"

"Right. My God. You're positively clairvoyant, Dad."

"I really don't think it's a matter of any clairvoyance, Melanie, from the way you were talking. Are you — is it sure?"

"Of course it's sure. But — well, that isn't the really hard thing. Maybe I should just wait."

"Wait," he said. "Wait for what?"

"Until you get used to everything else."

He said nothing. She was fretting on the other end, sighing and starting to speak and then stopping herself.

"I don't know," she said finally, and abruptly he thought she was talking to someone in the room with her.

"Honey, do you want me to put your mother on?"

"No, Daddy. I wanted to talk to you about this first. I think we should get this over with."

"Get this over with? Melanie, what're we talking about here?

Maybe I should put your mother on." He thought he might try a joke. "After all," he added, "I've never been pregnant."

"It's not about being pregnant. You *guessed* that."

He held the phone tight against his ear. Through the window, he saw his wife stand and stretch, massaging the small of her back with one gloved hand. *Oh, Mary.*

"Are you ready?" his daughter said.

"Wait," he said. "Wait a minute. Should I be sitting down? I'm sitting down." He pulled a chair from the table and settled into it. He could hear her breathing on the other end of the line, or perhaps it was the static wind he so often heard when talking on these new phones. "Okay," he said, feeling his throat begin to close. "Tell me."

"William's somewhat older than I am," she said. "There." She sounded as though she might hyperventilate.

He left a pause. "That's it?"

"Well, it's how much."

"Okay."

She seemed to be trying to collect herself. She breathed, paused. "This is even tougher than I thought it was going to be."

"You mean you're going to tell me something harder than the fact that you're pregnant?"

She was silent.

"Melanie?"

"I didn't expect you to be this way about it," she said.

"Honey, please just tell me the rest of it."

"Well, what did you mean by that, anyway?"

"Melanie, *you said* this would be hard."

Silence.

"Tell me, sweetie. Please?"

"I'm going to." She took a breath. "Dad, William's sixty — he's — he's sixty — sixty-three years old."

Ballinger stood. Out in the garden his wife had got to her knees again, pulling crabgrass out of the bed of tulips. It was a sunny near-twilight, and all along the shady street people were working in their little orderly spaces of grass and flowers.

"Did you hear me, Daddy? It's perfectly all right, too, because he's really a *young* sixty-three, and *very* strong and healthy, and look at George Burns."

"George Burns," Ballinger said. "George — George Burns? Melanie, I don't understand."

"Come on, Daddy, stop it."

"No, what're you telling me?" His mind was blank.

"I said William is sixty-three."

"William who?"

"Dad. My fiancé."

"Wait, Melanie. You're saying your fiancé, the man you're going to marry, *he's* sixty-three?"

"A young sixty-three," she said.

"Melanie. Sixty-three?"

"Dad."

"You didn't say six feet three?"

She was silent.

"Melanie?"

"Yes."

"Honey, this is a joke, right? You're playing a joke on me."

"It is not a — it's not that. God," she said. "I don't believe this."

"You don't believe —" he began. "You don't believe —"

"Dad," she said. "I told you —" Again, she seemed to be talking to someone else in the room with her. Her voice trailed off.

"Melanie," he said. "Talk into the phone."

"I know it's hard," she told him. "I know it's asking you to take a lot in."

"Well, no," Ballinger said, feeling something shift inside, a quickening in his blood. "It's — it's a little more than that, Melanie, isn't it? I mean it's not a weather report, for God's sake."

"I should've known," she said.

"Forgive me for it," he said, "but I have to ask you something."

"It's all right, Daddy," she said as though reciting it for him. "I know what I'm doing. I'm not really rushing into anything —"

He interrupted her. "Well, good God, somebody rushed into something, right?"

"Daddy."

"Is that what you call *him?* No, *I'm* Daddy. You have to call him *Grand*daddy."

"That is *not* funny," she said.

"I wasn't being funny, Melanie. And anyway, that wasn't my question." He took a breath. "Please forgive this, but I have to know."

"There's nothing you really *have* to know, Daddy. I'm an adult. I'm telling you out of family courtesy."

"I understand that. Family courtesy exactly. Exactly, Melanie, that's a good phrase. Would you please tell me, out of family courtesy, if the baby is his."

"Yes." Her voice was small now, coming from a long way off.

"I am sorry for the question, but I have to put all this together. I mean you're asking me to take in a whole lot here, you know?"

"I said I understood how you feel."

"I don't think so. I don't think you quite understand how I feel."

"All right," she said. "I don't understand how you feel. But I think I knew how you'd react."

For a few seconds, there was just the low, sea sound of long distance.

"Melanie, have you done any of the math on this?"

"I should've bet money," she said in the tone of a person who has been proven right about something.

"Well, but Jesus," Ballinger said. "I mean he's older than *I* am, kid. He's — he's a *lot* older than I am." The number of years seemed to dawn on him as he spoke; it filled him with a strange, heart-shaking heat. "Honey, nineteen years. When he was my age, I was only two years older than you are now."

"I don't see what that has to do with anything," she said.

"Melanie, I'll be forty-five *all the way* in December. I'm a *young* forty-four."

"I know when your birthday is, Dad."

"Well, good God, this guy's nineteen years older than your own father."

She said, "I've grasped the numbers. Maybe you should go ahead and put Mom on."

"Melanie, you couldn't pick somebody a little closer to my age? Some snot-nosed forty-year-old?"

"Stop it," she said. "Please, Daddy. I know what I'm doing."

"Do you know how old he's going to be when your baby is ten? Do you? Have you given that any thought at all?"

She was silent.

He said, "How many children are you hoping to have?"

"I'm not thinking about that. Any of that. This is now, and I don't care about anything else."

He sat down in his kitchen and tried to think of something else to say. Outside the window, his wife, with no notion of what she was about to be hit with, looked through the patterns of shade in the blinds and, seeing him, waved. It was friendly, and even so, all their difficulty was in it. Ballinger waved back. "Melanie," he said, "do you mind telling me just where you happened to meet William? I mean how do you meet a person forty years older than you are. Was there a senior citizen–student mixer at the college?"

"Stop it, Daddy."

"No, I really want to know. If I'd just picked this up and read it in the newspaper, I think I'd want to know. I'd probably call the newspaper and see what I could find out."

"Put Mom on," she said.

"Just tell me how you met. You can do that, can't you?"

"Jesus Christ," she said, then paused.

Ballinger waited.

"He's a teacher, like you and Mom, only college. He was my literature teacher. He's a professor of literature. He knows everything that was ever written, and he's the most brilliant man I've ever known. You have no idea how fascinating it is to talk with him."

"Yes, and I guess you understand that over the years that's what you're going to be doing a *lot* of with him, Melanie. A lot of talking."

"I am carrying the proof that disproves *you*," she said.

He couldn't resist saying, "Did *he* teach you to talk like that?"

"I'm gonna hang up."

"You promised you'd listen to something *I* had to tell *you*."

"Okay," she said crisply. "I'm listening."

He could imagine her tapping the toe of one foot on the floor: the impatience of someone awaiting an explanation. He thought a moment. "He's a professor?"

"That's not what you wanted to tell me."

"But you said he's a professor."

"Yes, I said that."

"Don't be mad at me, Melanie. Give me a few minutes to get used to the idea. Jesus. Is he a professor emeritus?"

"If that means distinguished, yes. But I know what you're —"

"No, Melanie. It means *retired*. You went to college."

She said nothing.

"I'm sorry. But for God's sake, it's a legitimate question."

"It's a stupid, mean-spirited thing to ask." He could tell from her voice that she was fighting back tears.

"Is he there with you now?"

"Yes," she said, sniffling.

"Oh, Jesus Christ."

"Daddy, why are you being this way?"

"Do you think maybe we could've had this talk alone? What's he, listening on the other line?"

"No."

"Well, thank God for that."

"I'm going to hang up now."

"No, please don't hang up. Please let's just be calm and talk about this. We have some things to talk about here."

She sniffled, blew her nose. Someone held the phone for her. There was a muffled something in the line, and then she was there again. "Go ahead," she said.

"Is he still in the room with you?"

"Yes." Her voice was defiant.

"Where?"

"Oh, for God's sake," she said.

"I'm sorry, I feel the need to know. Is he sitting down?"

"I *want* him here, Daddy. We both want to be here," she said.

"And he's going to marry you."

"Yes," she said impatiently.

"Do you think I could talk to him?"

She said something he couldn't hear, and then there were several seconds of some sort of discussion, in whispers. Finally she said, "Do you promise not to yell at him?"

"Melanie, he wants me to promise not to *yell* at him?"

"Will you promise?"

"Good God."

"Promise," she said. "Or I'll hang up."

"All right. I promise. I promise not to yell at him."

There was another small scuffing sound, and a man's voice came through the line. "Hello, sir." It was, as far as Ballinger could tell, an ordinary voice, slightly lower than baritone. He thought of cigarettes. "I realize this is a difficult —"

"Do you smoke?" Ballinger interrupted him.

"No, sir."

"All right. Go on."

"Well, I want you to know I understand how you feel."

"Melanie says she does, too," Ballinger said. "I mean I'm certain you both *think* you do."

"It was my idea that Melanie call you about this."

"Oh, really. That speaks well of you. You probably knew I'd find this a little difficult to absorb and that's why you waited until Melanie was pregnant, for Christ's sake."

The other man gave forth a small sigh of exasperation.

"So you're a professor of literature."

"Yes, sir."

"Oh, you needn't 'sir' me. After all, I mean I *am* the goddam kid here."

"There's no need for sarcasm, sir."

"Oh, I wasn't being sarcastic. That was a literal statement of this situation that obtains right here as we're speaking. And, really, Mr. . . . It's Coombs, right?"

"Yes, sir."

"Coombs, like the thing you comb your hair with."

The other man was quiet.

"Just how long do you think it'll take me to get used to this? You think you might get into your seventies before I get used to this? And how long do you think it'll take my wife who's twenty-one years younger than you are to get used to this?"

Silence.

"You're too old for my *wife*, for Christ's sake."

Nothing.

"What's your first name again?"

The other man spoke through another sigh. "Perhaps we should just ring off."

"Ring off. Jesus. Ring off? Did you actually say 'ring off'? What're you, a goddam limey or something?"

"I am an American. I fought in Korea."

"Not World War One?"

The other man did not answer.

"How many other marriages have you had?" Ballinger asked him.

"That's a valid question. I'm glad you —"

"Thank you for the scholarly observation, *sir*. But I'm not sitting in a class. How many did you say?"

"If you'd give me a chance, I'd tell you."

Ballinger said nothing.

"Two, sir. I've had two marriages."

"Divorces?"

"I have been widowed twice."

"And — oh, I get it. You're trying to make sure that that never happens to you again."

"This is not going well at all, and I'm afraid I — I —" The other man stammered, then stopped.

"How did you expect it to go?" Ballinger demanded.

"Cruelty is not what I'd expected. I'll tell you that."

"You thought I'd be glad my daughter is going to be getting social security before I do."

The other was silent.

"Do you have any other children?" Ballinger asked.

"Yes, I happen to have three." There was a stiffness, an overweening tone, in the voice now.

"And how old are they, if I might ask."

"Yes, you may."

Ballinger waited. His wife walked in from outside, carrying some cuttings. She poured water in a glass vase and stood at the counter arranging the flowers, her back to him. The other man had stopped talking. "I'm sorry," Ballinger said. "My wife just walked in here and I didn't catch what you said. Could you just tell me if any of them are anywhere near my daughter's age?"

"I told you, my youngest boy is thirty-eight."

"And you realize that if *he* wanted to marry my daughter I'd be upset, the age difference there being what it is." Ballinger's wife moved to his side, drying her hands on a paper towel, her face full of puzzlement and worry.

"I told you, Mr. Ballinger, that I understood how you feel. The point is, we have a pregnant woman here and we both love her."

"No," Ballinger said. "That's not the point. The point is that you, sir, are not much more than a goddam statutory rapist. That's the point." His wife took his shoulder. He looked at her and shook his head.

"What?" she whispered. "Is Melanie all right?"

"Well, this isn't accomplishing anything," the voice on the other end of the line was saying.

"Just a minute," Ballinger said. "Let me ask you something else. Really now. What's the policy at that goddam university concerning teachers screwing their students?"

"Oh, my God," his wife said as the voice on the line huffed and seemed to gargle.

"I'm serious," Ballinger said.

"Melanie was not my student when we became involved."

"Is that what you call it? Involved?"

"Let me talk to Melanie," Ballinger's wife said.

"Listen," he told her. "Be quiet."

Melanie was back on the line. "Daddy? Daddy?"

"I'm here," Ballinger said, holding the phone from his wife's attempt to take it from him.

"Daddy, we're getting married and there's nothing you can do about it. Do you understand?"

"Melanie," he said, and it seemed that from somewhere far inside himself he heard that he had begun shouting at her. "Jee-zus good Christ. Your fiancé was almost *my* age *now* the day you were *born*. What the hell, kid. Are you crazy? Are you out of your mind?"

His wife was actually pushing against him to take the phone, and so he gave it to her. And stood there while she tried to talk.

"Melanie," she said. "Honey, listen —"

"Hang up," Ballinger said. "Christ. Hang it up."

"Please. Will you go in the other room and let me talk to her?"

"Tell her I've got friends. All these nice men in their forties. She can marry any one of my friends — they're babies. Forties — cradle fodder. Jesus, any one of them. Tell her."

"Jack, stop it." Then she put the phone against her chest. "Did you tell her anything about us?"

He paused. "That — no."

She turned from him. "Melanie, honey. What is this? Tell me, please."

He left her there, walked through the living room to the hall and back around to the kitchen. He was all nervous energy, crazy with it, pacing. Mary stood very still, listening, nodding slightly, holding the phone tight with both hands, her shoulders hunched as if she were out in cold weather.

"Mary," he said.

Nothing.

He went into their bedroom and closed the door. The light

coming through the windows was soft gold, and the room was deepening with shadows. He moved to the bed and sat down, and in a moment he noticed that he had begun a low sort of murmuring. He took a breath and tried to be still. From the other room, his wife's voice came to him. "Yes, I quite agree with you. But I'm just unable to put this . . ."

The voice trailed off. He waited. A few minutes later, she came to the door and knocked on it lightly, then opened it and looked in.

"What," he said.

"They're serious." She stood there in the doorway.

"Come here," he said.

She stepped to his side and eased herself down, and he moved to accommodate her. He put his arm around her, and then, because it was awkward, clearly an embarrassment to her, took it away. Neither of them could speak for a time. Everything they had been through during the course of deciding about each other seemed concentrated now. Ballinger breathed his wife's presence, the odor of earth and flowers, the outdoors.

"God," she said. "I'm positively numb. I don't know what to think."

"Let's have another baby," he said suddenly. "Melanie's baby will need a younger aunt or uncle."

Mary sighed a little forlorn laugh, then was silent.

"Did you tell her about us?" he asked.

"No," she said. "I didn't get the chance. And I don't know that I could have."

"I don't suppose it's going to matter much to her."

"Oh, don't say that. You can't mean that."

The telephone on the bedstand rang, and startled them both. He reached for it, held the handset toward her.

"Hello," she said. Then: "Oh. Hi. Yes, well, here." She gave it back to him.

"Hello," he said.

Melanie's voice, tearful and angry: "You had something you said you had to tell *me*." She sobbed, then coughed. "Well?"

"It was nothing, honey. I don't even remember —"

"Well, I want you to know I would've been better than you were, Daddy, no matter how hard it was. I would've kept myself from reacting."

"Yes," he said. "I'm sure you would have."

"I'm going to hang up. And I guess I'll let you know later if we're coming at all. If it wasn't for Mom, we wouldn't be."

"We'll talk," he told her. "We'll work on it. Honey, you both have to give us a little time."

"There's nothing to work on as far as William and I are concerned."

"Of course there are things to work on. Every marriage —" His voice had caught. He took a breath. "In every marriage there are things to work on."

"I know what I know," she said.

"Well," said Ballinger. "That's — that's as it should be at your age, darling."

"Goodbye," she said. "I can't say any more."

"I understand," Ballinger said. When the line clicked, he held the handset in his lap for a moment. Mary was sitting there at his side, perfectly still.

"Well," he said. "I couldn't tell her." He put the handset back in its cradle. "God. A sixty-three-year-old son-in-law."

"It's happened before." She put her hand on his shoulder, then took it away. "I'm so frightened for her. But she says it's what she wants."

"Hell, Mary. You know what this is. The son of a bitch was her goddam teacher."

"Listen to you — what are you saying about her? Listen to what you're saying about her. That's our daughter you're talking about. You might at least try to give her the credit of assuming that she's aware of what she's doing."

They said nothing for a few moments.

"Who knows," Ballinger's wife said. "Maybe they'll be happy for a time."

He'd heard the note of sorrow in her voice, and thought he knew what she was thinking; then he was certain that he knew.

He sat there remembering, like Mary, their early happiness, that ease and simplicity, and briefly he was in another house, other rooms, and he saw the toddler that Melanie had been, trailing through slanting light in a brown hallway, draped in gowns she had fashioned from her mother's clothes. He did not know why that particular image should have come to him out of the flow of years, but for a fierce minute it was uncannily near him in the breathing silence; it went over him like a palpable something on his skin, then was gone. The ache which remained stopped him for a moment. He looked at his wife, but she had averted her eyes, her hands running absently over the faded denim cloth of her lap. Finally she stood. "Well," she sighed, going away. "Work to do."

"Mary?" he said, low; but she hadn't heard him. She was already out the doorway and into the hall, moving toward the kitchen. He reached over and turned the lamp on by the bed, and then lay down. It was so quiet here. Dark was coming to the windows. On the wall there were pictures; shadows, shapes, silently clamoring for his gaze. He shut his eyes, listened to the small sounds she made in the kitchen, arranging her flowers, running the tap. *Mary*, he had said. But he could not imagine what he might have found to say if his voice had reached her.

Weather

CARLA HEADED OUT to White Elks Mall in the late afternoon, accompanied by her mother, who hadn't been very glad of the necessity of going along, and said so. She went on to say what Carla already knew: that she would brave the August humidity and the discomfort of the hot car if it meant she wouldn't be in the house alone when Carla's husband came back from wherever he had gone that morning. "It's bad enough without me asking for more trouble by being underfoot," she said.

"Nobody thinks you're underfoot, Mother. You didn't have to come."

They were quiet after that. Carla had the Saturday traffic to contend with. Her mother stared out at the gathering thunderclouds above the roofs of the houses they passed. The wind was picking up; it would storm. Carla's mother was the sort of person who liked to sit and watch the scenery while someone else drove. It was something she got from growing up in South Carolina in the forties, when gentlemen did most of the driving. You hardly ever saw a lady behind the wheel of a car.

"I hope we get there before it starts to rain," she said.

Carla was looking in her side mirror, slowing down. "Go on, idiot. Go on by."

"We don't have an umbrella," her mother said.

Lightning cut through the dark mass of clouds to the east.

"I have to watch the road," Carla said, and then blew her horn at someone who had veered too close, changing lanes in front of them. "God, how I hate this town."

For a while there was only the sound of the rocker arms tapping in the engine and the gusts of wind buffeting the sides of the car. The car was low on oil — another expense, another thing to worry about. It kept losing oil. You had to check it every week or so, and it always registered a quart low. Something was leaking somewhere.

"This storm might cool us all off."

"Not supposed to," Carla said, ignoring the other woman's tone. "They're calling for muggy heat."

When they pulled into White Elks, Mother said, "I never liked all the stores in one building like this. I used to love going into the city to do my shopping. Walking along the street, looking in all the windows. And seeing people going about their business, too. It's reassuring — busy city street in the middle of the day. Of course we would never go when it was like this."

The rain came — big, heavy drops.

"Where're we going, anyway?"

"I told you," Carla said. "Record World. I have to buy a tape for Beth's birthday." She parked the car and they hurried across to the closest entrance — the Sears appliance store. Inside, they shook the water from their hair and looked at each other.

"It's going to calm down, sweetness."

"Mother, please. You keep saying that."

"It's true, though. Sometimes you have to say the truth, like a prayer or a chant. It needs saying, baby. It makes a pressure to be spoken."

Carla shook her head.

"I won't utter another syllable," said Mother.

At the display-crowded doorway of the record store, a man wearing a blue blazer over a white T-shirt and jeans paused to let the two of them enter before him.

"Thank you," Mother said, smiling. "Such a considerate young man."

But then a clap of thunder startled them and they paused,

watching the high-domed skylight above them flash with lightning. The tinted glass was streaked with water, and the wind
swept the rain across the surface in sheets. It looked as though
something were trying to break through the window and get at
the dry, lighted, open space below. People stopped and looked
up. Everybody was wearing the bright colors and sparse clothing
of summer — shorts and T-shirts, sleeveless blouses and tank
tops, even a bathing suit or two — and the severity of the storm
made them seem exposed, oddly vulnerable, as though they
could not possibly have come from the outdoors, where the
elements raged and the sunlight had died out of the sky. One
very heavy woman in a red jumpsuit with a pattern of tiny white
sea horses across the waistband said, "Looks like it's going to be
a twister," to no one in particular, then strolled on by. This was
not an area of Virginia that had ever been known to have a
tornado.

"What would a twister do to a place like this, I wonder,"
Mother said.

"It's a thunderstorm," Carla said.

But the wind seemed to gather sudden force, and there was
a banging at the roof in the vicinity of the window.

"Damn," Mother said. "It's violent, whatever it is."

They remained where they were, in front of the store entrance, looking at the skylight. Carla lighted a cigarette.

"Excuse me," the man in the blue blazer said. "Could you
please let me pass?"

She looked at him. Large, round eyes the color of water
under beams of sun, black hair, and bad skin. A soft, downturn-
ing mouth. Perhaps thirty or so. There was unhappiness in the
face.

"Can I pass, please?" he said impatiently.

"You're in his way," Carla's mother said. They both laughed,
moving aside. "We got interested in the storm."

"Maybe you'd both like to have a seat and watch to your
heart's content," the man said. "After all, this only happens to
be a doorway."

"All you have to do is say what you want," said Carla.

He went on into the store.

"And a good day to you, too," Carla said.

"I swear," Mother said. "The rudeness of some people."

They moved to the bench across the way and sat down. The bench was flanked by two fat white columns, each with a small metal ashtray attached to it. Carla smoked her cigarette and stared at the people walking by. Her mother fussed with the strap of her purse, then looked through the purse for a napkin, with which she gingerly wiped some rainwater from the side of her face. Above them, the storm went on, and briefly the lights flickered. A leak was coming from somewhere, and water ran in a thin, slow stream down the opposite wall. Carla smoked the cigarette automatically.

"I've always had this perverse wish to actually see a tornado," said Mother.

"I saw one when Daryl and I lived in Illinois, just before Beth was born. No thank you." Carla took a last drag on the cigarette, placed it in the mouth of the metal ashtray attached to the column, and clicked it shut. Then she opened it and clicked it shut again.

"You're brooding," Mother said. "Stop it."

"I'm not brooding," Carla said. She took another cigarette out of the pack in her handbag and lighted it.

"I didn't come with you to watch you smoke."

"We've established why you came with me, Mother."

"How you can put that in your lungs . . ."

"Leave me alone, will you?"

"I won't say another word."

"And don't get your feelings hurt, either."

"You're the boss. God knows, it's none of my business. I'm only a spectator here."

"Oh, please."

They were quiet. Somewhere behind them, a baby fussed. "What were you thinking about?" Mother said. "You were thinking about this morning, right?"

"I was thinking about how unreal everything is."

"You don't mean the storm, though, do you?"

"No, Mother, I don't mean the storm."

"We need the storm, though. The rain, I mean. I'm glad it's storming."

"I'm not surprised, since a minute ago you were wishing it was a tornado."

"I was doing no such thing. I was merely expressing an element of my personality. A — a curiousness, that's all. And that's not what I'm talking about. Let me finish. You never let me finish, Carla. You're always jumping the gun, and you've always done that. You did it to Daryl this morning, went right ahead and finished his sentences for him."

Carla shook her head. "I can't help it if I know what he's going to say before he says it."

"You didn't know what *I* was going to say."

Carla waited.

"I was going to say something about this morning."

"I don't want to talk about it."

They were quiet again. Mother stirred restlessly in her seat and watched the trickle of water run down the wall opposite where they sat. Finally she leaned toward the younger woman and murmured, "I was going to say it's just weather. This morning, you know. You're both going through a spell of bad weather. Daryl's still got some growing up to do, God knows. But all of them do. I never met a man who couldn't use a little growing up. And Daryl's a perfect example of that."

"I think I've figured out how you feel about him, Mother."

"No. I admit sometimes I think you'd be better off if he *did* move out. I promised I wouldn't interfere, though."

"You're not interfering," Carla said in the voice of someone who felt interfered with.

"I *will* say I don't like the way he talks to you."

"Oh, please, let's change the subject."

"I for one am happy to change the subject. You think I enjoy talking about it? You think I enjoy seeing you and that boy say those things to each other?"

"He's not a boy, Mother. He's your son-in-law, and you're stuck with him." Carla blew smoke. "At least for the time being."

"Don't talk like that. And I was just using a figure of speech."

"It happens to make him very mad."

"Yes, and he's not here right now."

She smoked the cigarette, watching the people walk by. A woman came past pushing a double stroller with twins in it.

"Look," said Mother. "How sweet."

"I see them." Carla had only glanced at them.

"You're so — hard-edged sometimes, Carla. You never used to be that way, no matter how unhappy things made you."

"What? I looked. What did you want me to do?"

"I swear, I don't understand anything anymore."

After a pause, Mother said, "I remember when you were that small. Your father liked to put you on his chest and let you nap there. Seems like weeks — just a matter of days ago."

Carla took a long drag of the cigarette, blew smoke, and watched it. She had heard it said that blind persons do not generally like cigarettes as much as sighted people, for not being able to watch the smoke.

"But men were more respectful in our day."

"Look, please —"

"I'll shut up."

"I'm sure it'll all be made up before the day's over."

"Oh, I know. You'll give in, and he'll say he forgives you. Like every other time."

"We'll forgive each other."

"I'm not uttering another word," Mother said. "I'm sure I cause tension by talking. It's no secret he hates me."

"He doesn't hate you. You drive him crazy."

"I drive him crazy? He sits in the living room plunking that guitar, even when the television is on, never finishing — have you ever heard him play a whole song? It would be one thing if he could play notes. But that constant strumming —"

"He's trying to learn. That's all. It's a project."

"It drives me right up the wall."

A pair of skinny boys came running from one end of the open space, one chasing the other and trying to keep up. Behind them a woman hurried along, carrying a handful of small flags.

"Do I drive *you* crazy?" Mother wanted to know.

"All the time," Carla said.

"I'm serious."

"Don't be. Let's not be serious, okay?"

"You're the one that's been off in another world all afternoon. I don't blame you, of course."

"Mother," Carla said. "Things are hard for him right now, that's all. He's not used to being home all day."

"If you ask me, he could've had that job at the shoe store."

"He's not a shoe salesman. He's an engineer. He's trained for something. That was what they all said when we were growing up, wasn't it? Train for something? Wasn't that what they said? Plan for the future and get an education so you'd be ready? Well, what if the future isn't anything like what you planned for, Mother?"

"But listen, it's like I said. You're both in a stormy period, and you have to wait it out, that's all. But the day your father ever called me stupid — I'd have shown him the door, let me tell you. I'd have slapped his face."

"Daryl didn't call me stupid. He said that something I said was the stupidest thing he ever heard. And what I said *was* stupid."

"Oh, listen to you."

"It was. I said the money he was spending on gas driving back and forth to coach Little League was going to cost Beth her college education."

"That's a valid point, if you ask me."

"Oh, come on. I was mad and I said anything. I wanted to hit at him."

"So? It's not the stupidest thing he ever heard. I'm certain that over the last month I've said three or four hundred things he thinks are more stupid."

Carla smiled.

"And he still shouldn't talk that way."

"We were having an argument."

"Well, like I told you. A storm. It shouldn't ruin your whole day."

Carla looked down, took the last drag of her cigarette.

"You have to set the boundaries a little. I mean, your father never —"

"I'm going into the record store, Mother."

"I know. I came with you, didn't I? You ought to get something for yourself. I hope you spend your own money on yourself for once. Get whatever Beth wants for her birthday and then get something for yourself."

"Beth wants a rap record, and I can't remember the name of it."

"My God," said Mother. "I don't like that stuff. I don't even like people who *do* like it."

"Beth likes it."

"Beth's thirteen. What does she know?"

"She knows what she wants for her birthday." Carla sighed. "I know what I have to get and how much it's going to cost and how much I'll hate having it blaring in the house all day, too. I just don't remember the name of it."

"Maybe it'll come to you."

"It'll have to."

"You could forget it, couldn't you?"

"It's the only thing she asked for."

"What if the only thing she asked for was a trip to Rome or — or a big truckload of drugs or something?"

Carla looked at her.

"Well?"

"The two go together so naturally, Mother. I always think of truckloads of drugs when I think of Rome."

"You know what I mean."

"Did you ever do that to me?" Carla asked. "Lie to me that way?"

"Of course not. I wouldn't dream of such a thing."

"How can you suggest I do it to Beth?"

"It was an idea. It had to do with self-preservation. If she hadn't been playing her music so loud this morning, Daryl and you might not've got into it."

Carla looked at her.

"You have my solemn vow."

Carla said, "You can't put this morning off on Beth."

Mother made a gesture, like turning a key in a lock, at her lips.

"The fact is, we don't need any excuses to have a fight these days."

"Now don't get down on yourself. You've had enough to deal with. I should never have moved in. I try to mind my own business —"

"You're fine. This has nothing to do with you. It was going on before you moved in. It's been going on a long time."

"Baby, it's nothing you can't solve. The two of you."

"Unreal," Carla said, bringing a handkerchief out of her purse. "It seems everything I do makes him mad."

"We're all getting on each other's nerves," said Mother.

"Let me have a minute here." Carla turned, facing the column, wiping her eyes with the handkerchief.

"Don't you worry, sweetness."

"We just have to get on the other side of it," Carla said.

"That's right. Daryl has to settle down and see how lucky he is. I won't say anything else about it. It's not my place to say anything."

"Mother, will you please stop that? You can say anything you want. I give you my permission. Let's just do what we came to do." Carla put the handkerchief back in her purse. "I don't want to think about anything else right now."

"You shouldn't have to, though you live in a house where you have to think of absolutely everything."

"That isn't true. It's not just Daryl, Mother."

"I'm sorry. I should keep my mouth shut."

Carla hesitated, looked around herself. She ran one hand through her hair and sighed again. "Sometimes I — I think — see, we were going to have a big family. We both wanted a lot of children. And maybe it's because I couldn't — God, never mind."

"Oh, no, you're imagining that. He's been out of work and that always makes tension. I mean Daryl's got a lot of things wrong with him, but he'd never blame you for something you can't help."

"But you read about tension over one thing making other tensions worse."

"That doesn't have anything to do with you," Mother said.

"When we had Beth, it — nothing about that pregnancy — you know, it was full term. Everything went so well."

"Carla, you don't really think he'd hold anything against you."

"He was so crestfallen the last time."

"Yes, and so were you."

"The thing is, we always pulled together before, when there was any trouble at all. We'd cling to each other. You remember when he was just out of college and there wasn't any work and he was doing all those part-time jobs? We were so happy then. Beth was small. We didn't have anything and we didn't want anything, really."

"You're older now. And you've got your mother living with you."

"No, that's what you don't understand. I told you, this was going on before you moved in. That's the truth. In fact, it got better for a little while, those first days after you moved in. It was like — it seemed that having you with us brought something of the old times back."

"Don't divide it up like that, sugar. It's still your time together. There's no old times or new times. That isn't how you should think about it. It's the two of you. And this is weather. Weather comes and changes and you keep on. That's all."

Carla put the handkerchief back in her purse. "Do I look like I've been crying?"

"You look like the wrath of God."

They laughed; they were briefly almost lighthearted. The crowd was moving around them, and though the thunder and lightning had mostly ceased, the rain still beat against the skylight. "So," said Carla, "on with the show."

"That's the spirit."

They walked into the store. The man in the blue blazer was standing by a rack of compact discs that were being sold at a clearance price. He'd already chosen several, and had them tucked under his arm. He was rifling through the discs, apparently looking for something specific that he would recognize on sight; he wasn't pausing long enough to read the titles. Concentrating, he appeared almost angry; the skin around his eyes was white. He glanced at the two women as they edged past him, and Carla's mother said "Excuse us" rather pointedly. He did not answer, but went back to thumbing through the discs.

The store was crowded, and there wasn't much room to move around. Carla and her mother made their way along the aisle to the audiotape section, where Carla recognized and selected the tape she had come for. It was in a big display on the wall, with a life-size poster of the artist.

"Looks like a mugger if you ask me," Mother said. She picked up a tape for herself, an anthology of songs from the fifties. Speakers were pounding with percussion, the drone of a toneless, shrill male voice.

"I think what we're hearing is what I'm about to buy," said Carla, pointing at the ceiling. "God help me."

There were two lines waiting at the counter, and the two women stood side by side, each on her own line. The man in the blazer stepped in behind Mother. He had several discs in his hands, and he began reading one of the labels. Carla glanced at him, so dour, and she thought of Daryl, off somewhere angry with her, unhappy — standing under the gaze of someone else, who would see it in his face. When the man glanced up, she sent a smile in his direction, but he was staring at the two girls behind the counter, both of whom were dressed in the bizarre getup of rock stars. The girls chattered back and forth, being witty and funny with each other in that attitude store clerks sometimes have when people are lined up waiting: as though circumstances had provided them with an audience, and that audience were entertained by their talk. The clerks took a long time with each purchase, running a scanner over the coded patch on the tapes and CDs and then punching numbers into the computer terminals. The percussion thrummed in the walls, and the lines moved slowly. When Mother's turn came, she reached for Carla. "Here, sweetness, step in here."

Carla did so.

"Wait a minute," the man said. "You can't do that."

"Do what?" Mother said. "She's waiting with me."

"She was in the other line."

"We were waiting together."

"You were in separate lines." The man addressed the taller of the two girls behind the counter. "They were in separate lines."

"I don't know," the girl said. Her hair was an unnatural shade of orange. She held her hands up as if in surrender, and bracelets clattered on her wrists. Then she moved to take Carla's tape and run the scanner over it.

"Oh, that's great," the man said. "Let stupidity and selfishness win out."

Mother faced him. "What did you say? Did you call my daughter a name?"

"You heard everything I said," the man told her.

"Yes I did," Mother said, and swung at his face.

He backpedaled but took the blow above the eye, so that he almost lost his balance. When he had righted himself, he stood straight, wide-eyed, clearly unable to believe what had just happened to him.

"Lady," the man said. "You —"

And Mother struck again, this time swinging her purse, so that it hit the man on the crown of the head as he ducked, putting his arms up to ward off the next blow. His CDs fell to the floor at his feet.

"Mother," Carla began, not quite hearing herself. "Good Lord."

"You don't call my daughter names and get away with it," Mother said to the man.

He had straightened again and assumed the stance of someone in a fight, his fists up to protect his face, chin tucked into his left shoulder.

"You think you can threaten me," Mother said, and poked at his face with her free hand. He blocked this and stepped back, and she swung the purse again, striking him this time on the forearm.

"Oh God," said Carla, barely breathing the words.

There was a general commotion in the crowd. Someone laughed.

"This isn't right," Carla said. "Let's stop this."

"Look at him. Big tough man. Going to hit a woman, big tough guy?"

"I want the police," the man said to the girl with the orange hair. "I absolutely demand to see a policeman. I've been assaulted and I intend to press charges."

"Look," Carla said. "Can you just forget about it? Here." She bent down to pick up the CDs he had dropped.

"Don't you dare," Mother said.

Carla looked at her.

"All right, I'll shut up. But don't you dare give him those."

Carla ignored her.

"I want to see a policeman."

"Here," Carla said, offering the discs.

Her mother said, "If he says another thing —"

The man looked past them. "Officer, I've been assaulted. And there are all these witnesses."

A security guard stepped out of the crowd. He was thin, green-eyed, blond, with boyish skin. Perhaps he had to shave once a week. But clearly he took great care with all aspects of his appearance: his light blue uniform was creased exactly, the shirt starched and pressed. His shoes shone like twin black mirrors. He brought a writing pad out of his pocket, and a ballpoint pen, the end of which he clicked with his thumb. "Okay, what happened here?"

"He called my daughter a name," said Mother. "I won't have people calling my daughter names."

"I'm pressing charges," said the man.

The security guard addressed him. "Would you tell me what happened?"

But everyone began to speak at once. The girl with the orange hair put her hands up again in surrender, and again the bracelets clattered. "None of my business," she said. "I don't believe in violence." She spoke in an almost metaphysical tone, the tone of someone denying a belief in the existence of a thing like violence. Carla was trying to get the officer's attention, but he was drawing her mother and the man out of the store, into the open area of shops, under the skylight. She followed. Mother and the man protested all the way, accusing each other.

"I've got a welt," the man said. "Right here." He pointed to his left eyebrow.

"I don't see it," said the officer.

"Do you have jurisdiction here?"

"I have that, yes. I have the authority."

"I've been attacked. And I want to file a complaint."

"This man verbally assaulted my daughter!"

"Just a minute," said the security guard. "Calm down. We're not going to get anywhere like this. I'll listen to you one at a time."

"This man verbally assaulted my daughter. And I slapped him."

"You didn't slap me. You hit me with your fist, and then you assaulted me with your purse."

"I didn't hit you with my fist. If I'd hit you with my fist, that would be an assault."

"Both of you be quiet." He stood there writing on the pad. "Let me have your names."

Mother and the man spoke at once.

"Wait a minute," the officer said. "One at a time."

"Please," said Carla. "Couldn't we just forget this?"

"I don't want to forget it," said the man. "I was attacked. A person ought to be able to walk into a store without being attacked."

"My sentiments exactly," said Mother. "You started it. You attacked my daughter verbally."

"Both of you be quiet or I'm going to cite you," the security guard said.

They stood there.

"What's your name, sir?"

"Todd Lemke."

The officer wrote it down on his pad. "Like it sounds?"

"One *e*."

"All right. You start."

"I was waiting in line, and this woman —" Lemke indicated Carla.

"You be careful how you say that," said Mother.

"Now, ma'am —" the security guard said.

"I won't let people talk about my daughter that way, young man. And I don't care what you or anybody else says about it." Her voice had reached a pitch Carla had never heard before.

"Please, ma'am."

"Well, he better watch his tone. That's all I have to say."

"Mother, if you don't shut up," Carla said. There were tears in her voice.

"What did I say? I merely indicated that I wouldn't tolerate abuse. This man abused you."

"Ma'am, I'm afraid I'm going to have to insist."

"Pitiful," Lemke was saying, shaking his head. "Completely pitiful."

"Who's pitiful?" Carla said. She moved toward him. She could feel her heart beating in her face and neck. "Who's pitiful?"

The security guard stood between them. "Now wait —"

"You watch who you call names," Carla said, and something slipped inside her. The next moment, anything might happen.

"I rest my case," Lemke was saying.

"There isn't any case," Carla said. "You don't have any case. Nobody's pitiful."

"They're making my case for me, Officer."

"— amazing disrespect —" Mother was saying.

"You're wrong about everything," Carla said. "Pity doesn't enter into it."

"Everybody shut up," the security guard said. "I swear, I'm going to run you all in for disturbing the peace."

"Do I have to say anything else?" Lemke said to him. "It's like I said. They make my case for me. Ignorant, lowlife —"

"I'm going to hit him again," said Mother. "You're the one who's ignorant."

"See? She admits she hit me."

"I'm going to hit you myself in a minute," the security guard said. "Now shut up."

Lemke gave him an astonished look.

"Everybody be quiet." The guard held his hands out and made a slow up-and-down motion with each word, like a conductor in front of an orchestra. "Let's — all — of — us — please — calm — down." He turned to Mother. "You and your daughter wait here. I'll come back to you."

"Yes, sir."

"We'll be here," Carla said.

"Now," he said to Lemke. "If you'll step over here with me, I'll listen to what you have to say."

"You're biased against me," Lemke said.

"I'm what?"

"You heard me. You threatened to hit me."

"I did not."

"I'm not going to get a fair deal here, I can sense it," Lemke said.

"We're not in a courtroom, sir. This is not a courtroom."

"I know what kind of report you'll file."

"Listen, I'm sure if we all give each other the benefit of the doubt —"

"This woman assaulted me," Lemke said. "I know my rights."

"Okay," the security guard said. "Why don't you tell me what you want me to do. Really, what is it that you think I should do here?"

Lemke stared into his face.

"I think he wants you to shoot me," Mother said.

"Mother, will you please stop it. Please."

"Her own daughter can't control her," Lemke said to the guard. Then he turned to Carla: "You shouldn't take her out of the house."

"I'm pregnant," Carla said abruptly, and began to cry. The tears came streaming down her cheeks. It was a lie; she had said it simply to cut through everything.

Her mother took a step back. "Oh, sugar."

Carla went on talking, only now she was telling the truth: "I've lost the last four. Do you understand, sir? I've miscarried four times and I need someone with me. Surely even you can understand that."

Something changed in Lemke's face. His whole body seemed to falter, as though he had been supporting some invisible weight and had now let down under it. "Hey," he stammered. "Listen."

"Why don't you all make friends," said the security guard. "No harm done, really. Right?"

"Right," Mother said. "My daughter had a — a tiff with her husband this morning, and he said some things. Maybe I over-reacted. I overreacted. I'm really sorry, sir."

Lemke was staring at Carla.

"I don't know my own strength sometimes," Mother was saying. "I'm always putting my foot in it."

"A misunderstanding," the security guard said.

Lemke rubbed the side of his face, looking at Carla, who was wiping her eyes with the back of one hand.

"Am I needed here anymore?" the security guard said.

Lemke said, "I guess not."

"There," said Mother. "Now, could anything have worked out better?"

"I have to tell you," Lemke said to Carla, and it seemed to her that his voice shook. "We lost our first last month. My wife was seven months pregnant. She's had a hard time of it since."

"We're sorry that happened to you," Mother said.

"Mother," said Carla, sniffling, "please."

"I hope things work out for you," Lemke said to her.

"Do you have other children?" Carla asked.

He nodded. "A girl."

"Us, too."

"How old?"

"Thirteen."

"Seven," Lemke said. "Pretty age."

"Yes."

"They're all lovely ages," Mother said.

"Thank you for understanding," Carla said to him.

"No," he said. "It's — I'm sorry for everything." Then he moved off. In a few seconds, he was lost in the crowd.

"I guess he didn't want his music after all," Mother said. Then: "Poor man. Isn't it amazing that you'd find out in an argument that you have something like that in common?"

"What're the chances," Carla said, almost to herself. Then she turned to Mother. "Do you think I could've sensed it somehow, or heard it in his voice?"

Mother smiled out of one side of her mouth. "I think it's a coincidence."

"I don't know," Carla said. "I feel like I knew."

"That's how I think I felt about you being pregnant. I had this feeling."

"I'm not pregnant," Carla told her.

Mother frowned.

"I couldn't stand the arguing anymore and I just said it."

"Oh, my."

"Poor Daryl," Carla said after a pause. "Up against me all by himself."

"Stop that," said Mother.

"Up against us."

"I won't listen to you being contrite."

Carla went back into the store, and when Mother started to follow, she stopped. "I'll buy yours for you. Let *me* get in line."

"I can't believe I actually hit that boy." Mother held out one hand, palm down, examining it. "Look at me, I'm shaking all over. I'm trembling all over. I've never done anything like that in my life, not ever. Not even close. I've never even yelled at anyone in public, have I? I mean, think of it. *Me*, in a public brawl. This morning must've set me up or something. Set the tone, you know. Got me primed. I'd never have expected this of me, would you?"

"I don't think anyone expected it," Carla said.

They watched the woman with the twin babies come back by them.

"I feel sorry for him now," Mother said. "I almost wish I hadn't hit him. If I'd known, I could've tried to give him the benefit of the doubt, like the officer said."

Carla said nothing. She had stopped crying. "Everybody has their own troubles, I guess."

She went to the counter, where people moved back to let her buy the tapes. It took only a moment to pay for them.

Mother stood in the entrance of the store looking pale and frightened.

"Come on, Sugar Ray," Carla said to her.

"You're mad at me," Mother said, and seemed about to cry herself.

"I'm not mad," Carla said.

"I'm so sorry. I can't imagine what got into me — can't imagine. But, sugar, I hear him talk to you that way. It hurts to hear him say those things to you and I know I shouldn't interfere —"

"It's fine," Carla told her. "Really. I understand."

Outside, they waited in the lee of the building for the rain to let up. The air had grown much cooler; there was a breeze blowing out of the north. The line of trees on the other side of the parking lot moved, and showed lighter green.

"My God," Carla said. "Isn't it — doesn't it say something

about me that I would use the one gravest sadness in Daryl's life with me, the one thing he's always been most sorry about — that I would use that to get through an altercation at the fucking mall?"

"Stop it," Mother said. "Don't use that language."

"Well, really. And I didn't even have to think about it. I was crying, and I saw the look on his face, and I just said it. It came out so naturally. And imagine, me lying that I'm pregnant again. Imagine Daryl's reaction to that."

"You're human. What do you want from yourself?"

Carla seemed not to have heard this. "I wish I *was* pregnant," she said. "I feel awful, and I really wish I was."

"That wouldn't change anything, would it?"

"It would change how I feel right now."

"I meant with Daryl."

Carla looked at her. "No. You're right," she said. "That wouldn't change anything with Daryl. Not these days."

"Now, sugar," Mother said, touching her nose with the handkerchief.

But then Carla stepped out of the protection of the building and walked away through the rain.

"Hey," Mother said. "Wait for me."

The younger woman turned. "I'm going to bring the car up. Stay there."

"Well, let a person know what you're going to do."

"Wait there," Carla said over her shoulder.

The rain was lessening now. She got into the car and sat thinking about her mother in the moment of striking the man with her purse. She saw the man's startled face in her mind's eye, and to her surprise she laughed, once, harshly, like a sob. Then she was crying again, thinking of her husband, who would not come home today until he had to. Across the lot her mother waited, a blur of colors, a shape in the raining distance. Mother put the handkerchief to her face again, and seemed to totter. Then she stood straight.

Carla started the car and backed out of the space, aware that the other woman could see her now. She tried to master herself, wanting to put the best face on, wanting not to hurt any more feelings and to find some way for everyone to get along, to bear the disappointments and the irritations. As she pulled toward the small waiting figure under the wide stone canopy, she caught herself thinking, with a sense of depletion — as though it were a prospect she would never have enough energy for, no matter how hard or long she strove to gain it — of what was constantly required, what must be repeated and done and given and listened to and allowed, in all the kinds of love there are.

Her mother stepped to the curb and opened the door. "What were you doing?" she said, struggling into the front seat. "I thought you were getting ready to leave me here."

"No," Carla said. "Never that." Her voice went away.

Her mother shuffled on the seat, getting settled, then pulled the door shut. The rain was picking up again, though it wasn't wind-driven now.

"Can't say I'd blame you if you left me behind," Mother said. "After all, I'm clearly a thug."

They were silent for a time, sitting in the idling car with the rain pouring down. And then they began to laugh. It was low, almost tentative, as if they were both uneasy about letting go entirely. The traffic paused and moved by them, and shoppers hurried past.

"I can't believe I did such an awful thing," Mother said.

"I won't listen to you being contrite," Carla said, and smiled.

"Touché, sugar. You have scored your point."

"I wasn't trying to score points," Carla told her. "I was only setting the boundaries for today." Then she put the car in gear and headed them through the rain, toward home.

High-Heeled
Shoe

DORNBERG, out for a walk in the fields behind his house one morning, found a black high-heeled shoe near the path leading down to the neighboring pond. The shoe had scuffed places on its shiny surface and caked mud adhering to it, but he could tell from the feel of the soft leather that it was well made, the kind a woman who has money might wear. He held it in his hand and observed that his sense of equilibrium shifted; he caught himself thinking of misfortune, failure, scandal.

The field around him was peaceful, rife with the fragrances of spring. The morning sun was warm, the air dry, the sky blue. Intermittently, drowsily, the cawing of crows sounded somewhere in the distance, above the languid murmur of little breezes in the trees bordering the far side of the pond. A beautiful, innocent morning, and here he stood, holding the shoe close to his chest in the defensive, wary posture of the guilty — the attitude of someone caught with the goods — nervously scraping the dried mud from the shoe's scalloped sides.

The mud turned to dust and made a small red cloud about his head, and when the wind blew, the glitter of dust swept over him. He used his shirttail to wipe his face, then walked a few paces, automatically looking for the shoe's mate. He thought he saw something in the tall grass at the edge of the pond, but when he got to it, stepping in mud and catching himself on thorns to make his way, he found the dark, broken curve of a beer bottle. The owner of the pond had moved last fall to Alaska, and there were signs posted all over about the penalties for trespassing, but no one paid any attention to them. Casual littering went on. It was distressing. Dornberg bent down and picked up the shard of glass. Then he put his hand inside the shoe and stretched the leather, holding it up in the brightness.

He felt weirdly dislodged from himself.

Beyond the pond and its row of trees, four new houses were being built. Often the construction crews, made up mostly of young men, came to the pond to eat their box lunches and, sometimes, to fish. On several occasions they had remained at the site long after the sun went down; the lights in the most nearly finished house burned; other cars pulled in, little rumbling sports cars and shiny sedans, motorcycles, even a taxi now and again. There were parties that went on into the early morning hours. Dornberg had heard music, voices, the laughter of women, all of which depressed him, as though this jazzy, uncomplicated gaiety — the kind that had no cost and generated no guilt — had chosen these others over him. The first time he heard it, he was standing at the side of his house, near midnight, having decided to haul the day's garbage out before going to bed (how his life had lately turned upon fugitive urges to cleanse and purge and make order!). The music stopped him in the middle of his vaguely palliative task, and he listened, wondering, thinking his senses were deceiving him: a party out in the dark, as if the sound of it were drifting down out of the stars.

Some nights when sleep wouldn't come, he had stared out his window at the faint shadows of the unfinished houses and, finding the one house with all its windows lighted, had quietly made his way downstairs to the back door and stood in the chilly open frame, listening for the music, those pretty female voices — the tumult of the reckless, happy young.

Today, a Saturday, he carried what he had found back to his own recently finished house (some of the men on the construction crew were in fact familiar to him, being subcontractors who worked all the new houses in the area). The piece of glass he dropped in the trash can by the garage door, and the shoe he brought into the house with him, stopping in the little coat porch to take off his muddy boots.

His wife, Mae, was up and working in the kitchen, still wearing her nightgown, robe, and slippers. Without the use of dyes or rinses, and at nearly forty-seven years of age, her hair retained that rich straw color of some blondes, with a bloom of light brown in it. She'd carelessly brushed it up over her ears and tied it in an absurd ponytail which stood out of the exact middle of the back of her head. She was scouring the counter with a soapy dishcloth. Behind her, water ran in the sink. She hadn't seen him, and as he had done often enough lately, he took the opportunity to watch her.

This furtive attention, this form of secret vigilance, had arisen out of the need to be as certain as possible about predicting her moods, to be ready for any variations or inconsistencies of habit — teaching himself to anticipate changes. For the better part of a year, everything in his life with her had been shaded with this compunction, and while the reasons for it were over (he had ended it only this week), he still felt the need to be ever more observant, ever more protective of what he had so recently allowed to come under the pall of doubt and uncertainty.

So he watched her for a time.

It seemed to him that in passages like this — work in the house or in the yard, or even in her job at the computer store — her face gleamed with a particular domestic heat. Curiously, the sense of purpose, the intention to accomplish practical tasks, made her skin take on a translucent quality, as though these matters required a separate form of exertion, subjecting the sweat glands to different stimuli.

She saw him now and stepped away from the counter, which shined.

"Look at this." He held up the shoe.

She stared.

"I found it out by the pond." Somehow, one had to try to remember the kind of thing one would have done before everything changed; one had to try to keep the old habits and propensities intact.

"Whose is it?" she asked him.

"Someone in a hurry," he said, turning the shoe in his hand.

"Well, I certainly don't want it."

"No," he said. "Just thought it was odd."

"Somebody threw it away, right?"

"You wonder where it's been."

"What do these girls do to be able to drive those fancy foreign jobs, anyway?"

"The daughters of our landed neighbors."

"Playing around with the workforce."

"Maybe it's encouraged," he said.

"Are you okay?" she asked.

The question made him want to get outside in the open again. "Sure. Why?"

"It's odd," she said. "A high-heeled shoe. You look a bit flustered."

"Well, honey, I thought a shoe, lying out in the back — I thought it *was* odd. That's why I brought it in."

"Whatever you say." She had started back to work on the kitchen.

Again, he watched her for a moment.

"What," she said. "You're not imagining something awful, are you? I'll bet you looked around for a body, didn't you."

"Don't be absurd," he said.

"Well, I thought of it. I've become as morbid as you are, I guess."

"I'll get busy on the yard," he said.

"You sure you're okay?"

He tried for teasing exasperation: "Mae."

She shrugged. "Just asking."

Was it going to be impossible, now that everything was over, now that he had decided against further risk, to keep from making these tiny slips of tone and stance? At times he had wondered if he were not looking for a way to confess: Darling, I've wronged you. For the past nine months I've been carrying on with someone at work — lunch hours, afternoon appointments, that trip to Boston (she met me there), those restless weekend days when I went out to a matinee (the motels in town have satellite movies which are still playing in the theaters). Oh, my darling, I have lavished such care on the problem of keeping it all from you that it has become necessary to tell you about it, out of the sheer pressure of our old intimacy.

Outside, he put the shoe in the trash, then retrieved it and set it on the wooden sill inside the garage. He would throw it away when it was not charged with the sense of recent possession, a kind of muted strife: he could not shake the feeling that the wearer of the shoe had not parted with it easily. He felt eerily proprietary toward it, as though any minute a woman might walk down the street in the disarming, faintly comical limp of a person bereft of one shoe, and ask him if he had its mate. He conjured the face: bruised perhaps, smeared and drawn, someone in the middle of the complications of passion, needing to account for everything.

They had been married more than twenty-five years, and the children — two of them — were gone: Cecily was married and living in New York, and Todd was in his first year of college out in Arizona. Cecily had finished a degree in accounting, and was putting her husband through business school at Columbia. They were planners, as Dornberg's wife put it. When the schooling was over, they would travel, and when the travel was done, they'd think about having children. Everything would follow their carefully worked-out plan. She did not mean it as a criticism, particularly; it was just an observation.

"I have the hardest time imagining them making love," she'd said once.

This was a disconcerting surprise to Dornberg. "You mean you try to imagine them?"

"I just mean it rhetorically," she said. "In the abstract. I don't see Cecily."

"Why think of it at all?"

"I didn't say I dwelled on it."

He let it alone, not wanting to press.

"Come here," she said. "Let's dwell on each other a little."

The hardest thing during the months of what he now thought of as his trouble was receiving her cheerful, trustful affection, her comfortable use of their habitual endearments, their pet names for each other, their customary tenderness and gestures of attachment. He wondered how others bore such guilt: each caressive phrase pierced him, each casual assumption of his fidelity and his interest made him miserable, and the effort of hiding his misery exhausted him.

The other woman was the kind no one would suppose him to be moved by. Even her name, Edith, seemed far from him. Brassy and loud in a nearly obnoxious way, she wore too much makeup and her brisk, sweeping gestures seemed always to be accompanied by the chatter of the many bracelets on her bony wrists. She had fiery red hair and dark blue, slightly crossed eyes — the tiny increment of difference made her somehow more attractive — and she had begun things by stating bluntly that she wanted to have an affair with him. The whole thing had been like a sort of banter, except that she had indicated, with a touch to his hip, that she was serious enough. It thrilled him. He couldn't catch his breath for a few moments, and before he spoke again, she said, "Think it over."

This was months before the first time they made love. They saw each other often in the hallways of the courthouse, where he worked as an officer on custody cases (he had seen every permutation of marital failure, all the catastrophes of divorce) and she was a secretary in the law library. They started looking for each other in the downstairs cafeteria during coffee breaks and lunch hours, and they became part of a regular group of people who congregated in the smoking lounge in the after-noons. Everyone teased and flirted, everyone seemed younger than he, more at ease, and when she was with him, he felt the gap between him and these others grow narrower. Her voice and manner, her easy affection, enveloped him, and he felt as though he moved eloquently under the glow of her approval.

Of course, he had an awareness of the aspects of vulgarity surrounding the whole affair, its essential banality, having come as it did out of the fact that over the past couple of years he had been suffering from a general malaise, and perhaps he was bearing middle age rather badly: there had been episodes of anxiety and sleeplessness, several bouts of hypochondria and depression, and a steady increase in his old propensity toward gloom. This was something she had actually teased him about, and he had marveled at how much she knew about him, how exactly right she was to chide him. Yet even in the unseemly, forsaken-feeling last days and hours of his involvement with her, there remained the simple reprehensible truth that for a time his life had seemed somehow brighter — charged and brilliant under the dark blue gaze she bestowed on him, the look of appreciation. Even, he thought, of a kind of solace, for she *was* sympathetic, and she accepted things about his recent moods that only irritated Mae.

Perhaps he had seen everything coming.

Once, they stood talking for more than an hour in the parking lot outside the courthouse, she leaning on her folded arms in the open door of her small blue sports car, he with the backs of his thighs against the shining fender of someone's Cadillac. He had gone home to explain his lateness to Mae, feeling as he lied about being detained in his office the first real pangs of guilt, along with a certain delicious sense of being on the brink of a new, thrilling experience.

The affair commenced less than a week later. They went in her car to a motel outside the city. The motel was off the main road, an old establishment with a line of rooms like a stopped train — a row of sleeper cars. She paid for the room (she was single and had no accounts to explain to anyone), and for a while they sat on opposing beds and looked at each other.

"You sure you want to do this?" she said.

"No." He could barely breathe. "I've never done anything like this before."

"Oh, come on," she said.

"I haven't," he told her. "I've been a good husband for twenty-five years. I love my wife."

"Why are you here, then?"

"Sex," he said. "I can't stop thinking of you."

She smiled. "That's what I like about you. You're so straight with me."

"I'm scared," he said.

"Everybody is," she told him, removing her blouse. "Except the stupid and the insane."

There was a moment, just as they moved together, when he thought of Mae. He looked at the shadow of his own head on the sheet, through the silky, wrong-colored strands of her hair, and the room spun, seemed about to lift out of itself. Perhaps he was dying. But then she was uttering his name, and her sheer difference from Mae, her quick, bumptious energy and the strange, unrhythmical otherness of her there in the bed with him — wide hips and ruddiness, bone and breath and tongue and smell — obliterated thinking.

Later, lying on her side gazing at him, she traced the line of his jaw. "No guilt," she said.

"No."

"I love to look at you, you know it?"

"Me?"

"I like it that the pupils of your eyes don't touch the bottom lids. And you have long eyelashes."

He felt handsome. He was aware of his own face as being supple and strong and good to look at in her eyes.

Not an hour after this, seeing his own reflection in the bathroom mirror, he was astonished to find only himself, the same plain, middle-aged face.

Saturday was the day for household maintenance and upkeep. The day for errands. While he ran the mower, hauling and pushing it back and forth in the rows of blowing grass, he felt pacified somehow. He had forgotten the shoe, or he wasn't thinking about it. He knew Mae was inside, and he could predict with some accuracy what room she would be working in. Between loads of laundry, she would run the vacuum, mop the floors, and dust the furniture and knickknacks — every room in the house. Toward the middle of the morning, she would begin to prepare something for lunch. This had been the routine for all the years since the children left, and as he worked in the shaded earth which lined the front porch, digging the stalks of dead weeds out and tossing them into the field beyond the driveway, he entertained the idea that his vulnerability to the affair might be attributed in some way to the exodus of the children; he had felt so bereft in those first weeks and months of their absence.

But then, so had Mae.

He carried a bag of weeds and overturned sod down to the edge of the pond and dumped it, then spread the pile with his foot. Somewhere nearby was the *tunk tunk* of a frog in the dry knifegrass. The world kept insisting on itself.

She called him in to lunch. He crossed the field, and she waited for him on the back deck, wearing faded jeans and a light pullover, looking, in the brightness, quite flawlessly young — someone who had done nothing wrong.

"Find another shoe?" she asked him.

He shook his head. "Got rid of some weeds. It's such a pretty day."

"Why did you save the other one?"

He walked up on the deck, kicking the edge of the steps to get dried mud from his boots. "I guess I did save it."

"It was the first thing I saw when I went through the garage to put the garbage out."

"I don't know," he said.

The breeze had taken her hair and swept it across her face. She brushed at it, then opened the door for him. "You seem so unhappy. Is there something going on at work?"

"What would be going on at work? I'm not unhappy."

"Okay," she said, and her tone was decisive. She would say no more about it.

He said, "It just seemed strange to throw the thing away."

"One of the workmen probably left it," she said. "Or one of their girlfriends."

The kitchen smelled of dough. She had decided to make bread, had spent the morning doing that. In the living room, which he could see from the back door, were the magazines and newspapers of yesterday afternoon. The shirt he had taken off last night was still draped over the chair in the hallway leading into the bedroom. He suddenly felt very lighthearted and confident. He turned to her, reached over and touched her cheek. "Hey," he said.

She said, "What."

"Let's make love."

"Darling," she said.

They lay quiet in the stripe of shadow which fell across the bed. During their lovemaking he had felt a chill at his back, and as he'd often romantically strived to do when he was younger, he tried to empty his mind of anything but her physical being — the texture of her skin, the contours of her body, the faint lavender-soaped smell of her; her familiar lovely breathing presence. But his mind presented him with an image of the other woman, and finally he was lost, sinking, hearing his wife's murmuring voice, holding her in the shivering premonition of disaster, looking blindly at the room beyond the curve of the bed, as though it were the prospect one saw from high bluffs, the sheer edge of a cliff.

"Sweet," she said.

He couldn't speak. He lay back and sighed, hoping she took the sound as an indication of his pleasure in her. Part of him understood that this was all the result of having put the affair behind him; it was what he must weather to survive.

"Cecily called while you were weeding," she said.

He waited.

"I wanted to call you in, but she said not to."

"Is anything wrong?"

"Well," his wife said, "a little, yes."

He waited again.

She sighed. "She didn't want me to say anything to you."

"Then," he said, "maybe you shouldn't."

This made her turn to him, propping herself on one elbow. "We always tell each other everything."

He could not see through the cloudy, lighter green of her eyes in this light. Her questioning face revealed nothing.

"Don't we?" she said.

"We do."

She put one hand in his hair, combed the fingers through. "Cecily's afraid Will has a girlfriend at school. Well, he has a friend at school that Cecily's worried about. You know, they have more in common, all that."

"Do you think it's serious?" he managed.

"It's serious enough for her to worry about it, I guess. I told her not to."

He stared at the ceiling, with its constellations of varying light and shadow.

"Will's too single-minded to do any carrying on," she said. "He probably doesn't even know the other girl notices him."

"Is that what you told Cecily?"

"Something like that."

"Did you tell her to talk to Will about it?"

"Lord, no."

"I would've told her to talk to him."

"And put ideas in his head?"

"You don't mean that, Mae."

"I guess not. But there's no sense calling attention to it."

"I don't know," he said.

"It's not as if he's saving old shoes or anything."

"What?"

She patted his chest. "Just kidding you."

* * *

"Is it such an odd thing, putting that shoe in the garage?" he said.

They were in the kitchen, sitting at the table with the day's newspaper open before them. She had been working the crossword puzzle. The light of early afternoon shone in her newly brushed and pinned-back hair.

"Well?" he said.

She only glanced at him. "I was teasing you."

He got up and went out to the garage, took the shoe down from its place on the sill, and carried it to the garbage cans at the side of the house. The air was cooler here, out of the sun, like a pocket of the long winter. He put the shoe in the can and closed it, then returned to the kitchen. She hadn't moved from where she sat, still looking at the puzzle.

"I threw it away," he said.

Again, her eyes only grazed him. "Threw what away?"

"The shoe."

She stared. "What?"

"I threw the shoe away."

"I was just teasing you," she said, and a shadow seemed to cross her face.

He took his part of the paper into the living room. But he couldn't concentrate. The clock ticked on the mantel, the house creaked in the stirring breezes. Feeling unreasonably ill-tempered, he went back into the kitchen, where he brought the feather duster out of the pantry.

"What're you doing?" she said.

"I'm restless."

"Is it what I told you about Cecily?"

"Of course not." He felt the need to be forceful.

She shrugged and went back to her puzzle.

"Is something bothering you?" he asked.

She didn't even look up. "What would be bothering me?"

"Cecily."

"I told her it was nothing."

"You believe that?"

"Sure. I wouldn't *lie* to her."

In the living room, he dusted the surfaces, feathered across the polished wood of the mantel and along the gilt or black edges of photographs in their frames: his children in some uncannily recent-feeling summer of their growing up, posing arm in arm and facing into the sunlight; his own parents staring out from the shade of a porch in the country fifty years ago; Mae waving from the stern of a rented boat. When he was finished, he set the duster on the coffee table and lay back on the sofa. Could he have imagined that she was hinting at him? He heard her moving around in the other room, opening the refrigerator, pouring something.

"Want some milk?" she called.

"No, thanks," he called back.

"Sure?"

"Mae. I said no thanks."

She stood in the arched entrance to the room and regarded him. "I don't suppose your restlessness would take you to the dining room and family room as well."

"No," he said.

"Too bad."

When she started out, he said, "Where're you going?"

"I'm going to lie down and read awhile. Unless you have other ideas."

"Like what?" he said.

"I don't know. A movie?"

"I don't feel like it," he told her.

"Well, you said you were restless."

He could think of nothing to say. And it seemed to him that he'd caught something like a challenge in her gaze.

But then she yawned. "I'll probably fall asleep."

"I might go ahead and get the other rooms," he offered.

"Let it wait," she said, her voice perfectly friendly, perfectly without nuance. "Let's be lazy today."

He had ended the affair with little more than a hint; that was all it had taken. The always nervy and apparently blithe Edith had nevertheless more than once voiced a horror of being anyone's regret or burden, was highly conscious of what others thought about her, and while she obviously didn't mind being involved with a married man, didn't mind having others know this fact, she would go to lengths not to be seen in the light of a changed circumstance: the woman whose passion has begun to make her an object of embarrassment.

The hint he had dropped was only a plain expression of the complications he was living with. It happened without premeditation one afternoon following a quick, chaste tussle in the partly enclosed entrance of an out-of-business clothing store in the city. They'd had lunch with five other people, and had stayed behind to eat the restaurant's touted coffee cake. They were casually strolling in the direction of the courthouse when the opportunity of the store entrance presented itself, and they ducked out of sight of the rest of the street, embracing and kissing and looking out at the row of buildings opposite, feeling how impossible things were: they couldn't get a room anywhere now, there wasn't time. They stood apart, in the duress of knowing they would have to compose themselves. The roofs of the buildings were starkly defined by gray scudding clouds — the tattered beginning of a storm.

"It's getting so I feel like I can't keep up," he said.

Her eyes fixed him in their blue depths. "You're not talking about you and Mae, are you."

"I don't know what I'm talking about."

"Sure you do," she said. Then she took his hands. "Listen, it was fun. It was a fling. It never meant more than that."

"I don't understand," he told her.

Edith smiled. It was a harsh, knowing smile, the look of someone who knows she's divined the truth. "I think we both understand," she said. Then she let go of him and walked out into the increasing rain.

Two days later she took another job, at one of the district courts far out in the suburbs; she told everyone they knew that she had wanted out of the city for a long time, and indeed it turned out that her application to the new job was an old one, predating the affair. The opportunity had arisen, and she'd been thinking about it for weeks. This came out at the office party to bid her farewell. He stood with her and all the others, and wished her the best of luck. They were adults, and could accept and respect each other; it was as if everything that had happened between them was erased forever. They shook hands as the celebrating died down, and she put her arms around his neck, joking, calling him sexy.

The dark was coming later each night.

He went out on the deck and watched the sky turn to shades of violet and crimson, and behind him Mae had begun to prepare dinner. There were lights on in the other house. Two cars had pulled up. Dornberg heard music. As he watched, a pair drove up on a motorcycle — all roaring, dust-blown, the riders looking grafted to the machine like some sort of future species, with an insectile sheen about them, and a facelessness: the nylon tights and the polished black helmets through which no human features could be seen. When the motorcycle stopped, one rider got off, a woman — Dornberg could tell by the curve of the hips — who removed her helmet, shook her hair loose and cursed, then stalked off into the light of the half-finished porch, holding the helmet under her arm like a football. Her companion followed, still wearing his helmet.

Inside Dornberg's house, Mae made a sound, something like an exhalation that ended on a word. He turned, saw that she was standing in the entrance of the living room, in the glow of the television, gesturing to him.

"What?" he said, moving to the screen door.

"Speaking of your high-heeled shoe. Look at this."

He went in to her. On television, a newsman with an over-bright red tie was talking about the body of a woman that had been found in a pile of leaves and mud in a wooded section of the county. Dornberg listened to the serious, steady, reasonable news voice talking of murder. The picture cut away and the screen was blank for an instant, and when he heard the voice pronounce the name Edith before going on to say another last name, the name of some other girl, his heartbeat faltered. On the screen now was a photograph of this unfortunate woman, this coincidence, not *his* Edith, some poor stranger, twenty-five years old, wearing a ski sweater, a bright, college-picture smile, and brown hair framing a tanned face. But the moment had shocked him, and the shock was still traveling along the nerves in his skin as Mae spoke. "You don't suppose —"

"No," he said, before he could think. "It's not her."

His wife stared at him. He saw her out of the corner of his eye as he watched the unfolding story of the body that was in tennis shoes and jeans — the tennis shoes and part of a denim cuff showing as men gently laid it down in a fold of black plastic.

"Tennis shoes," he managed. But his voice caught.

She still stared at him. On the screen, the newsman exuded professional sincerity, wide-eyed, half frowning. Behind him, in a riot of primary colors and with cartoonish exaggeration, was the representation of a human hand holding a pistol, firing.

Mae walked into the kitchen.

He called after her. "Need help?"

She didn't answer. He waited a moment, trying to decide how he should proceed. The damage done, the television had shifted again, showing beer being poured into an iced glass in light that gave it impossibly alluring hues of amber and gold. Already the world of pure sensation and amusement had moved on to something else. He switched the TV off, some part of him imagining, as always, that it went off all over the country when he did so.

In the kitchen, she had got last night's pasta out, and was breaking up a head of lettuce.

"What should I do?" he asked, meaning to be helpful about dinner, but he was immediately aware of the other context for these words. "Should I set the table?" he added quickly.

"Oh," she said, glancing at him. "It's fine." The look she had given him was almost shy; it veered from him and he saw that her hands shook.

He stepped to the open back door. By accident, then, she

knew. All the months of secrecy were done. And he could seek forgiveness. When he understood this, his own guilty elation closed his throat and made it difficult to speak. Outside, in the dusk beyond the edge of the field, from the lighted half-finished house, the sound of guitar music came.

"Think I'll go out on the deck," he told her.

"I'll call you when it's ready." Her voice was precariously even, barely controlled.

"Honey," he said.

"I'll call you."

"Mae."

She stopped. She was simply standing there, head bowed, disappointment and sorrow in the set of her jaw, the weary slope of her shoulders, waiting for him to go on. And once more he was watching her, this person who had come all the long way with him from his youth, and who knew him well enough to understand that he had broken their oldest promise to each other — not the one to be faithful so much as the one to honor and protect, for he had let it slip, and he had felt the elation of being free of the burden of it. It came to him then: the whole day had been somehow the result of his guilty need to unburden himself, starting with the high-heeled shoe. And there was nothing to say. Nothing else to tell her, nothing to soothe or explain, deflect or bring her closer. In his mind the days ahead stretched into vistas of quiet. Perhaps she might even decide to leave him.

"What are you thinking?" he managed to ask.

She shrugged. Nothing he might find to say in this moment would be anything he could honestly expect her to believe.

"Are you okay?" he said.

Now she did look at him. "Yes."

"I'll be out here."

She didn't answer.

He stepped out. The moon was rising, a great red disk above the trees and the pond. A steady, fragrant breeze blew, cool as the touch of metal on his cheek. The music had stopped from the other house, though the lights still burned in the windows.

Behind him, only slightly more emphatic than usual, was the small clatter of plates and silverware being placed. He watched the other house for a while, in a kind of pause, a stillness, a zone of inner silence, like the nullity of shock. Yet there was no denying the stubborn sense of deliverance which breathed through him.

When something shattered in the kitchen, he turned and saw her walk out of the room. He waited a moment, then quietly stepped inside. She had broken a wine glass; it was lying in pieces on the counter where it had fallen. He put the smaller pieces into the cupped largest one and set it down in the trash, then made his way upstairs and along the hall toward the bedroom. He went slowly. There seemed an oddly tranquilizing aspect about motion itself. It was as if he were being pulled back from disaster by the simple force of sensible actions: cleaning up broken glass, climbing stairs, mincing along a dimly lighted hallway.

She had turned the blankets back on the bed but was sitting at her dressing table, brushing her hair.

"Aren't you going to eat?" he said.

"I broke one of the good wine glasses."

"I'm not hungry either," he told her.

She said nothing.

"Mae. Do you want to talk about it?"

Without looking at him, she said, "Talk about what?"

He waited.

"We only have two left," she said. "I just hate to see the old ones get broken."

"Never again," he said. "I swear to you."

"It happens," she told him. "And it's always the heirlooms."

"How long have you known?" he said.

"Known?"

Again, he waited.

"You've been so strange all day. What're you talking about?"

He understood now that the burden had been returned to him, and he was not going to be allowed to let it slip.

"I guess I'll go back down and watch some television," he said.

She kept brushing her hair.

Downstairs, he put the uneaten dinner away, then turned the television on and stood for a minute in the uproar of voices and music — a huge chorus of people singing about a bank. Finally he walked out on the deck again. From the unfinished house came the hyperbolic percussion of an electronic synthesizer. Shadows danced in the windows, people in the uncomplicated hour of deciding on one another. A moment later, he realized that Mae had come back downstairs. She was standing in the kitchen in her bathrobe, pouring herself a glass of water. She glanced at him, glanced in his direction; he was uncertain if she could see him where he stood. She did not look unhappy or particularly distressed; her demeanor was somehow practical, as though she had just completed an unpleasant task, a thing that had required effort but was finished, behind her. Seeing this sent a little thrill of fear through him, and then he was simply admiring her in that light that was so familiar, the woman of this house, at evening.

Quietly, feeling the need, for some reason, to hurry, he stepped down into the grass and walked out of the border of the light, toward the pond. He did not go far, but stood very still, facing the column of shimmering moonlight on the water and the four bright, curtainless windows in that house where the music grew louder and louder. He no longer quite heard it. Though the whole vast bowl of the night seemed to reverberate with drums and horns, he was aware only of the silence behind him, listening for some sound of his wife's attention, hoping that she might call him, say his name, remind him, draw him back to her from the darkness.

Tandolfo
the Great

"TANDOLFO," he says to his own image in the mirror over the bathroom sink. "She loves you not, oh, she doesn't, doesn't, doesn't."

He's put the makeup on, packed the bag of tricks — including the rabbit that he calls Chi-Chi, and the bird, the attention getter, Witch. He's to do a birthday party for some five-year-old on the other side of the river. A crowd of babies, and the adults waiting around for him to screw up — this is going to be one of those tough ones.

He has fortified himself, and he feels ready. He isn't particularly worried about it. But there's a little something else he has to do first. Something on the order of the embarrassingly ridiculous: he has to make a delivery.

This morning at the local bakery he picked up a big pink wedding cake, with its six tiers and scalloped edges and its miniature bride and groom on top. He'd ordered it on his own; he'd taken the initiative, planning to offer it to a young woman he works with. He managed somehow to set the thing on the back seat of the car, and when he got home he found a note from her announcing, excited and happy, that she's engaged. The man she'd had such difficulty with has had a change of heart; he wants to get married after all. She's going off to Houston to live. She loves her dear old Tandolfo with a big kiss and a hug always, and she knows he'll have every happiness. She's so thankful for his friendship. Her magic man. Her sweet clown. She actually drove over here and, finding him gone, left the note for him, folded under the door knocker — her notepaper with the tangle of flowers at the top. She wants him to call her, come by as soon as he can, to help celebrate. *Please*, she says. *I want to give you a big hug.* He read this and then walked out to stand on the sidewalk and look at the cake in its place on the back seat of the car.

"Good God," he said.

He'd thought he would put the clown outfit on, deliver the cake in person, an elaborate proposal to a girl he's never even kissed. He's a little unbalanced, and he knows it. Over the months of their working together at Bailey & Brecht department store, he's built up tremendous feelings of loyalty and yearning toward her. He thought she felt it, too. He interpreted gestures — her hand lingering on his shoulder when he made her laugh; her endearments, tinged as they seemed to be with a kind of sadness, as if she were afraid for what the world might do to someone so romantic.

"You sweet clown," she said. She said it a lot. And she talked to him about her ongoing sorrows, the man she'd been in love with who kept waffling about getting married, wanting no commitments. Tandolfo, a.k.a. Rodney Wilbury, told her that he hated men who weren't willing to run the risks of love. Why, he personally was the type who'd always believed in marriage and children, lifelong commitments. It was true that he had caused difficulties for himself, and life was a disappointment so far, but he believed in falling in love and starting a family. She didn't hear him. It all went right through her, like white noise on the radio. For weeks he had come around to visit her, had invited her to watch him perform. She confided in him, and he thought of movies where the friend stays loyal and is a good listener, and eventually gets the girl: they fall in love. He put his hope in that. He was optimistic; he'd ordered and bought the cake, and apparently the whole time, all through the listening and being noble with her, she thought of it as nothing more than friend-ship, accepting it from him because she was accustomed to being offered friendship.

Now he leans close to the mirror to look at his own eyes through the makeup. They look clear enough. "Loves you ab-solutely not. You must be crazy. You must be the Great Tan-dolfo."

Yes.

Twenty-six years old, out-of-luck Tandolfo. In love. With a great oversized cake in the back seat of his car. It's Sunday, a cool April day. He's a little inebriated. That's the word he pre-fers. It's polite; it suggests something faintly silly. Nothing could be sillier than to be dressed like this in broad daylight and to go driving across the bridge into Virginia to put on a magic show. Nothing could be sillier than to have spent all that money on a completely useless purchase — a cake six tiers high. Maybe fifteen pounds of sugar.

When he has made his last inspection of the clown face in the mirror, and checked the bag of tricks and props, he goes to his front door and looks through the screen at the architectural shadow of the cake in the back seat. The inside of the car will smell like icing for days. He'll have to keep the windows open even if it rains; he'll go to work smelling like confectionery delights. The whole thing makes him laugh. A wedding cake. He steps out of the house and makes his way in the late after-noon sun down the sidewalk to the car. As if they have been waiting for him, three boys come skating down from the top of the hill. He has the feeling that if he tried to sneak out like this at two in the morning, someone would come by and see him anyway. "Hey, Rodney," one boy says. "I mean, Tandolfo."

Tandolfo recognizes him. A neighborhood boy, a tough. Just the kind to make trouble, just the kind with no sensitivity to the suffering of others. "Leave me alone or I'll turn you into spa-ghetti," he says.

"Hey guys, it's Tandolfo the Great." The boy's hair is a bright blond color, and you can see through it to his scalp.

"Scram," Tandolfo says. "Really."

"Aw, what's your hurry, man?"

"I've just set off a nuclear device," Tandolfo says with grave seriousness. "It's on a timer. Poof."

"Do a trick for us," the blond one says. "Where's that scurvy rabbit of yours?"

"I gave it the week off." Someone, last winter, poisoned the first Chi-Chi. He keeps the cage indoors now. "I'm in a hurry. No rabbit to help with the driving."

But they're interested in the cake now. "Hey, what's that? Jesus, is that real?"

"Just stay back." Tandolfo gets his cases into the trunk and hurries to the driver's side door. The three boys are peering into the back seat. To the blond boy he says, "You're going to go bald, aren't you?"

"Hey man, a cake. Can we have a piece of it?" one of them says.

"Back off," Tandolfo says.

Another says, "Come on, Tandolfo."

"Hey, Tandolfo, I saw some guys looking for you, man. They said you owed them money."

He gets in, ignoring them, and starts the car.

"Sucker," the blond one says.

"Hey man, who's the cake for?"

He drives away, thinks of himself leaving them in a cloud of exhaust. Riding through the green shade, he glances in the rear-view mirror and sees the clown face, the painted smile. It makes him want to laugh. He tells himself he's his own cliché — a clown with a broken heart. Looming behind him is the cake, like a passenger in the back seat. The people in the cake store had offered it to him in a box; he had made them give it to him like this, on a cardboard slab. It looks like it might melt.

He drives slow, worried that it might sag, or even fall over. He has always believed viscerally that gestures mean everything. When he moves his hands and brings about the effects that amaze little children, he feels larger than life, unforgettable. He learned the magic while in high school, as a way of making friends, and though it didn't really make him any friends, he's been practicing it ever since. It's an extra source of income, and lately income has had a way of disappearing too quickly. He has been in some travail, betting the horses, betting the sports events. He's hung over all the time. There have been several polite warnings at work. He has managed so far to tease everyone out of the serious looks, the cool study of his face. The fact is, people like him in an abstract way, the way they like distant clownish figures: the comedian whose name they can't remember. He can see it in their eyes. Even the rough characters after his loose change have a certain sense of humor about it.

He's a phenomenon, a subject of conversation.

There's traffic on Key Bridge, and he's stuck for a while. It becomes clear that he'll have to go straight to the birthday party. Sitting behind the wheel of the car with his cake behind him, he becomes aware of people in other cars noticing him. In the car to his left, a girl stares, chewing gum. She waves, rolls her window down. Two others are with her, one in the back seat. "Hey," she says. He nods, smiles inside what he knows is the clown smile. His teeth will look dark against the makeup.

"Where's the party?" she says.

But the traffic moves again. He concentrates. The snarl is on the other side of the bridge, construction of some kind. He can see the cars in a line, waiting to go up the hill into Roslyn and beyond. Time is beginning to be a consideration. In his glove box he has a flask of bourbon. More fortification. He reaches over and takes it out, looks around himself. No police anywhere. Just the idling cars and people tuning their radios or arguing or simply staring out as if at some distressing event. The smell of the cake is making him woozy. He takes a swallow of the bourbon, then puts it away. The car with the girls in it goes by in the left lane, and they are not looking at him. He watches them go on ahead. He's in the wrong lane again; he can't remember a time when *his* lane was the only one moving. He told her once that he considered himself of the race of people who gravitate to the non-moving lanes of highways, and who cause green lights to turn yellow merely by approaching them. She took the idea and ran with it, saying she was of the race of people who emit enzymes which instill a sense of impending doom in marriageable young men.

"No," Tandolfo/Rodney said. "I'm living proof that isn't so. I have no such fear, and I'm with you."

"But you're of the race of people who make mine relax all the enzymes."

"You're not emitting the enzymes now. I see."

"No," she said. "It's only with marriageable young men."

"I emit enzymes that prevent people like you from seeing that I'm a marriageable young man."

"I'm too relaxed to tell," she said, and touched his shoulder. A plain affectionate moment that gave him tossing nights and fever.

Because of the traffic, he's late to the birthday party. He gets out of the car and two men come down to greet him. He keeps his face turned away, remembering too late the breath mints in his pocket.

"Jesus," one of the men says, "look at this. Hey, who ordered the cake? I'm not paying for the cake."

"The cake stays," Tandolfo says.

"What does he mean, it stays? Is that a trick?"

They're both looking at him. The one spoken to must be the birthday boy's father — he's wearing a party cap that says DAD. He has long, dirty-looking strands of brown hair jutting out from the cap, and there are streaks of sweaty grit on the sides of his face. "So you're the Great Tandolfo," he says, extending a meaty red hand. "Isn't it hot in that makeup?"

"No, sir."

"We've been playing volleyball."

"You've exerted yourselves."

They look at him. "What do you do with the cake?" the one in the DAD cap asks.

"Cake's not part of the show, actually."

"You just carry it around with you?"

The other man laughs. He's wearing a T-shirt with a smiley face on the chest. "This ought to be some show," he says.

They all make their way across the lawn, to the porch of the house. It's a big party, bunting everywhere and children gathering quickly to see the clown.

"Ladies and gentlemen," says the man in the DAD cap. "I give you Tandolfo the Great."

Tandolfo isn't ready yet. He's got his cases open, but he needs a table to put everything on. The first trick is where he releases the bird; he'll finish with the best trick, in which the rabbit appears as if from a pan of flames. This always draws a gasp, even from the adults: the fire blooms in the pan, down goes the "lid" — it's the rabbit's tight container — the latch is tripped, and the skin of the lid lifts off. Voilà! Rabbit. The fire is put out by the fireproof cage bottom. He's gotten pretty good at making the switch, and if the crowd isn't too attentive — as children often are not — he can perform certain sleight-of-hand tricks with some style. But he needs a table, and he needs time to set up.

The whole crowd of children is seated in front of their parents, on either side of the doorway into the house. Tandolfo is standing on the porch, his back to the stairs, and he's been introduced.

"Hello boys and girls," he says, and bows. "Tandolfo needs a table."

"A table," one of the women says. The adults simply regard him. He sees light sweaters, shapely hips, and wild hair; he sees beer cans in tight fists, heavy jowls, bright ice-blue eyes. A little row of faces, and one elderly face. He feels more inebriated than he likes, and tries to concentrate.

"Mommy, I want to touch him," one child says.

"Look at the cake," says another, who gets up and moves to the railing on Tandolfo's right and trains a new pair of shiny binoculars on the car. "Do we get some cake?"

"There's cake," says the man in the DAD cap. "But not that cake. Get down, Ethan."

"I want that cake."

"Get down. This is Teddy's birthday."

"Mommy, I want to touch him."

"I need a table, folks. I told somebody that over the telephone."

"He did say he needed a table. I'm sorry," says a woman who is probably the birthday boy's mother. She's quite pretty, leaning in the door frame with a sweater tied to her waist.

"A table," says still another woman. Tandolfo sees the birthmark on her mouth, which looks like a stain. He thinks of this woman as a child in school, with this difference from other children, and his heart goes out to her.

"I need a table," he says to her, his voice as gentle as he can make it.

"What's he going to do, perform an operation?" says DAD.

It amazes Tandolfo how easily people fall into talking about him as though he were an inanimate object or something on a television screen. "The Great Tandolfo can do nothing until he gets a table," he says with as much mysteriousness and drama as he can muster under the circumstances.

"I want that cake out there," says Ethan, still at the porch railing. The other children start talking about cake and ice cream, and the big cake Ethan has spotted; there's a lot of confusion and restlessness. One of the smaller children, a girl in a blue dress, approaches Tandolfo. "What's your name?" she says, swaying slightly, her hands behind her back.

"Go sit down," he says to her. "We have to sit down or Tandolfo can't do his magic."

In the doorway, two of the men are struggling with a folding card table. It's one of those rickety ones with the skinny legs, and it probably won't do.

"That's kind of shaky, isn't it?" says the woman with the birthmark.

"I said, Tandolfo needs a sturdy table, boys and girls."

There's more confusion. The little girl has come forward and taken hold of his pant leg. She's just standing there holding it, looking up at him. "We have to go sit down," he says, bending to her, speaking sweetly, clownlike. "We have to do what Tandolfo wants."

Her small mouth opens wide, as if she's trying to yawn, and with pale eyes quite calm and staring she emits a screech, an ear-piercing, non-human shriek that brings everything to a stop. Tandolfo/Rodney steps back, with his amazement and his inebriate heart. Everyone gathers around the girl, who continues to scream, less piercing now, her hands fisted at her sides, those pale eyes closed tight.

"What happened?" the man in the DAD cap wants to know. "Where the hell's the magic tricks?"

"I told you, all I needed is a *table*."

"What'd you say to her to make her cry?" DAD indicates the little girl, who is giving forth a series of broken, grief-stricken howls.

"I want magic tricks," the birthday boy says, loud. "Where's the magic tricks?"

"Perhaps if we moved the whole thing inside," the woman with the birthmark says, fingering her left ear and making a face.

The card table has somehow made its way to Tandolfo, through the confusion and grief. The man in the DAD cap sets it down and opens it.

"There," he says, as if his point has been made.

In the next moment, Tandolfo realizes that someone's removed the little girl. Everything's relatively quiet again, though her cries are coming through the walls of one of the rooms inside the house. There are perhaps fifteen children, mostly seated before him, and five or six men and women behind them, or kneeling with them. "Okay, now," DAD says. "Tandolfo the Great."

"Hello, little boys and girls," Tandolfo says, deciding that the table will have to suffice. "I'm happy to be here. Are you glad to see me?" A general uproar commences. "Well, good," he says. "Because just look what I have in my magic bag." And with a flourish he brings out the hat that he will release Witch from. The bird is encased in a fold of shiny cloth, pulsing there. He can feel it. He rambles on, talking fast, or trying to, and when the time comes to reveal the bird, he almost flubs it. But Witch flaps his wings and makes enough of a commotion to distract even the adults, who applaud and urge the stunned children to follow suit. "Isn't that wonderful," Tandolfo hears. "Out of no-where."

"He had it hidden away," says the birthday boy, managing to temper his astonishment. He's clearly the type who heaps scorn on those things he can't understand, or own.

"Now," Tandolfo says, "for my next spell, I need a helper from the audience." He looks right at the birthday boy — round face, short nose, freckles. Bright red hair. Little green eyes. The whole countenance speaks of glutted appetites and sloth. This kid could be on Roman coins, an emperor. He's not used to being compelled to do anything, but he seems eager for a chance to get into the act. "How about you," Tandolfo says to him.

The others, led by their parents, cheer.

The birthday boy gets to his feet and makes his way over the bodies of the other children to stand with Tandolfo. In order for the trick to work, Tandolfo must get everyone watching the birthday boy, and there's a funny hat he keeps in the bag for this purpose. "Now," he says to the boy, "since you're part of the show, you have to wear a costume." He produces the hat as if from behind the boy's ear. Another cheer goes up. He puts the hat on the boy's head and adjusts it, crouching down. The green eyes stare impassively at him; there's no hint of awe or fascination in them. "There we are," he says. "What a handsome fellow."

But the birthday boy takes the hat off.

"We have to wear the hat to be onstage."

"Ain't a stage," the boy says.

"Well, but hey," Tandolfo says for the benefit of the adults. "Didn't you know that all the world's a stage?" He tries to put the hat on him again, but the boy moves from under his reach and slaps his hand away. "We have to wear the hat," Tandolfo says, trying to control his anger. "We can't do the magic without our magic hats." He tries once more, and the boy waits until the hat is on, then simply removes it and holds it behind him, shying away when Tandolfo tries to retrieve it. The noise of the others now sounds like the crowd at a prizefight; there's a contest going on, and they're enjoying it. "Give Tandolfo the hat. We want magic, don't we?"

"Do the magic," the boy demands.

"I'll do the magic if you give me the hat."

"I won't."

Nothing. No support from the adults. Perhaps if he weren't a little tipsy; perhaps if he didn't feel ridiculous and sick at heart and forlorn, with his wedding cake and his odd mistaken romance, his loneliness, which he has always borne gracefully and with humor, and his general dismay; perhaps if he were to find it in himself to deny the sudden, overwhelming sense of the unearned affection given this lumpish, slovenly version of stupid complacent spoiled satiation standing before him — he might've simply gone on to the next trick.

Instead, at precisely that moment when everyone seems to pause, he leans down and says, "Give me the hat, you little prick."

The green eyes widen.

The quiet is heavy with disbelief. Even the small children can tell that something's happened to change everything.

"Tandolfo has another trick," Rodney says, loud, "where he makes the birthday boy pop like a balloon. Especially if he's a fat birthday boy."

A stirring among the adults.

"Especially if he's an ugly slab of gross flesh like this one here."

"Now just a minute," says DAD.

"*Pop*," Rodney says to the birthday boy, who drops the hat and then, seeming to remember that defiance is expected, makes a face. Sticks out his tongue. Rodney/Tandolfo is quick with his hands by training, and he grabs the tongue.

"Awk," the boy says. "Aw-aw-aw."

"Abracadabra!" Rodney lets go and the boy falls backward onto the lap of one of the other children. More cries. "Whoops, time to sit down," says Rodney. "Sorry you had to leave so soon."

Very quickly, he's being forcibly removed. They're rougher than gangsters. They lift him, punch him, tear at his costume — even the women. Someone hits him with a spoon. The whole scene boils over onto the lawn, where someone has released Chi-Chi from her case. Chi-Chi moves about wide-eyed, hopping between running children, evading them, as Tandolfo the Great cannot evade the adults. He's being pummeled, because he keeps trying to return for his rabbit. And the adults won't let him off the curb. "Okay," he says finally, collecting himself. He wants to let them know he's not like this all the time; wants to say it's circumstances, grief, personal pain hidden inside seeming brightness and cleverness. He's a man in love, humiliated, wrong about everything. He wants to tell them, but he can't speak for a moment, can't even quite catch his breath. He stands in the middle of the street, his funny clothes torn, his face bleeding, all his magic strewn everywhere. "I would at least like to collect my rabbit," he says, and is appalled at the absurd sound of it — its huge difference from what he intended to say. He straightens, pushes the grime from his face, adjusts the clown nose, and looks at them. "I would say that even though I wasn't as patient as I could've been, the adults have not comported themselves well here," he says.

"Drunk," one of the women says.

Almost everyone's chasing Chi-Chi now. One of the older boys approaches, carrying Witch's case. Witch looks out the air hole, impervious, quiet as an idea. And now one of the men, someone Rodney hasn't noticed before, an older man clearly wearing a hairpiece, brings Chi-Chi to him. "Bless you," Rodney says, staring into the man's sleepy, deploring eyes.

"I don't think we'll pay you," the man says. The others are filing back into the house, herding the children before them.

Rodney speaks to the man. "The rabbit appears out of fire."

The man nods. "Go home and sleep it off, kid."

"Right. Thank you."

He puts Chi-Chi in his compartment, stuffs everything in its place in the trunk. Then he gets in the car and drives away. Around the corner he stops, wipes off what he can of the makeup; it's as if he's trying to remove the stain of bad opinion and disapproval. Nothing feels any different. He drives to the suburban street where she lives with her parents, and by the time he gets there it's almost dark.

The houses are set back in the trees. He sees lighted windows, hears music, the sound of children playing in the yards. He parks the car and gets out. A breezy April dusk. "I am Tandolfo the soft-hearted," he says. "Hearken to me." Then he sobs. He can't believe it. "Jeez," he says. "Lord." He opens the back door of the car, leans in to get the cake. He'd forgot how heavy it is. Staggering with it, making his way along the sidewalk, intending to leave it on her doorstep, he has an inspiration. Hesitating only for the moment it takes to make sure there are no cars coming, he goes out and sets it down in the middle of the street. Part of the top sags from having bumped his shoulder as he pulled it off the back seat. The bride and groom are almost supine, one on top of the other. He straightens them, steps back and looks at it. In the dusky light it looks blue. It sags just right, with just the right angle expressing disappointment and sorrow. Yes, he thinks. This is the place for it. The aptness of it, sitting out like this, where anyone might come by and splatter it all over creation, makes him feel a faint sense of release, as if he were at the end of a story. Everything will be all right if he can think of it that way. He's wiping his eyes, thinking of moving to another town. Failures are beginning to catch up to him, and he's still aching in love. He thinks how he has suffered the pangs of failure and misadventure, but in this painful instance there's symmetry, and he will make the one eloquent gesture — leaving a wedding cake in the middle of the road, like a sugar-icinged pylon. Yes.

He walks back to the car, gets in, pulls around, and backs into the driveway of the house across the street from hers. Leaving the engine idling, he rolls the window down and rests his arm on the sill, gazing at the incongruous shape of the cake there in the falling dark. He feels almost glad, almost, in some strange inexpressible way, vindicated. He imagines what she might do if she saw him here, imagines that she comes running from her house, calling his name, looking at the cake and admiring it. He conjures a picture of her, attacking the tiers of pink sugar, and the muscles of his abdomen tighten. But then this all gives way to something else: images of destruction, of flying dollops of icing. He's surprised to find that he wants her to stay where she is, doing whatever she's doing. He realizes that what he wants — and for the moment all he really wants — is what he now has: a perfect vantage point from which to watch oncoming cars. Turning the engine off, he waits, concentrating on the one thing. He's a man imbued with interest, almost peaceful with it — almost, in fact, happy with it — sitting there in the quiet car and patiently awaiting the results of his labor.

Evening

HE WAS UP HIGH, reaching with the brush, painting the eaves of the house, thinking about how it would be to let go, simply fall, a man losing his life in an accident — no humiliation in that. He paused, considering this, feeling the wobbly lightness of the aluminum ladder, and then he heard the car pull in. His daughter Susan's red Yugo. Susan got out, pushed the hair back from her brow. She looked at him, then waved peremptorily and set about getting Elaine out of the car seat. It took a few moments. Elaine was four, very precocious, feisty, and lately quite a lot of trouble.

"I want my doll."

"You left it at home."

"Well, I want it."

"Elaine, *please*."

Their contending voices came to him, sounds from the world; they brought him back. "Hello," he called.

"Tell Granddaddy hello."

"Don't want to."

Elaine followed her mother along the sidewalk, pouting, her thumb in her mouth. Even the sight of Granddaddy on a ladder in the sky failed to break the dark mood. Her mother knelt down and ran a handkerchief over the tears and smudges of her face.

"I'll be right down," he said.

"Stay," said his daughter in a tired voice.

He could see that she looked disheveled and overworked, someone not terribly careful about her appearance: a young woman with a child, going through the turmoil following a divorce. He had read somewhere that if you put all the world's troubles in a great pile and gave everyone a choice, each would probably walk away with his own.

"Mom inside?" his daughter asked.

"She went into town. I don't think she'll be gone long."

"What're you doing up there?"

"Little touch-up," he said.

"When did she leave?"

He dipped the brush into the can of paint. "Maybe ten minutes ago. She went to get something for us to eat."

"Is the door open?"

"Go on in," he said. "I'll be down in a minute."

"It's okay," she said. "Finish what you're doing. You don't have a lot of light left."

"Susan, I wouldn't get it all if I had a whole day."

"Stay there," she told him, and went on inside with Elaine, who, a moment later, came back out and stood watching him, her hands clasped behind her back.

"You're up high," she said.

"Think so?"

"Granddaddy?"

"Just a minute, honey."

He waited, listening. Susan was on the phone. He could not distinguish words, but he heard anger in the tone, and of course he was in the usual awkward position of not knowing what was expected, how he should proceed.

"I can come up if I want to, right?" Elaine said.

"But I'm not staying," he told her, starting down.

"Are you going to bring me up there?" she said.

He said, "It's scary here. The wind's blowing, and it's so high an eagle tried to build a nest in my hair."

"An eagle?"

"Don't you know what an eagle is?"

"Is it like a bird?"

When he had got to the ground, he laid the paint can, with the paintbrush across the lidless top, on the bottom step of the porch, then turned and lifted her into his arms. Everything, even this, required effort: the travail of an inner battle which he was always on the point of losing.

"Goodness," he said. "You're getting so big."

She was a solid, dark-eyed girl with sweet-smelling breath, and creases appeared on her cheeks when she was excited or happy.

"Is an eagle like a bird or not?"

"An eagle," he said, turning with her, "is exactly like a bird. And you know why?" A part of him was watching himself: a man stuffed with death, charming his granddaughter.

She stared at him, smiling.

"Because it *is* a bird," he said, extending his arms so she rode above his head.

"Don't," she called out, but she was still smiling.

He brought her back down. "I want a kiss. You don't have a kiss for me?"

"No," she said in the tone she used when she meant to be shy with him.

"Are you in a bad mood?"

She shook her head, but the smile was gone.

"You don't even have a kiss for me?"

She sighed. "Well, Granddaddy, I can't because I'm just exhausted."

"You poor old thing," he said, resisting the temptation to suppose she had half-consciously divined something from merely looking into his eyes.

"Put me down now," she said. "Okay?"

He did so, kissed the top of her head, the shining hair. She went off into the yard, stopping to examine the white blooms of clover dotting that part of the lawn. It was her way. She enjoyed being watched, and this was a ritual the two of them had often played out together. He would observe her and try to seem puzzled and curious, and occasionally she would glance his way, obviously wanting to make certain of his undivided attention. Sometimes they would play a game in which they both narrowly missed each other's gaze. They would repeat the pattern until she began to laugh, and then all the motions would become exaggerated.

Now she held her dress out from her sides, facing him. "Granddaddy, what do you think of me?"

Pierced to his heart, he said, "I think you're so beautiful."

She sighed. "I know."

Behind him, in the house, he heard Susan's voice.

"Mommy's mad at Daddy again," Elaine said.

She stood there thinking, and then she did something he recognized as a characteristic gesture, a jittery motion she wasn't quite aware of: her long, dark hair hung down on either side of her face, and occasionally she reached up with her left hand and tucked the strands of it behind the ear on that side of her head. The one ear showed.

In the house, Susan was shouting into the phone. "I don't care about that. I don't care."

"Daddy was cussing," Elaine said. "It made Mommy cry."

Susan's voice came from inside the house. "I don't care what anybody has or hasn't got."

"Granddaddy," Elaine said. "You're not watching me."

"Okay, baby," he said, "I'm watching you."

"See my dress?"

"Beautiful," he said.

"Granddaddy, are you coming with me?" Again, she tucked the strands of hair behind the one ear. He walked over to her and, when she reached for it, gave her his hand.

"Where are we going?"

"Oh, for a walk."

She took him in a wide circle, around the perimeter of the front yard.

"Isn't this nice," she said.

A girl the bulk of whose life would be led in the next century. The thought made him pause.

"Granddaddy, come on," she said impatiently. "Men are so slow."

"I'm sorry," he told her. "I'll try to do better."

Her mother's voice came to them from the house. "You can do without a radio in your car."

"Mommy wants to see Grandmom," Elaine said.

"What about me?" he said, meaning to try teasing her.

"Grandmom," Elaine said with an air of insistence.

There had been times during the months of his daughter's recent troubles when he had sensed a kind of antipathy in her attitude toward him which was almost abstract, as though in addition to other complications she had come to view him only in light of his gender. He had even spoken to his wife about this. "I suppose since I'm a representative of the same sex to which her ex-husband belongs, I'm guilty by association."

"Stop that," his wife said. "She's upset, and she wants to talk to her mother. There's nothing wrong with that. Besides, don't you think it's time you stopped interpreting everything to be about you?"

"Oh, no," he said. "I'm clearly not in this at all. I'm the ineffectual, insensitive Daddy kept in the dark."

"Come on, William."

His wife's name was Elizabeth. But for almost forty years he had been calling her Cat, for the first three letters of her middle name, which was Catherine. Some of their friends did so as well, and she signed her cards and letters with a cartoon cat, long-whiskered and smiling, a decidedly wicked look in its eye. She had even had the name printed on the face of the checkbook: it read *William and Cat Wallingham*. They were one of the few married couples in Stuart Circle Court these days. "The only traditional couple," William would say, "in this cul-de-sac." And in what his wife and daughter would indicate was his way of joking at the wrong time and with the wrong words, he would go on to point out that this was almost literally true. The college nearby, where he had spent the bulk of his working life as an administrator, had begun to expand in recent years, and the neighborhood seemed always to be shifting; houses were going up for sale, or being rented. The tenants came and went without much communication. Living arrangements seemed confused or uncertain. And there were no older couples nearby anymore.

The only other married people in the cul-de-sac, as far as they knew, were a stormy young couple who had already been through two trial separations, but who were quite helplessly in love with each other. The young woman had confided in Cat. Occasionally William saw this woman working in her small fenced yard — an attractive, slender girl wearing tight jeans and a smock, looking not much out of high school. He almost never saw the husband, whose job required travel. But it was often the case that they were in the middle of some turbulence or other, and sometimes Cat talked about them as if they were part of the family, important in her sphere of concerns. Last year, William would come home from work (it was the last one hundred days before his retirement; he had been counting them down on a calendar fixed to the wall in the den) and find Cat sitting in the living room with the young neighbor, teary-eyed, embarrassed to have him there, already getting up to excuse herself and go back to her difficult life.

When his daughter's marriage began to break, William found himself thinking of this couple across the way, their tumultuous separations and reconciliations, their fractious union that was apparently so . . . well, glib, and also, in some peculiar emotional way, serviceable. Or at least it seemed so from the distance of the other side of the street. He had felt a kind of amusement about them, waffling back and forth, ready to walk away from each other with the first imagined slight or defection, no matter their talk of love, their supposed passion. And during the crucial beginning of Susan's divorce, he'd found it hard to take her crisis seriously. It had felt so much the same, coming in to find Susan sitting there with the moist eyes and the hand-kerchief squeezed into her fist, showing the same anxiousness to get away from him. Perhaps Susan still held this all against him; and he knew he had seemed badly insensitive. In fact he had bungled everything, since he rather liked Susan's husband and honestly believed that the two of them were better together than apart. He had made these feelings known, and now that she was in the process of getting the divorce, she had distanced herself from him.

"Granddaddy," Elaine said, pulling him, then letting go. "I don't want to go for a walk anymore." She ran across the yard to the largest of two willow trees, under which there was an inner tube hung on a rope. Parting the drooping branches, she entered the shade there, and in a moment she'd put her head and chest through the inner tube. She lifted her small feet and suspended herself, swinging, obviously having forgotten him. He waited a minute, and when he was certain she was occupied, went into the house. It was cool in the dim hallway. Susan made a shadow at the other end, still talking on the phone. She did not look up as he approached.

"I know that," she said. "I know."

He waited.

"I don't care what he says. It's been late every month, and this is not amicable. This has ceased to be amicable."

He went back out onto the porch. Elaine had lost interest in the swing, was standing with her hands on it, staring out at the road, singing to herself. He walked along the front of the house to where the porch ended in flagstone stairs. His wife had planted rose bushes here, and they climbed the trellis he'd erected, forming a thorny arch under which he stood.

Part of his daily portion of trouble was that he had been having difficulty in the nights: his dreams were pervaded with a nameless dread. When he drifted off, it was with the knowl-edge that he would be awake with the dawn, feeling nothing of his old appetite for the freshest hours of the day, finding himself sapped of energy, vaguely fearful, sick at heart, and more gloomy than the day before.

"Get busy doing something," his wife had told him. "You were never the type to sit around and let things get the best of you."

No. Yet he couldn't bring himself to say the word aloud.

"I'm going to make an appointment for you."

"I'm not going to any damn head doctors. There's nothing wrong with me that I can't take care of myself."

He could not put his finger on exactly where or how this present misery had begun to take hold, but it had moved in him with the insidious incremental growth of a malignancy. The first inkling of it had come to him nearly a year ago, on his seventy-fourth birthday, when the thought occurred to him, almost casually, as though it concerned someone else, that he had gone beyond the age at which his father's life ended. He had the thought, marked it with little more than mild interest — he might even have mentioned it to Cat — and then he experienced a sudden, fierce gust of desolation, a taste of this awful gloom. The recognition had come, and what followed it had felt like a leveling force inside him. But that feeling passed, and there had been good days — wonderful days and good weeks — between then and now. He would not have believed that the thing could seep back, that it could blossom slowly in him, changing only for the worse. Tonight, it was nearly insupportable.

One of the tenets of the religion he had practiced most of his adult life was that if one kept up the habits of faith, then faith would be granted. He had hoped the same was true of just going through the days.

Susan came out and slammed the door shut behind her.

"Everything okay?" he managed.

She stirred, seemed to notice him, then looked out at the street. "I hate this time of day."

He thought she would go on to say more, and when she didn't, he searched for some response. But she had already left him, was striding over to Elaine. Perhaps she might be about to leave, and how badly he wanted not to be alone! When she lifted Elaine and put her back on the inner tube, he hurried over to them, eager to be hospitable. Elaine sat in the swing with her chubby legs straight out and demanded that she be pushed higher, faster. Susan obliged her. "Only for a little while," she said.

"Mom should be here any minute," William said.

"Where'd she go, anyway?"

"She was going to get some Chinese. Neither of us felt like doing anything in the kitchen. I had this — touching up to do."

"I don't want to get in the way of dinner," she said.

"Don't be absurd."

"Mommy, push me higher."

"I'm doing the best I can, Elaine."

"You didn't like the swings when you were Elaine's age," he said. "Do you remember?"

"I was a-f-r-a-i-d," Susan said. "I don't want her to be that way."

"Stop spelling," Elaine said.

"You be quiet and swing."

William said, "Do you remember when I used to push you in this swing?"

She touched his arm. "Do you know how often you ask me that kind of question?"

"You don't recall it, though."

"Do you recall asking me this same question last week?"

"Well," he said, "I guess I don't. No."

She frowned. "I'm teasing you."

"Well?" he said. "*Do* you remember?"

"I don't remember," she told him. "You dwell on things too much."

He said, "You sound like your mother."

"It's true. You've always been that way."

This irritated him. "Since the beginning of Time," he said.

"Men are such babies. Can't you take a little teasing?"

"Well, if I'm going to be asked to represent a whole sex every time I do any damn thing at all, I guess not."

"Oh, and I suppose you never talk about women that way."

"I always thought such talk was disrespectful."

"Okay, I won't tease, then. All right?"

They said nothing for a few moments.

"Was that Sam you were talking to on the phone?"

"At first."

"Higher," Elaine said.

"Hold on," said Susan.

He walked back to the porch and sat down on the bottom step, watching the two of them in the softening shade of the tree. The sun was nearing the line of dark horizon to the west, and through the haze it looked as though its flames were dying out. It was enormous, bigger than it ever seemed in midday. His daughter, still standing under the filamentous shade of the willow tree, turned to look at him, apparently just noticing that he had walked away from her. He put both hands on his knees, trying to appear satisfied and comfortable. But his heart was sinking. She walked over to stand before him. "Did you and Mom have a fight or something?" she asked.

"Not that I know of."

"Ha."

"We never fight anymore."

"Maybe you should."

"I can't think why." He smiled at her.

"You bicker all the time instead of fighting."

He said, "What's the difference, I wonder?" A moment later he said, "Are the two of you talking about me?"

"I didn't say that."

"What's there to talk about?" he said.

"Dad."

"We've been married almost forty years," he said. "What's there to talk about?"

"Are you saying you're bored?"

"Jesus," he said. "Are *we* going to have a fight?"

"I'm just asking."

"Is your mother bored?" he said.

"You don't think she'd tell me a thing like that, do you?"

"I was just asking."

"To tell you the truth, she doesn't talk about you at all."

"Well," he said, "I wouldn't. You know, there's not much to say."

"Do you still love each other?" his daughter asked suddenly. "Sam and I lasted five years and I can't imagine why. It's kind of hard to believe in married love, you know."

"Can't judge the rest of the world by what happens to you," he said. "Married love takes a little more work, maybe."

"Why do I feel like you're talking about me and not Sam."

"I'm not," he said. "I didn't have anybody specific in mind."

As they watched, the young woman from across the street drove up. She got out of the car and made her way over to them, having obviously come from her job at the college: she wore a bright flower-print dress and high heels. She was carrying a package.

"Cat's not here?" she said, pausing. She had addressed Susan.

"She'll be back soon," William said.

The young woman hesitated, then came forward. "Could you give her this for me? It's a scarf and earrings."

"Why don't you give it to her?" William said, smiling at her. "Sit here and wait with us."

"No, I've really — I've got to go."

Susan took the package from her.

"There's a — I put a card with it."

"Very good," Susan said. "It'll make her happy."

"We're moving," the young woman said. "He got a job back home. I get to go home."

"I'm sure she'll want to see you before you go."

"Oh, of course. We won't be leaving until December."

"Thank you," William said as the young woman went back along the walk.

They watched her cross to her house and go in, and then Susan said, "You know the trouble with us?"

"What," he said.

"We'd never inspire that kind of gratitude in anyone."

"I'm too old to start trying," he said.

She shrugged. "Anyway, you haven't answered my question."

"Which question is that?"

"Whether or not you and Mom are still in love."

He looked at her. "It's an aggressive, impolite, prying question, and the answer to it is none of your business."

"Then I guess you've answered it."

"Goodness gracious," he said with what he hoped was an ironic smile. "I don't think so."

Somewhere beyond the roof of the porch, birds were calling and answering one another, and over the hill someone's lawn mower sent up its incessant drone of combustion. The air smelled of grass, and of the paint he'd been using. A jet rumbled across the rim of the sky, and for a time everything else was mute. As the roar passed, his granddaughter's voice came faintly to him from the yard, talking in admonitory tones to an imaginary friend.

"That kid's imagination," Susan said. "Something else."

They were quiet. William noticed that the bottom edge of the sun had dipped below the burnished haze at the horizon.

"I thought you said she'd be here any minute."

"She just went to get some carry-out," William said. "But you know how she can be."

"We really don't talk about you, Dad."

"Okay," he said.

"We talk about my divorce, and about men who don't pay their child support, and we talk about how I'm sort of sick of living alone all the damn time — you know?" She seemed about to cry. It came to him that he was in no state of mind for listening to these troubles, and he was ashamed of himself for the thought.

He said, "She'll be home soon."

His daughter looked away from him. "You know the thing about Mom?"

"What," he said, aware that he had faltered.

"She knows how to blot out negative thoughts."

"Yes," he said.

"She thinks about other people more than she thinks about herself."

He did not believe this required a response.

"You and I," his daughter said, turning toward him, "we're selfish types."

He nodded, keeping his own eyes averted.

"We're greedy."

In the yard, Elaine sang brightly about dreams — a song she had learned from one of her cartoon movies, as she called them.

"I wouldn't be surprised if Mom ran off and left us," Susan said. "At least I wouldn't blame her."

"Well," William said.

They waited a while longer, and Elaine wandered over to sit on her mother's lap. "Mommy, I'm thirsty."

"What if she did leave us?" Susan said.

He turned to her.

"I wonder what we'd do," she said.

"I guess we'd deserve it." He reached over and touched Elaine's hair.

"No, really," she said. "Think about it. Think about the way we depend on her."

"I've never said I could take a step without her," said William.

"There you are."

"She doesn't mind your confiding in her, Susan. She doesn't mind anyone's confidence. Christ, that girl across the street —" He halted.

"Well," she said, holding up the package. "She gets the pretty scarf and earrings for her efforts."

"That's true," he said. For an instant, he thought he could feel the weight of what he and this young woman, his only child, had separately revealed to Cat; it was almost palpable in the air between them.

The light was fading fast.

"Granddaddy?" Elaine had reached up and taken hold of his chin.

"What?"

"I said I want to go inside."

Susan said, "We heard you, Elaine."

"God," said Elaine. "Why didn't he answer me."

"Be quiet."

"We can go in, sweetie," William said.

"I'm getting worried," said Susan.

He stood. "Let's go in the house. She'll pull in any minute with fifty dollars' worth of food." But he was beginning to be a little concerned, too.

Inside, Susan turned on a lamp in the living room, and the windows, which had shown the gray light of dusk, were abruptly dark, as if she had called the night into being with a gesture. They sat on the couch and watched Elaine play with one of the many dolls Cat kept for her here.

"You don't suppose she had car trouble," Susan said.

"Wouldn't she call?"

"Maybe she can't get to a phone."

"She was just going to China Garden."

"Did she say anything else? Is there anything else she needed?"

He considered a moment. "I can't recall anything."

In fact, her departure had been a result of his hauling out the ladder and paint cans. He had thought to follow her advice and get himself busy, moving in the fog of his strange apathy, and when he had climbed up the ladder, she came out on the porch. "Good God, Bill," she said.

"I'm putting myself to work," he told her.

"I don't feel like cooking," she said, almost angrily.

"No," he said. "Right."

She stared at him.

"It's a few cracks. This won't take long."

"I'm getting very tired, William."

"This won't take long."

"Don't fall."

He said, "No."

"If I go out to get us something to eat, will you eat?"

"I'll eat something."

"Is this going to be to enjoy, or merely to survive?"

"Cat."

"I'll go to China Garden okay?"

"You sure you feel like Chinese?"

"Just do me a favor and don't fall," she said.

And he had watched, from his shaky height, as she drove away.

Now he turned to his daughter, who sat leaning forward on the sofa as though she were about to rise. "Is that the car?"

They moved to the front door and looked out. The driveway was dark.

"Maybe we should call the police and see if there's been any accidents," Susan said.

"It's only been a little over an hour," said William. "Maybe it's taking longer to prepare the food."

She stopped. "Let's go there."

"Susan."

"No, really. It's only ten minutes away. We'll see her there and then we can relax."

"Let's wait a few more minutes."

She moved past him and into the living room, where Elaine sat staring at her own reflection in the blank television screen.

"It's time to put the dolls away," Susan said to her.

"I'm still playing with them."

"Is there something," William began. "Do you want to talk?"

"I came to visit. There wasn't anything."

"Well," William said, "you had all that difficulty on the phone."

"Fun and games," she said.

He was quiet.

"Why don't you put the ladder away," she said. "And the paint. If she pulls up and sees it's still there, it might scare her."

"Why would it scare her?"

"Oh, come on, Daddy. You haven't been much like yourself the last few weeks, right?"

He turned from her and went out onto the porch. It was full dark now, and the crickets and night bugs had started their racket. Perhaps Cat had found it necessary to confide in her daughter about him. If that were so, his place in the house was lonely indeed.

He was ashamed; his mind hurt.

The moon was half shrouded in a fold of cumulus, and beyond the open place in the cloud, a single star sparkled. He took the ladder down, set it along the base of the house, then closed the paint can and put the brush in its jar of turpentine. Twice he saw Susan at the door, looking out for her mother. And when Cat finally drove in, Susan rushed out to her, letting the screen door slam. The car lights beamed onto the corners of the house, and he felt the burst of energy from Susan's relief, the flurry and confusion of his wife's return. Cat emerged from the car and held up two packages. He was at the dim end of the yard as she came up the walk.

"What're you doing?" she asked. "Come eat."

How he admired her! "Putting things away," he said. He had meant it to sound cheerful.

"I hope you're hungry."

He was not hungry. Cat and Susan went up the steps of the porch and into the house, Susan leading the way, talking about the absurd county caseworkers and their failures, their casual attitude about laws broken, restraining orders left unheeded. He walked around to the garage and put the paint can and the glass jar on a shelf. The night was cool and fragrant. From inside the house, he heard Elaine shout a word and his wife's high-pitched laughter.

Now they were calling him from the porch. They were all three standing in the light there.

"I'm here," he said. "I was putting the paint in the garage."

"You'd better be hungry, old man," Cat said from the top step, in her way of commanding him, and out of the long habit of her affection. "I've got a lot of good food here."

"A feast," Susan said.

"Tell me you're hungry," said Cat.

"I'm famished," he said, taking the step toward them. Trying again, gathering himself.

Billboard

I'D BEEN THINKING about burning my once goddam intended Betty's house down for about a week. Playing with the idea and looking at it in my head. This wave of thinking it through, like a push under the chest bone, like I'd really do it. There'd be the sweet revenge of it. After what they did to me. My own brother and my fiancée. One day things are normal as they have been for six years and then bang, Eddie and Betty are absent. Poof. Gone. The two of them.

Well, I let the rage seep down into me through the days. Kept getting this dream: I'm on a big billboard with a cigarette in my fingers, and it says "Alive with pleasure." Big letters six feet tall. My face ten times bigger than that. Handsome as all hell. In the dream, I go by this thing on my way to Betty's, on my way to exacting some payback from her and little brother. I'm flying, doubled up on this motor scooter, a tiny mother that squeaks like an un-oiled wagon. I'm headed over there, knowing the whole thing and living absa-fucking-lutely in the middle of it. I'm flying along on the scooter and there the thing is, up in front of me, bigger than life. This damn billboard with me on it looking like absolute Hollywood.

I'm roiling around in broken glass under my skin, right? But it's like Betty's waiting for me anyway, and not in New York fucking my brother. I'm going to bring her over to the billboard and park and wait for her to look up. Hey Betty, look who's alive with pleasure. Only, in the dream I can't find her house. It's gone. Everything's where it was, trees and bushes and all that, but no house. Nothing. Empty ground. A burn place. Gone, just like Betty. Girl I loved. My own brother. I'm driving all over the county, and then I know again that she's gone off with him and I've burned the house down and for the rest of that dream I'm looking hard for both of them even knowing I'm asleep — like it might be fun to kill them both in there where it doesn't matter.

And I start wondering if it means something I'm on a fucking scooter, so I start asking questions in a general way about it. Without explaining the whole thing. I find myself telling it to Susanna at work. Worked in the stereo department at the Walgreen's together. Turns out, I'm given a strong opinion from Susanna, who I've known since high school. A vague irritation through all the years. Susanna. "Everything means something," she says importantly.

We've been doing a lot of this kind of talking, and I don't think it means anything. Other than I've got murder in my heart.

"How did you find out?" Susanna asks me.

Took my poor mother telling me. Woman hated confrontations, and here she was wringing her hands, with her hair up in that beehive she always wore. Giving me the bad news. Sixty-three then and still slim, with that way of trying to soften the blow about the whole experience of life on this planet, if you know what I mean. Like she figured all along from the day I was born that I was going to get the shit knocked out of me. It felt that way.

"Larry," she says, "you got something else you want to do tonight?"

Like that.

"What're you getting at?" I say, though I guess some part of me knows this isn't going to be pleasant. There's too much pain in her face.

"Betty's gone with Eddie. They headed north, son. Getting married."

"Eddie?" I say. "Betty?"

She nods like it's news they're dead.

Well, I figured they might as well be. I could see the two of them strolling all over New York together. Honeymooners. Betty wearing clothes I bought her, since I had the job. Betty listening to tapes I made for her.

I don't know how I could've let Susanna in on all this, but I did. Fact is, she was always there, like the walls of a damn room or something. Around, you know. This aggravating somebody you don't have to be careful with.

"You know what I think your dream means?" she says. "I think it means maybe you got a big head."

And I say, "Jesus Christ, Susanna."

And she says, "Well, there it is. It's only your head in the picture, right?"

"I don't know why I tell you anything," I say. We're being fairly good-natured under the circumstances.

"Well, it is your head, right? Big as a house?"

"It's my face."

"Well, your face is on your head."

"It's a picture. Like the one out on Interstate Twenty-nine."

"That's Jeff Bridges, id'n it?"

"This is a dream," I say.

"No, the real one. Id'n that Jeff Bridges?"

I figure Susanna's trying to work me a little, the way she does. When she's like that, talking to her can be like trying to give complicated instructions to a foreigner.

"I know what it means," she says. "You're not as big as you wish you were. That's why you're on the scooter."

"No," I say. "I owned a scooter last year."

"You never rode it," she says.

"Doesn't matter whether I rode it or not," I say.

Susanna's tall. Smart. Back then, she was very skinny and not much at all up top, which she suffered for all through high school. She carried herself in a sort of hunched way, like something was bothering her in her heart. Looking at her, you got the feeling that if she melted she'd go on a long, long time. A river of Susanna. Everywhere I went at work, there she was. I'd known her, ten years? twelve years? An aggravation, generally, but we both hated Grimes, who owned the store. Compared to Grimes, she was all sweetness and light.

Anyway, she says, "I don't think your dream means anything."

And I tell her, "You said before that you thought everything means something."

"Only if you want it to," she says.

"Bullshit," I say.

"The fact that you say bullshit could mean something," she says.

And I say, "A repeated dream means something."

And she says, "You're mad at Eddie."

"Raging," I tell her.

"He fell in love," she says. "Poor guy."

"He snuck around behind my back."

"I think it's like in the movies," she says. "Romantic, like it should have music playing behind it. And they'll have Betty's nice house to live in, if you don't go off the deep end."

"Shut up, Susanna."

"Do you love her?"

"She was engaged to me," I say. "Of course I love her."

"Did you tell her that? I mean, obviously you didn't provide something she needed."

"Yeah, I just trusted her and gave her anything she wanted."

This goes on all day in the store. Nobody comes in. Mr. Grimes is going to go bust. "Put up a billboard," I tell him. "You have to advertise."

"I heard that," Susanna says. "You're dreaming again."

In the stockroom there's some boxes to break up, so I break them up. I wreck them. Boom. Boom, with a hammer from the hardware section. Splitting Eddie's skull. Splitting Betty's. Boom, little brother. Boom, Betty-bye. In my head I'm watching her house go up like any movie fire I ever saw. I'm *her*, come home with my new husband to find everything destroyed.

"I heard you back there," Susanna says.

"I wasn't striving for quiet."

And she says, "Tell me more about your dream."

There's nothing else to tell. So I say that.

"You never find her house, right?"

"Right," I say.

And she says, "Want to go somewhere tonight?"

"Why would I want to do that?"

"Maybe it'll help," she says. "Get your mind off things."

No. And I wish Betty was home so I could take Susanna over there. Have Betty see me pull up with long Susanna in the car. Another girl. But Betty's house is empty. Because Betty's in New York giving it to my goddam little brother.

And the next thing I do is walk over to the hardware section for a gas can. My blood's going a mile a minute.

"You're asking for trouble," Susanna says, behind me.

"Look," I say. "Go find somebody else to bother."

"I'm the voice of your conscience," she says.

"Fuck off," I say.

"Okay." She sings it. "I'm the voice of your future. I'm the voice of consequences — time in jail, trials and fines and Betty's policeman brother. Boo."

"I'm going to cut my lawn," I say.

But then when it's closing time she's all primed to come with me. So I tell her no. "I usually cut the grass alone," I tell her. "I'm weird that way."

She says, "I know what you're thinking of doing, Larry. You said you dreamed it was all burned. And it's just like you. It's got television written all over it."

And she does know. I can see that much. I may not know when my fiancée of six years standing is getting set to run off with my brother, but I can see when somebody's figured out my intentions. "What'll you do if I don't take you?" I say.

"It would be a real crisis of conscience for me," she says.

I don't have any desire to listen to more of this kind of talk, so I take her with me and we drive to the Gulf station and fill the can up with high-test. I think I might tie her up somewhere and let her spend the night worrying about creatures in the wild, bears and raccoons and insects, I know how scared she is of snakes. But it feels almost normal with her sitting there on the passenger side, waiting for me to get back in. She smiles like it's perfectly okay to go out in the woods and burn a house down with every fucking thing in it. We head for Betty's place, a cottage in an acre of trees past the graveyard. The gas is smelling up the inside of the car, and Susanna opens her window and sticks her head out.

"You know, this is against the law."

"I'm stunned and disappointed," I say.

"I can't hear you," she says. "The wind."

I yell, "I said I know it's against the law."

And she says, "Sorry, I can't hear you."

There's clearly something intentional about how she can't hear me.

We get to the turnoff to Betty's. There's the billboard. We look at it.

"Jeff Bridges," she says.

"It doesn't say so."

"Well, it's not you, Larry."

"I didn't say it was."

She stares at it. "He doesn't look like a smoker."

"He's just somebody in a picture," I say.

And she says, "Yeah, but look. His teeth are white."

"It's a Hollywood guy," I tell her. "They have special white stains. Dyes they use so their teeth look like that."

She's not buying any of it. "They're people, no different from you and me."

"They have better dentists," I tell her. "Better everything."

"I used to think that, too," she says.

"Well, it's true."

"They're like anybody else."

"Yeah," I say. "Anybody else with an ocean of money and all the sex they want."

"You can have all the sex you want," she says. And pauses a

little, giving me this look. "Just close your eyes and fantasize."
Then she sings it: "Close your eyes and fantasize."

"Shut up, Susanna. I'm in no mood."

"Just teasing," she says. "Gyah."

She sits there staring at Jeff Bridges.

"Hey, Larry," she says, "you remember when you went off to
join the air force?"

"No. It slipped my mind until you mentioned it. Was I ever
in the air force?"

"You remember how you kissed Betty and then shook hands
with little Eddie, how old was he?"

"Fourteen."

"Think of it," Susanna says. "It's all gone so fast."

"What about it?"

"Well, you're not as hurt as you are mad. I think you'd be
more hurt if you really loved Betty."

I ignore this. I pull into the road toward Betty's house. It's
dawning on me that I'm really going to burn it to the ground.
Of course I don't have the slightest trouble finding it.

"Okay," I say.

And Susanna says, "I was going to tell you something else
about when you joined the air force."

"I don't want to hear it."

"He looked up to you," she says. "You were big as any hero
to him. He told me. I did too, you know."

"Great," I tell her. "I'll give you an autograph." Real sarcastic.

She says, "What happened to you though?"

I get out of the car and reach into the back seat for the gas
can. The house is back in the trees.

"Larry," she says. "Wait for me."

I don't stop. She's coming along behind me, and then she's
next to me. "Maybe we can run away after this," she says.

I'm not sure I hear her right. When I stop, she stops.

"They'll be after you," she says. It's like she's being shy now,
toeing the ground, not looking at me.

"How're they going to know?" I ask.

"I'll tell them?" She smiles.

"Wait a minute," I say. "Let me sit down so I can get it straight. You want us to run away together or you'll tell on me?"

"I know it's ridiculous."

I walk on back to the car and put the can in the trunk, with this ache like I knew I'd probably never go through with it anyway. And — but, see — I'm totally at a loss, too. Totally *thwarted*, which is one of her words. It comes to me that I might tie her to a tree and let the ants crawl, I confess it. Let the ants thwart her around a little bit. But I don't, of course. Because the truth is I'm not half so bad when it's something other than breaking up boxes with a hammer. So we ride without a word back to town and she asks me will I take her home. I do. She asks me in. I can't believe it.

"No," I say.

"We've had some kind of breakthrough," she says. "What do you think?"

"I think I'll get drunk," I say. "Jesus."

And she says, "I guess this means we're not running away."

"I wouldn't think so," I say.

"I like the romance of it, I must admit," she says.

"Romance," I tell her.

"Well," she says, "I'd have to supply it all. I know that."

Her mother's already waiting in the open doorway of the house.

"Time to go," I tell her. "Romance and all."

"I don't suppose you want to kiss me," she says.

And I say, "I never asked for any charity."

"I'm not interested in charity," she says. "It wasn't out of charity that I asked."

"Right," I say.

"So?" she says.

"What," I say.

And she says, "You can't be serious. I'm offering you riches."

I don't have an answer for this.

"Wonderful date," she says. "We looked at a billboard. We didn't burn a house down."

Her mother put on the floodlamps around the yard, and in that light she looks almost pretty. The truth is, I never minded her face. "Well," she says. "I had fun." And she smiles.

"Fun," I say.

"I have fun with you," she says. "I really do. Even looking at billboards and not burning houses. You have nice clear eyes and when you're not crazy you make me laugh. And it doesn't even bother me that you didn't turn out to be so great."

"What was I supposed to turn out to be?" I say.

She shrugs. "Different from us, I guess. You were heading off into the sun."

I watch her fool with the top button of her blouse.

"Poor Larry," she says. "Trying to bear up under the beams of love."

"You," I say, "are truly the oddest person around."

She's looking at me with this expression like she might say something really serious. Then she smiles. "I know," she says. "It's ridiculous."

She gets out, and I watch her go up the walk. She's attractive in a kind of stretched way. Long Susanna. The bigger-than-life girl.

"Ought to put you on that goddam billboard," I say. "You'd sell some cigarettes." I really mean it to be kind. And it's the first kind thought I've had in days. And I'm thinking, well, maybe we have got to some new place, who knows? Nobody likes to be alone. And could be that's it in the dream: I'm all alone up there in that bigger-than-life picture. I have my shortcomings but I'm not stupid.

"See you tomorrow?" she says.

"If I don't kill myself or hurt somebody," I tell her.

"I think we're safe," she says.

Ah hell. Susanna. Imagine it. Close your eyes and fantasize. Susanna, of all people. Because we didn't burn a damn house down. Because I didn't turn out to be any different.

When I get home, my mother's sitting out on the front porch.

"Well?" she says.

"I went out with Susanna." I can hear the surprise in my own voice. Susanna. I almost have to say the name again.

"That's good, son. Eddie called. Wanted to talk to you."

"No," I said. "Not for a long time."

"I'm sure he'll understand," she says.

"Yeah," I say. "Everybody understands." I go in the house. Eddie. Nothing excuses it. Not one thing in it makes a bit of sense to me. But I'm actually quiet inside. And I can breathe all the way out.

"I like Susanna," she says from the other side of the screen door. "Always have."

"I could never really stand her," I say.

"Well, you never know," says my mother. It's clear from her voice that she's already got hopes of some kind, and never mind what I just said. Just then, I don't think I could've told what holds the trees in place, if I ever did know.

"Ma?" I say. "You know what Susanna says? She says it's ridiculous."

"Eddie and Betty running off?" she says.

"No. She thinks that's romantic."

"Oh, well — that's Susanna, all right."

"Do you think it's ridiculous?" I say. "Susanna and me?" But she doesn't answer, and maybe I didn't get it out so she could hear me. I'm sitting in my chair by the window and it's like I can feel the planet spinning, because I just can't believe it. Susanna, of all people. Long Susanna. Irritating, talk-too-much, get-in-my-way Susanna.

Jesus. The damn God's honest truth. Right there in front of me. And then the more I think about it, the more it starts to be funny. I'm laughing, sitting in the chair, and after a while my mother says from the porch, "Give it time, son. It'll all heal with time."

I don't even have the strength to tell her.

The Person I Have
Mostly Become

Fridays my mother cleans at the Wiltons', and last week she said the lady, Mrs. Wilton, asked her if she knew anyone, meaning me, who can give an estimate on some remodeling work. My mother likes to tell people what I can do with a hammer and nails, so I didn't have any trouble believing this. I can hear her clear as if I'm standing there, her voice with the cigarettes in it, telling Mrs. Wilton about her carpenter son.

She came home all excited. Sure that she'd found me a job. I was sitting in my chair on the porch, and wasn't in much of a cheerful mood. She said it's not like me, which is true enough. My boy, Willy, who's almost eleven years old and ought to know better, had left his brand-new baseball glove out in the yard so the dog could get to it. Dog's not even our own, this German shepherd pup the people next door are going to start a kennel with. Thing chewed a hole in the thumb; I'd been trying to get Willy interested in baseball, and to tell the truth, Willy'd rather play soldier with plastic dolls. So I was giving him words about the baseball glove, wondering to myself if they called him sissy in school and wanting, even if I don't know exactly how to go about it, to at least be there for him — tending to him and giving a damn what happens to him — like my father never was, or did, for me. And to tell you the real truth, I was mad at him about this first baseman's mitt that I couldn't afford in the first place being left out all night, so when my mother walked up announcing that she'd got me a job, this whole other area of worry came in on me — as if you could forget a thing like being out of work.

"You'd never let a little thing like that bother you, son," she said.

"Okay," I said. "But it shouldn't have happened."

"Well, things'll be better now."

Willy hung back by the door while she went on about the job. He wanted to know, too. But I was a little sore at him, couldn't help this feeling that he'd begun to depend on her to smooth things over when he was being disciplined. This wasn't the first time she'd stepped between us, and Willy is smart. There's no excuse for it, but being in the kind of mess we're in doesn't leave a lot in the way of patience. Maybe she should've stepped between us a time or two. But sometimes it feels like you put so much into a child, into the raising of him, you love him so hard, there's not much left for liking him, particularly. "Get inside," I said to him, feeling low and mean, and out of control some way, watching him go on in.

"Are you listening?" my mother said.

"I'm listening, Ruth. The lady wants an estimate."

"Paint and carpentry, too. She wants a ceiling redone, and some molding put up, and wallpaper. The library needs redoing, and the whole porch has to be rebuilt and painted, and all the eaves have to be done, too. This is your job if you play your cards right."

Nothing ever stops her. She moved to the door and caught Willy, who had come back and was standing there. She put her arms around him and asked how's her little man.

"I told you to get inside," I said to him.

"Yes, sir."

He shuffled through the kitchen.

"Are you riding him again?" she said to me, but she was smiling. From the kitchen I could hear Janet rattling dishes. She'd come in from work and insisted that she would put dinner on, as she always does when things are getting her down. Lately she hasn't been very good about hiding the strain she feels with Ruth here, and there's no place for Ruth to go, not to mention the fact that Ruth is also bringing in a good part of the income. These days, she and Janet make the money, and I generally keep the house.

You have to know that I've been all over the area looking: busboy, clerk, salesman, janitor, anything. The last three houses I worked on are still empty in that big meadow south of here, and the builder — Teddy Aubrey — still owes me money. He's down to selling Oldsmobiles in Charlottesville. Went bust as a builder after the first of the year. One of the new houses that he did manage to sell he never finished, and the people who live there don't have any screens, are stuck with a dirt-and-weed patch for a lawn. No hydroseeding, because Baylor, who does hydroseeding around here, refused to do it unless Aubrey could pay him cash up front.

Which is what I should've done. I worked two months in the last one, flooring and drywall and painting, even some plumbing, and I never got paid a penny for it. I went over to the new house last week and asked the owners if I could hydroseed for them; I'd charge half what Baylor charges. Just enough above cost to pay my rent. Anything. But they don't have ready cash, either.

"I can't take blood from a stone," Aubrey tells me over the phone. "I'm having to bring my kids home from college. I don't know what I'm going to do."

Well, he's selling cars, is what he's doing. And he *still* drives a Lincoln. I get cards from him saying, "Come on in!"

"When the big ones go down, they bring all the little ones down with them," Ruth said.

"I wouldn't characterize Teddy Aubrey as big," I told her. "Nor me as being so small, either." I meant it as a joke, I was always joking and kidding around before. This didn't come out sounding like any joke, though.

She said, "I was talking about the real estate companies, baby."

When I was a kid, we lived in a nice house in the country. Central air before anyone else had it. Swimming pool. Extra rooms, the whole thing. My father worked high up for the space program. Top-level executive, and he traveled all the time. Ruth had somebody in every week to help out with the housekeeping: this big Mexican lady with a partially cut-off ear, who was always blessing the house with her rosary. I wondered about that sudden place where her ear just stopped, especially after my father went off to start a new life. The ear looked like it had been snipped with scissors, a planned cut, part of some ritual or other, but then I heard my mother say it was the result of a fight between the Mexican lady and her husband, who still lived with her. Knowing this, I was always tempted to ask how it happened, but I never let on that I had noticed it.

When I say my father went off to start a new life somewhere else, I mean *as* someone else, too: a man with a new name, a new identity, in another state, or maybe even in another country, who knows? I was afraid of him a lot of the time and wasn't so sad to realize he wasn't coming back, except that we started having money problems. We wound up moving to this little place in the north end of the county, living with Ruth's older brother and his new wife, who never dressed in anything but a nightgown and robe. Someone had told her once that she looked like that movie star, Katharine Hepburn, and it must've gone to her head. She wore her hair in the style of those old movies, and she hurried through the house with that ratty robe flowing behind her, constantly in some kind of uproar, like a person playing a scene. She loved piano music. It was always on in the house, always coming from their room during the nights, and we knew it was part of the act. But she liked to have a good laugh, too, and she didn't mind helping us out. We tolerated each other's ways, and we shared the bills, and had some fun in the evenings. By then I was working in the summers as an apprentice to Mr. Hall, who was contracting with Aubrey for almost everything. Then Mr. Hall retired and I took over, and for a while there I had a pretty steady source of income, even in the winter months. That was our life for a time. It was what I ended my growing up in. And when the changes came, they came quick.

First I got married and moved out. And we had Willy almost right away. Nobody ever talks about how scary that is, having a child. Being a father. At least nobody talked to me about it. I was plenty scared, but I loved that baby so much it hurt. Then when Willy was three, my uncle and his wife got a divorce, and while she moved to Hollywood (none of us asked why), he went north, to Boston, to live. He left the house for my mother, and she called and asked me to move back in with Janet and Willy.

"There's so much room," she said. "It's lonesome here." But we were happy where we were, though we fought a lot over dumb things, the way people do when they're finding out how to be with each other all the time.

"We'll come visit you," I told my mother.

So we'd go over for weekends. We'd play with Willy, and watch him and laugh. We'd look at old movies on TV or have a few rounds of gin rummy while he slept. I would read something to Willy before he went to bed every night. It got so he knew the stories by heart, and then as he got older and was in school, he would read them to me. He would tell me how things went at school. I'd come in from being with him and the two women would be dealing cards, laughing and teasing each other. We might as well have lived over there.

But then, a couple years ago, things started to go sour for Ruth's brother up in Boston, and he had to let go of the house in Virginia. This was right before the real estate business fell through the floor around here. Anyway, Mom had to move in with us. It was supposed to be temporary. And it's a different thing when you *have* to live together.

Nobody, but nobody, thought things would dry up so suddenly. Up until two years ago, the main industry in this poor county was building houses. Now it was coming down all around, and we didn't see it coming. There had been slumps and setbacks before, but business always bounced back. This time, it got so Teddy Aubrey couldn't pay me for work I'd already done, though he kept promising he'd catch up, and I believed him because I couldn't afford not to. For a while I was doing jobs on pure spec — working for nothing in the hope of some new development. But every shift in the winds brought more bad news, and as you know, the bill collectors and the banks never have been too notable for understanding when you can't pay what you owe.

The reason I bring this up is so you'll understand what we came from, and where we had been, and maybe you'll know how much it hurt me every time I saw that woman come walking up the sidewalk with her hair tied back like that, wearing sweat clothes and no makeup, and with other people's dirt on her hands. She'd raised me; she'd never trained herself for anything else. She'd been led to believe by everybody and everything that she would never have to work outside the house if she didn't want to. She'd taken to smoking again. Her cough was back. I hated that, and so every day I was out looking for any kind of work. Even handyman stuff, which I did get now and then — forty dollars here, fifty dollars there. Enough for a couple days' worth of groceries, or for part of a payment.

Don't get me wrong. There are plenty of people worse off than we are. I'm not asking for sympathy, really. What I'm trying to do is explain.

The night she came home with the news about Mrs. Wilton and the remodeling job, we celebrated. We had beer in Ruth's old champagne glasses, toasting Mrs. Wilton and her big old house. Janet already had herself worked into thinking it'd last into the summer. Five thousand dollars net, at least. She hugged Willy and teased him about the baseball glove, and after dinner she asked Ruth, "How about a game of gin rummy?"

We hadn't played cards since the first days after Ruth moved in with us. Ruth looked at my wife and nodded with the best smile — a smile like the good days we'd had. It made me happy, and when I said I'd watch TV, for a second there I couldn't quite find my voice.

I went in and watched the ball game, with the sound up fairly loud, in case Willy didn't know it was on. He stayed in the kitchen with the women.

"Hey," I said. "Willy?" I was feeling good. I thought all I had to do was show him how glad I was.

He came to the doorway.

"Ball game's on," I said to him, like one man talking to another.

"I heard it," he said. One thing I hate is when a man doesn't look you in the eye. When I was nine, I was playing third base in the Little League and looking straight back at people.

"Come here," I said.

"I don't want to watch the game, Dad."

I got up and turned the TV off, and when I got to the kitchen he was standing by his grandmother's chair.

"Get your mitt," I said.

"I don't want to," he said. Still not looking at me.

"Stand up straight, son."

And Janet said, "Leave him alone about it, will you?"

"I wanted to throw the ball around," I said.

"Okay," Willy said. Whining.

"No," I told them. "The hell with it."

"Go throw the ball around with your son," Ruth said.

So we went out into the yard. My heart wasn't in it. I felt wrong, and my boy looked like somebody being punished. He was scared of the ball, I could tell. No matter how easy I lobbed it. After a few minutes of this I said, "Okay, I'm beat."

"Sure?" he said.

"Really."

He was a little too quick going up on the porch, and I guess he sensed it, because he stopped at the door. For that second he stood in the same stance as he did when I was mad at him before. Even the same look on his face. "If you want to, we can play catch some more," he said.

"That's all right," I told him, and I patted his skinny shoulder. My boy. "You go on in," I said.

I sat on the porch and listened to them inside, Ruth and Janet playing their cards, Willy making little war sounds with his mouth, his toy men. It was a pretty twilight. The sun came through the leaves and there was a breeze stirring. I could hear the traffic way out on Route 29, and birds were singing, too. I felt sad, and it was as if I could turn around in myself and look at the feeling. I thought about how things go on, and other changes come. Hard times arrive sooner or later for everybody. Ruth's parents went through the Depression.

I was thinking about this when Ruth came out.

"What about cards?" I said.

"Janet's using the powder room. Thought I'd come out and smoke a cigarette."

Janet doesn't let her smoke in the house. She lighted up. Nobody enjoys a cigarette like my mother. "So," she said. "We'll go over to Mrs. Wilton's at nine o'clock tomorrow. That's when I told her."

"We?" I said.

"I told her I'd bring you over and introduce you."

"How bad did you brag on me, Ruth?"

"I'm not bragging." She blew smoke, then she looked down at her tennis shoes. "I need new shoes."

"Yes, ma'am," I said.

"These are comfortable, though."

"They're falling apart."

"They're like an old pair of slippers," she said, crossing one over the other. She leaned on the railing and smoked. Then she sighed, and when she started talking again there was something else in her voice: she was someone remembering a thing with pain. Except it wasn't quite that, either, because I heard no regret in it, and she didn't seem sad. "You know, I used to say that was how your father and I were, a nice old comfy worn pair of slippers. It used to make me feel good saying it. Imagine."

"I think I remember you saying it," I told her.

"It was a joke we had," she said. "Nothing original or anything." I was quiet.

Then she said, "He never was much of a father to you."

"No," I said.

And she said, "I think you're doing the right thing with Willy."

"Well," I said, "I wish I knew for sure sometimes."

Inside, Janet was shuffling the cards. "Mom?" she said.

"Be right there," Ruth said. She flicked the cigarette out on the lawn and leaned down to kiss me on the cheek. For a second I had this funny sense of what she must've been like when she was young, a girl, before her husband took everything she had to give him and then left her. "I feel good this evening," she said to me. "I think it's going to work out fine."

Mrs. Wilton lives in those hills south of here. A big gray house with about four different entrances. I couldn't go with Ruth at nine o'clock because Willy messed around in his room and wound up missing the school bus and I had to drive him, so Ruth called Mrs. Wilton and set up a visit for later in the morning. I got Willy in the car and we headed out, neither one of us much in the mood for talk. He stared out his side. I had yelled at him for putting everything on his mother, and then Janet got miffed at me for coming down on him too hard. It was a sunny morning, and I felt like hell.

"I don't mean to be too hard on you," I said to Willy.

Nothing. It made me mad.

"You hear what I said?"

"Yes."

"Well?"

"I don't know."

I took hold of his shoulder so he looked at me, and then I pointed out the windows of the car. "That's the world out there, son. They don't care whether you make it or not. You understand? They'd just as soon walk over you as look at you. And it's my job to make you ready for it. Get you so you can walk out in it and not get knocked down." I was almost yelling now. But I was right. I didn't mean for him to do any daydreaming while I told him, and what I was telling him was the truth. "I need you to be tough," I said. I said, "I don't want you coming back to me when you've been out there and saying you didn't know, that I didn't tell you."

"Okay," he said. And he started to cry.

"I'm not yelling at you," I said. "I'm telling you the truth."

"Yes, sir." He was giving me this look, like a scared rabbit.

"Dammit," I said. "Sit up straight." It was like everything I'd been through came rushing up behind my eyes, and I wanted to hit him. "Sit up," I said. "And stop blubbering. You baby."

He sat straight, looking at me out of the corner of his eye, ready to duck, as if all he ever had from me was getting hit. I have never hit him, or anyone else for that matter. I can't explain it any better than this. In my mind, I saw myself reach over and smack him. I was that close. I didn't even like him in that minute. "Quit being such a baby about it," I said. "Stop crying right now. NOW!"

"Yes, sir."

And he was trying to stop. He had wet all over his face — tears, and stuff from his nose. He kept sniffling, and his hands went up to his mouth. I thought he might've gagged.

"Okay, I'm sorry," I said. "I didn't mean to yell at you."

Then I was just driving, and he was leaning over against the window, still sniffling. We went on that way for a while, and when I looked at his back, I felt something drop down inside me, like a big collapsing wall.

"They don't care about you out there," I told him when I could get my voice again. But it sounded empty now, and I knew something else had happened. I wished I had another mind, some other set of memories.

When we pulled into the school parking lot, I put my hand on his arm. "You all right now?" I said. I couldn't find any other voice to use with him; it was like I was a drill sergeant. He nodded, and I could see that all he wanted was to get away from me. I told him again, "I didn't mean to hurt your feelings. It just got me going."

"Yes, sir," he said. That little scared kid's crying voice.

"All right," I said, and let him go. He got out, dropped a book, and bent over to get it — a boy out in front of a big brick and aluminum building, going through a bad morning in his life.

I watched him walk on into the school, and then I drove back to the house, so sick at heart and full of rage that I drove past it.

Ruth was waiting on the porch. "Daydreaming?" she said.

I went on up and into the kitchen, where Janet sat drinking coffee. "What," she said when I looked at her.

"Nothing," I said.

"We should go," Ruth said from the door.

"In a minute," I said.

"What happened?" Janet asked.

I have never been able to get anything past her. After we'd been married a year, I got into a little hugging-kissing thing with this woman at the end of a party I'd gone to alone, and when I got home Janet knew the whole thing. I don't mean that she saw lipstick on me or smelled the perfume or anything; she knew from me, from the way I was with her, that something was different. Now she sat there with her coffee and waited for me to tell her.

"Maybe I'm not cut out to be a father," I said.

"Poor baby," she said.

I knew she was right about that, too. I'm not always a son of a bitch. I said, "All right."

"Did you yell at him?" she said.

I couldn't answer this.

"You did, didn't you. You got on him some more."

"I told him I was sorry," I said.

She stood and poured the rest of her coffee down the sink. "I won't have you yelling at him."

"No," I said.

"Good gracious," Ruth said from the door. "He's just like you were, baby. You could dream the year away if somebody didn't get after you and get you going."

"Ruth, please," Janet said.

"Fine. Fine. I'll be out at the end of the sidewalk."

We both watched her go on into the sunlight. "Patience," Janet said. It was as if she had said it to herself.

I said, "I don't have any left."

"Ha," she said. "Maybe we can laugh it all off."

"I didn't mean it that way."

She got her purse and put it over her shoulder, then stood at the door, watching Ruth, who was moving Willy's bike off the sidewalk. "I hope she's got you something, I'll tell you that. Because lately I've been thinking of taking my son out of here."

"He's my son, too."

She turned, faced me, and when she spoke it was in a quick voice I didn't know. "We sound like a soap opera, don't we?"

"I love him," I said. "I love you, too."

Ruth called from the sidewalk. "We really ought to get over there."

"I'll do better," I said. I didn't want to think about what she'd do when she'd had enough of all this. "Please," I said.

She kissed my cheek, and then I saw that she was going to cry. "I took chicken out for dinner," she said.

"I'll make it," I told her.

"Ruth wants to make her southern fried."

We went out and joined my mother, who had opened the car door and was waiting with her hands on her hips.

"Conference over?" Ruth said.

We got in, and we took Janet to work. Nobody said much. Janet kissed me and nodded goodbye to Ruth, and we watched her walk up the steps and into the building. She likes the job, that's one lucky thing. You could see her step getting lighter the closer she got to the door.

"Okay," Ruth said as we pulled away. "So tell me."

"Nothing to tell," I said.

"She hates having me around, I know."

"It's the whole situation," I said. "It's not just you."

She said, "I don't blame her."

I didn't know what she was thinking, but I didn't want her to worry about it. "It's me," I said. "Janet's unhappy with me."

"Well, it's going to be better now," she said. "We'll have you working again. There'll be more money."

We went on south, and all the way she talked about what a

nice woman Mrs. Wilton was. Not like so many people who have money. Mrs. Wilton looked right at you when she talked and never put on any airs. She had a great laugh, and she liked to tell stories on herself. She'd love me if I got to telling my stories, and all I had to do was relax and be myself. Forget everything and just be who I really was. Her husband was some sort of expert in the fitness business, and owned a few spas in the area. The house was a beautiful old Victorian. Ruth couldn't wait for me to see it.

I went the long way, so we could go past the school. "I thought I'd drive by," I said. "Wave to Willy, maybe."

There were a lot of kids out on the playground, four or five groups of them. I slowed down to look for Willy, but couldn't see him in the middle of all that running and playing, all the colors.

"I don't see him," Ruth said.

I said, "No."

And everything must have been in my voice, because she said, "It's going to be okay, son."

"I want him to know I give a damn what happens to him in life," I said. "I didn't have that when I was his age."

"Not from your father."

"That's what I meant," I said.

She didn't say anything else. She quietly directed me to the Wilton house. It was what she said it was, too, a big old gray clapboard place more than a hundred years old and, for all its nice tall rooms and big porches and balconies, needing a lot of work. Mrs. Wilton stood in her doorway as we came up the walk. I was surprised how young she was — mid-thirties, maybe. Maybe even younger than that. Pretty, with brown hair and dark eyes and a tanned look to her skin. She held the door open for us, and Ruth said my name to her. We shook hands. I noticed her hands were rough-feeling, almost like a man's. She was wearing jeans and a sweatshirt.

"So," she said. "Your mother says you're a good man with a hammer and nails."

"I do my best," I said.

"He's a real craftsman," Ruth said.

We were standing in the foyer of the house, and Mrs. Wilton turned and started through to what looked like a library.

"Why don't I just run the sweeper upstairs while you-all talk?" Ruth said.

"But you were here yesterday."

"But you had the rugs out on the porch," Ruth said. "Won't take a minute."

My shoes sounded on the hardwood floor as I followed Mrs. Wilton, and Ruth said, "Baby, you watch those big heavy shoes on my fresh-waxed floor."

My fresh-waxed floor.

I never felt lower, never felt worse all my life. We went into the library and Mrs. Wilton started talking about her book-shelves and what she wanted done — the painting and the crown molding and the wiring, the track lighting, measurements and kinds of wood and designs, and I didn't hear most of it. I couldn't look her in the face, couldn't really say anything when she asked questions. I heard Ruth running the vacuum in the upstairs hall.

"Look, is something wrong?" Mrs. Wilton said.

"Yes," I said. I was utterly unable to help myself. "All sorts of things are wrong." I wanted to go on and say how my mother once had a cleaning lady of her own, and it wasn't always like this with us. But I couldn't even speak then, for what was going through me, the whole thing, the whole disaster of the last couple of years.

"Explain," she said.

I might have shrugged, I don't know.

"Is there something about all this that bothers you?"

I could see what she was thinking: what sort of lazy, ignorant type I am, maybe the sort who beats up on his children or his wife or both, a sullen, inexpressive man with dirt under his fingernails and a collection of destructive habits.

"Well?" she said. There was something wrong with the way she said this, like she could demand an answer right now.

"I want to do the work," I said. "Whatever you want me to do, I'll do." But I wasn't able to get the sullenness out of my voice.

"You don't sound like you really want anything."

"What do you expect me to do," I said, "jump up and down for you?" I couldn't help myself. It was out of me before I could stop it. This woman who was so comfortable having my mother running a vacuum in her upstairs hallway. She looked at me for a minute, then led the way out to the front porch. Ruth was at the top of the stairs as we came through the foyer. "He'll do a real good job," she called down to us.

Out on the porch, Mrs. Wilton said, "There are one or two other carpenters and contractors I'm talking to, you know. I told your mother I was. I only agreed to let you provide an estimate."

I didn't say anything.

"Do you want to continue with this?" she said.

I said, "What did I do?"

"You haven't done anything. You can take some notes down, can't you?"

I said, "Whatever you say."

"No," she said. "Well, I guess there isn't any point."

"I've got an idea what this will take," I told her. "I can write up an estimate." I couldn't look at her.

Ruth rattled the sweeper on the stairs, making her way down. Probably we were both trying to think what we would say to her, how we would break it to her.

"If you'd let me do the work," I said, "I'll do a good job."

"Well, write me an estimate," she said.

But it was clear that everything about me had scared her, and she wasn't about to go with me. She took a step back and looked me up and down. "The truth is, I've already pretty well committed to someone else."

Ruth came out then, all smiles. I wished I was dead. She took my hand and faced Mrs. Wilton. "He doesn't like to brag about himself, you know."

"You were both very nice to come out," Mrs. Wilton said.

Ruth squeezed my hand. "Yes, so. Next week then?"

"For cleaning," Mrs. Wilton said. "Oh, yes. Could you come on Tuesday?"

"Tuesday's fine," Ruth said, and she sounded a little out of breath. "Are you two finished with everything?" She looked at me and then back at Mrs. Wilton.

"Yes, I'm afraid we are," Mrs. Wilton said.

"That was fast. You-all are more efficient than I am."

Then we were quiet. It was embarrassing.

"So," Ruth said. "We won't keep you another minute." And she started down off that porch. I felt like a child being led. Ruth turned and waved. "Bye."

Mrs. Wilton waved back.

In the car, we didn't talk. I drove back out to the highway and on toward home, and the wind blew into the open windows of the car. Ruth had lighted a cigarette. Finally she said, "Boy, that was quick."

I couldn't think of anything to tell her.

"What happened?" she said.

I told her Mrs. Wilton had already taken estimates from contractors I couldn't begin to compete with; I said I would write up an estimate anyway. I said I spoke up to save the woman a lot of unnecessary inconvenience, that she appreciated my honesty, and that she promised to call me as soon as she knew for certain what she would want done. And there were other jobs, too — other jobs might come up. She'd give my name to her friends. I said, bright as I could, that things were looking up.

What would you say? I would like to know what you would find to tell her about it. Would you be able to say that hearing her talk about someone else's floor as if it was her own had set you off? That it had made you angry and sick inside, because you had once felt that you liked people and you had always wanted to be kind and you didn't have that anymore, and because it reminded you of all this? Reminded you of where you were and where Ruth was, no more real to Mrs. Wilton than that poor Mexican woman with a cut ear had been to you when you were young and fortunate? That it had made you see yourself as you were now, grabbing at anything, any little hope that all this might somehow change for the better? That maybe you can learn to stop being this person you have ended up being — that man who makes his wife think of leaving him and frightens his own son? And if you could find a way to tell her all of this, what would you then say? If you were that man and she had asked you and you had spoken at all, you had found that you could say one thing, anything, anything at all?

The Natural
Effects of Divorce

IN EARLY OCTOBER, Tilson's mother telephoned to say she was coming north from Miami to be with him and the baby — meaning Donny of course, though Donny was seven years old and making a show of being grown up about everything. Tilson tried gently to talk his mother out of the journey, and he felt a surge of the old annoyance with her when she persisted. He could not quite suppress it in his voice. "Do me a favor," he said, "and listen to me. You don't have to come up here."

"Honey?" she said.

"Hey," he managed. "Listen. Mom." He took a breath and forced a softer tone, expressing concern about the trouble she would put herself to, traveling north. "And really, I'm okay," he told her.

"Well of course you're okay. It's mostly Donny I'm concerned about."

"Donny's okay, too."

"That's what he shows to you, Arthur. Now really. Don't be heroic." She spoke without a trace of uncertainty, in that tone which told him she meant business. "I'll tell Herb he can do without me for a few days, and I'll head on up there. In fact it's Herb's idea. So there. I'll take the train up. And speaking of trains, we'll go ride that scenic train through the mountains. The one your father and I took back when it was the only train to Cumberland."

"Mom."

"You have to think of yourself, too, Arthur. You're no good to the child if you're not yourself."

Of course I'm not myself, he wanted to tell her. My wife just headed out with her new love to start life all over in another state three thousand miles away, and I have a little boy who by agreement of the courts is to stay with me only during the school year and who cannot understand, any more than I can, really, why any of it is happening. He said, "How are things where you are?"

"Oh, perfect," she said. "Couldn't be more wonderful."

He had seen her with her new husband, and observed the casual impatience with which the man addressed her. It rankled him, as it had always rankled him when his father was alive. He had himself been nettled by her tendency in all sorts of hard circumstances to parade a forced radiance about things, as though adversity might actually conform to one's wishes and would go away only if one had the energy to insist on it enough. If anybody had that kind of energy, Constance Wayne Tilson — now Macklin — did. In her own son's cool estimation of her, she was a woman who refused to look upon the facts of existence — not out of avoidance, but out of a determination to remain cheerful, as if to do otherwise were to be somehow indecorous.

Indeed, it seemed to him that she was quite unable to strike any modulation in the way she greeted experience. Many times in his growing up, he had observed that she was changing the visible reality to suit this trait of hers, especially where his father was concerned: the old man had been prone to prodigious rages and shows of temper, and through every tempest, every complication of that uneasy union, she had somehow managed to put the best face on — at times seeming almost blithe about it all, as though there were nothing unusual about having a big, gesticulating, wild-eyed man shouting oaths at her, and as if others, witnesses all, would believe her pleasant countenance and decide upon the true, deep happiness of her marriage, thereby ignoring what could only have been the evidence of their own eyes.

"Arthur," she said over the hum of long distance, "don't you want to see me?"

And he stopped — a man standing in a kitchen with such detached thoughts about his mother. "We'd love to see you," he said a little too loudly. "Of course we would."

"I won't stay long. A week."

"Don't be silly," Tilson said, feeling heartless. "We'll probably kidnap you and keep you."

"That would be nice." Something had gone out of her voice. "A week, though. We'll see."

"Mom?" he said.

"I'll leave right away," she told him. "I've already made the reservations."

Perhaps it was not really so odd that in the guilty moment of realizing his own neglect of her feelings, he had stumbled on the part of himself that wanted her there. And as he made plans to pick her up at the station, he caught himself basking in the practical aspects of the idea, like someone walking out into warm sunlight. Everything she'd said — including times and the names of stopovers, and what she would bring to wear — caused a surprising stir of gratitude and anticipation.

He was tired of everything, distressed and lonely and sleepless. It would be good to see her.

Good, in fact, for anything to change. These days, his whole existence seemed bounded by what was unfinished, and at night he tossed and worried over what he couldn't get to: the steadily increasing accumulation of clutter in the house; dirty dishes, unwashed clothes, unpaid bills; work piling up on his desk at the office. All day, each day, he was locked in a sort of automatic motion — hurrying from one frantic minute to the next, buried in responsibilities and expectations and requirements — and often by the time he picked Donny up in the afternoon, he was too tired even for talk. But Donny almost always *needed* talk, chattering on about California, where his mother had gone, though he carefully avoided talking directly about her. Donny had been monitoring the weather in California through the television news in the evenings; he liked summer in Virginia; he was going to miss everything. Mostly now, though, he talked about school, the foibles of his elderly teacher, the work, the frustrations and little conflicts among friends. Even as he assumed the posture and comportment of an older boy, sitting there in the car, Tilson knew it was all child worry: it would all change with time, centered as it was around a juvenile idea of popularity and what that meant, and how it felt to seek it in light of having to spend the summer thousands of miles away.

Of course he knew, too, that the boy had other anxieties, which he was keeping to himself. Just after the breakup and before anything had been decided about custody, Donny had taken to harboring things. He was very sad and troubled those weeks, when it was too hot to do much of anything and he'd had too much time alone, sitting in front of the portable fan in his room, brooding about how his mother had gone off to have another baby with somebody else — somebody with other children and, as Donny put it (his pale cheeks looking gaunt with worry), another divorced wife. Tilson and his son had suffered each other's pain, really, and though they had managed to establish a routine when school started, there were zones of confusion and unhappiness which were barely hidden by the round of tasks they were called on to perform every day. It was going to be good to have someone come in and nurse them a little.

Donny, however, disagreed.

"I'm happy with *you*," he said to his father. "I don't need to see Gammie."

"Gammie needs to see you," Tilson said.

"Is it going to be a long visit?" Donny asked in a tone of deep exhaustion.

"A week," he said. "Stop whining."

"I'm not whining."

"Look, we'll have fun. She wants to take us on that scenic train through the mountains."

"What scenic train?"

"It's an old-fashioned steam engine. We went on it once when you were smaller. You were three."

"All of us? I don't remember."

"There's a tunnel, and you weren't ready for it. And your mother held you on her lap all the way. When we went into the tunnel, you said it was dark in your eyes. You've heard me tell that story, Donny."

"Gammie talks to me like I'm a baby," Donny said.

"Well, when she talks to you that way, I'll correct her, okay?" Tilson was barely able to conceal the irritability he felt.

"I'm sorry," the boy said.

"No," said Tilson, "that's perfectly okay. That's a perfectly acceptable concern. You have every right . . ." He trailed off. He had heard something of his own explanations to his wife, in the days before she packed up and left. "You'll see," he told his son. "It's going to be fine."

Was there some generalized anger in him about women now? At work he found himself growing impatient and sardonic with them, and their voices grated on his nerves. This morning at breakfast he experienced an unpleasant shock to discover a new resemblance between his son and his wife — something that he hadn't noticed before about the set of the small mouth, the measured way the boy returned his gaze — and he could not help seeing the resemblance as a defect.

"What is it?" he said, leaning on the kitchen counter with his cup of coffee.

Donny was sitting in his place at the table. "Nothing."

"Don't pout," Tilson said. "You look like you're pouting."

"I'm not pouting."

"All right, tell me a story, then."

"What story?"

"The story about the little boy who wasn't pouting."

"Dad."

Tilson waited for him to say more, but the boy just sat there holding a Pop-Tart in one hand, a glass of milk in the other.

"We'll have a good time," Tilson said.

And Donny began to cry.

"Hey," he said. "Come on. Tell Dad."

The boy was concentrating on the milk. Tilson sat down next to him and waited.

"Donny."

The boy swallowed. "Nothing. I just don't like anything."

"It'll change," Tilson said. "We were doing so much better. You'll — we'll get used to it."

"I don't want anyone to come."

"Oh," he said. "That." He took his son's wrist. "I promise it'll be okay."

"Mommy's really not ever coming back here, is she."

"Well, we know that, son. We've been through that."

The boy said nothing.

It came to Tilson that something about Constance's impending visit had caused his son to feel all the more acutely the harsh finality of the divorce. He thought of how it would be with the boy gone through the coming summer, living so far away.

"It's going to be okay," he said. But Donny's shrug sent a shiver of pain through him. He stood, breathed, made himself pat the boy's shoulder, then got busy clearing the table.

Constance arrived Friday afternoon, wearing a dark blue dress with a darker blue sash around the waist. Over this she had draped a clear vinyl raincoat with enormous red-striped pockets; the thing was freakishly shiny in the gray light of the station. Tilson thought there was something glittering in her hair, then saw that it was sequins in the scarf she wore. She put her arms around him, and he breathed the strong fragrance of her perfume mingled with smoke from her cigarette.

"My darling," she said, then stood back and regarded him. "You look thin."

"You do, too," he told her.

She did. The bones of her face stood out more. She smiled at him, and her dark red lipstick gleamed. Donny was standing with his arms folded across his chest, watching everything with the wariness of someone inclined to reserve judgment. Constance turned to the boy as though finally allowing herself the luxury. "Let me get my hands on this little soldier," she said, reaching, with the lighted cigarette, to put her arms around him. The cigarette was filterless, and Tilson looked at the stain of her lipstick on the end of it.

Donny permitted himself to be hugged.

"Don't I get a kiss?" Constance asked.

The boy nodded, then offered his mouth, and Constance kissed it, casually wiping the smear of lipstick away with a napkin she'd produced from one of the striped pockets of the vinyl coat. "There," she said. "You've grown up since I saw you."

"Not so much," Donny said, pleasantly enough.

"Well," Constance said to them both. "I've already got reservations for the train ride." She leaned down to look into Donny's eyes. "It's an old-fashioned steam engine and it goes right through the Cumberland Gap. It's awfully pretty this time of year, with the leaves turning. You can see for miles and miles."

Donny's smile was automatic.

Tilson said, "Let's get your bags."

"I never learned how to travel light," said Constance. "I've got all these suitcases and my overnight bag. But what a nice journey I had. You know me and trains."

Tilson's father had been an airline pilot, and for the more than twenty-five years Constance and he were together, her fear of flying, her adamant refusal even to talk about ever getting on an airplane, had been a continuing source of contention between them. Her own father had worked as an engineer on the C & O Railroad until his retirement in 1953, and she liked telling stories about him. She would say that because of him she had always preferred the railroads — the lore, the sights and sounds, the history — and about airplanes she freely admitted that she was something of a snob: air travel lacked the aesthetic grace of passing countryside, the sleepy rush of bells sloughing off in the night as one glided through the sparse lights of a town on the plains, the steady rhythmic chatter of the rails. She had read many books about it, and if a movie or a television show or a book had a train in it, she was interested. Indeed, she'd met her present husband, Herb, on an express to Boston, the year Tilson graduated from college. Having set out to visit him on Parents' Weekend that spring, she'd got into a conversation with her seatmate — Herb — who was on his way to the same small college to visit his own son. This little coincidence struck Constance like fate. She later told Tilson that she'd felt a stir in her blood almost immediately, even before Herb had done much more than say his name and the name of his son. And though Herb was plodding and careful of speech and very nervous, it wasn't long before he volunteered, with all the tentative, badly concealed distress of someone accustomed to disappointments in such casual talk, that he owned a collection of electric trains.

She was thrilled. She told him so. And later she told her son that while she was never as interested as Herb was in these miniature toy railroads — they were finally somewhat of an affront to the real thing — she had nevertheless cultivated a pleasure in them for his sake. But then of course everything was for Herb's sake, including the move to Miami three years ago, just as her son's life began, without his knowledge, to unravel. The fact was that everything about Tilson's mother annoyed Tilson's wife, who was never so glad to see anyone go, and who was in the process of going herself, though perhaps even she herself didn't quite know it yet.

Tilson had lain awake the night before his mother was due to arrive and wondered if some of the discomfort he had experienced over the years concerning his own reluctance to be in Constance's company had somehow been the side effect of living with a woman who felt little more than scorn for her.

No.

He couldn't pin that on his ex-wife. He had felt this way long before her advent in his life, had felt something of it on that weekend Constance had traveled to Boston to see him, and had made such a spectacle of herself, mooning over a man like Herb. Poor Herb, with his engineer's cap and his rounded features that looked always faintly silly, as if he were about to make a funny face — Herb had only to give that smile of particular satisfaction when his little trains were running, and all his dignity was gone. Tilson had never been able to think of the man without feeling an urge to sarcasm.

They went from the station to a steak house for dinner. Constance explained that she had made reservations long distance for the nine o'clock run of the scenic train, and talked about what they would do up in the mountains, all the sights there were to see; her animation worked a kind of spell in Tilson. A familiar turmoil. He found himself trying to interrupt her, cut her off, and when Donny rudely broke in on her to demand more ice water, he did turn from her to attend to the boy.

Later, at the house, after he had sent Donny to bed and Constance had gone to tuck him in — ignoring the boy's muttered protestations that he was quite able to do it for himself — the two adults sat in the dark of the porch, in the balmy autumn dusk, while the lights came on in the city beyond the end of the street. It had been Tilson's habit to sit out here and read, but tonight he felt crowded and vaguely cross. Constance smoked and sighed and sipped iced tea; her movements divided his attention, and he could see that she wanted to talk. In one of the houses across the way, someone shouted at children to be quiet. A car went by, bass notes pounding in the radio, louder than the engine. The car went on, and the quiet after it had gone seemed almost supernatural.

Constance blew smoke. "Arthur," she said, "I didn't think about how maybe you wouldn't want to go on the train. I know I can be a little overbearing at times. But it seemed like such an excellent idea. Those beautiful mountains, this time of year."

"It's fine," said Tilson, without being able to muster the necessary note of enthusiasm.

"Still," she said, "I guess I should've asked you what you thought. I'm always assuming things. Herb and his boy say —" She stopped.

Presently he said, "What do Herb and his boy say?"

"What? Oh, that." Again, she blew smoke. "Listen. I wondered, coming up here, if you were . . . seeing anyone else now."

"Nobody special," he said.

"You haven't been out with anyone, have you?"

He hadn't. Friends had offered; he'd felt too much at loose ends, and there was Donny to think about.

"Well?" she said.

"I can't just turn around and do that."

"Nobody has to be alone. It doesn't say that anywhere."

"No," he said. "Right."

"It's not good for you to be alone." There was a tension in her voice, and he turned to look at her. She cleared her throat and went on. "You have to get on with living."

"I'm doing okay," he told her.

"If you ask me, you deserved better from a wife."

He said nothing.

"Depression can explain a lot of things. But not being cheap. Not going off and leaving your husband and child."

"It's done," he murmured. He was worried about Donny hearing any of this.

"I thought you were too easy with her, though."

"Mom," he said. "Somebody starts going to bed at five o'clock in the afternoon and then staying in bed — you get scared. You weren't here. It was clinical. It was real, and for a long time I was afraid she might do something to herself."

"She certainly got well fast enough."

"I wish her the best," Tilson said. "The best of everything. The world on a platter, like somebody's head."

"I can't believe they let her have any part of that boy in there."

He shrugged. He had indeed argued about the custody ruling, had considered it grossly unfair that under the circumstances he be asked to give the child up for any amount of time. Yet he had not wanted Donny subjected to more questioning from the forces of authority and justice. The boy had been injured enough by such questioning. In this he agreed with his ex-wife: you do not ask a child to define his feelings in such a way, with such official-feeling seriousness, even if it is official, and serious.

"In my day, she would've been shunned for doing such a thing," Constance said. "It's disgraceful."

"What," he said, "falling in love?"

"She was in a marriage!"

"Quiet," he said.

"I know each couple's different," she went on, more softly. "But it felt like she never gave you — I don't know — she never seemed to be quite there for either one of you. I could have predicted that she'd run off like that. Didn't you ever want to throw up your hands and just smack her one?"

He gave no answer to this.

"Well, you're a grown man."

A moment later, he said, "Pretty night."

"Yes. It's still hot in Florida, you know. Of course you know. I was just thinking about how lonesome poor Herb will be to-night."

"He has his boy."

"I don't like him much, Herb's son. There's something — I don't know — sarcastic about him. The two of them when they're together. I wish he'd get a job and move on. I'm always like the third wheel."

He simply stared at her. But then she smoked and sighed again and lay her head back on the chair. Inside the house, Donny stirred from his bed. They heard him go into the bath-room and run water, then come out and go back into his room.

"Such a grown boy," said Constance. "I can't believe what happens to them in a year." And she began to cry.

"Mom?" he said, sitting forward.

"Oh, me. I'm just being sentimental. I always wanted us to be a happy family."

"We're happy," he told her, not really hearing himself.

"Look at me. God. Reach me my purse, will you?"

Her purse was on the coffee table in the house. He went in

and picked it up, and he saw Donny standing in the hallway, a thin shadow, facing him. "Hey," he murmured.

"Hey." The boy stepped out of sight, and Tilson turned and went out onto the porch. His mother was sitting up in the chair, her hand with the cigarette in it resting on one knee. "I'm okay," she said.

He sat down and put her purse at her side in the chair. "You mustn't worry about us," Tilson said.

"I'm not." She seemed about to cry again.

"We'll get through it," he told her.

She nodded, smoking. She hadn't opened the purse. "I must look a mess," she said.

"You were going to tell me something about Herb." He was merely trying to make conversation now.

"I was?" She thought a moment. "We've always had a lot of fun together."

"I'm glad."

"I still love your father, of course. But it's different with Herb. I must say, he's more considerate of my feelings."

"I always thought Dad treated you like hell," Tilson said. "To tell you the truth of it. I mean, speaking of wondering why someone didn't smack somebody." He felt as if he had thrown her words back in her face, and he hadn't wanted to.

"Let's talk about something else," she said. "Your father isn't here to defend himself."

He was at a loss.

"I know you're unhappy, Arthur. But that's no reason to take it out on someone who isn't even here to —"

He interrupted her. "We've established that Dad isn't here to defend himself."

"He was a good father to you. And we may have had our difficulties, but it was a good marriage."

"And I *didn't* have a good marriage," Tilson said.

"Well, that wasn't your fault."

This seemed to require no response.

"But about your father. I don't know what you think about

me now, but it wasn't always — difficult. And I had you to think about, too, remember."

"Let's forget it."

"And I've been happy with Herb," she said, beginning to cry again. "It's not everyone who would tell his wife to go ahead and leave him for a few days to look after her son. At our stage in life."

"No, right," Tilson said.

She put the cigarette out and then lighted another. He saw that her hands shook.

"I didn't mean to upset you," he said.

"I'm not upset." She blew smoke. "I don't know what I'm saying. I don't know the truth anymore."

He watched the progress of an airplane across the sky, and thought of his father. There had been nights when he was a boy and had gazed at airplane lights trailing down from the stars, knowing his father was out there, thirty thousand feet above the earth, held up by complicated processes which Tilson could not understand and was vaguely afraid of.

He remembered that often he did not want his father to come home.

"Every marriage," his mother said, sniffling, "is like a covered dish. There's no guessing what really goes on. I always thought the thing to do was to make the best of it, and that's what I tried to do."

Again, they were quiet. She finished the cigarette, then stood. "Oh hell, I don't seem to be able to say anything right. Straight out. Nothing comes out like the — like I mean it to. I've said things all wrong here, Arthur. I — you see, I was wondering if I couldn't stay with you a little longer than a week."

He stood, too. "What is it," he said. "Tell me."

"I — well, I've missed you. You know —"

He waited. There was more. He could see it in her face.

She sat down again and clasped her hands over her knees. "I don't know quite how to say this."

"Are you and Herb —"

She was shaking her head. "He's a good man. He is. He does the very best with what he's given. And we were happy, too, until that boy showed up. We had good quiet times when it was the two of us. There was almost never any unpleasantness."

"You've left him," Tilson said.

"It's just for a time. Until he sees — until he sees how much he really does need me." She began to cry again, and he took a step toward her, put one hand on her shoulder. "I didn't have anywhere else to go," she said.

"Of course," he said.

"And you were — you were going through all this, the both of you. I thought if maybe I could help."

"Don't," he said. "Don't worry about anything."

She opened the purse, brought out a handkerchief, and held it tight to her face for a few moments, trembling. He sat down in his chair and waited.

"Are you going to stay out here?" she asked, gathering herself. "It's getting chilly."

"I'm fine," he said. "Do you want me to come inside with you?"

"That won't — that's all right."

"I'm sorry," he told her.

She rose to her feet again. "Don't brood, darling. That's no good."

"I'm not brooding. Let's both not brood."

She leaned over and kissed his forehead. "Good night, my dear handsome boy." Then she went inside.

He slept poorly. At some point during the night he heard his son get up again, and later Constance had a small coughing fit in the hall. He saw the light and thought to ask if she needed anything. But then he was asleep. He had a dream about his wife. It wasn't a particularly bad dream — they were in a room with others, talking, and he wanted to go but couldn't find a break in the conversation in which to let this be known — and even so, he felt very bad after he woke and remembered it.

Later, when he made his way downstairs, he was startled to

discover Donny asleep on the sofa in the living room. He took the boy's hand and said his name, and Donny sat up and shivered once.

"Did you have a bad dream or something?" Tilson said.

"I don't want to go," Donny told him. "I hate trains."

"Be quiet. For heaven's sake, she'll hear you."

"I don't care."

"You will care. You will learn to think of someone besides yourself. Please."

Donny glared at him.

"Gammie's here to stay," Tilson said.

The boy's mouth dropped open.

"Close your mouth," Tilson said. "Stop this now."

He went out on the porch. It was cool and cloudless. The sun wasn't quite up. He sat in the chair but couldn't be still. He heard Donny moving around in the room behind him, and he began to worry that the boy might do or say something which would be impossible to smooth over or correct; the fact was, Tilson lacked the energy for such a pass. Back inside, he found the boy sitting with his legs gathered under him on one end of the couch, staring into space.

"Son."

"I don't want to go anywhere," Donny said.

Abruptly the texture of his skin, his solid, ruddy presence itself, aggravated Tilson. "Oh, come on, Donny. You're old enough to know better than this."

The boy said nothing.

"You're going," Tilson told him. "That's that. And if you say anything more about it, you'll spend all day tomorrow in your room."

"I don't care," Donny muttered.

"This is your last warning," Tilson said, low. "I mean it."

His mother was coming down the stairs. They watched her bone-thin legs, saw the bright red skirt she wore, the shiny black belt. Constance put one hand on the railing and leaned down to look at them. "Am I interrupting anything?"

"Good morning," Tilson said, striving for a casual tone.

She came into the room and stood before them in the skirt. Her blouse was a bright shade of pink. There were frills down the front of it. "What do you think? Be honest."

"Very nice," he said. These were the clothes of a much younger woman. The skirt came to well above the knees, and the frills of the blouse had a feathery softness that made her look puffy, almost pigeon-chested. He kept the smile on his face, and Donny shifted on the couch, suddenly interested in the toes of his left foot.

"Donny, what do you think?"

"Nice," he said, without looking up.

"Well," said Constance, turning her attention to the weather outside the open door. She stood at the screen and inhaled. "A beautiful, beautiful fall day."

"It's a little nippy," Tilson said. "We'll need to wear jackets."

"Let's eat at that diner on the way," said his mother.

"I'm not hungry," Donny said.

"The mountain air will make you hungry."

"I don't think so."

"Give it a chance," said Tilson with a definiteness he meant for his son to understand. "You'll see."

The boy said little as they prepared for the trip, but he went along with it all. He went out and sat in the car to wait for them, jacket wrapped around his middle, hands folded in his lap. Tilson followed Constance down the walk to the car, and her heels clattered on the pavement, a cheery, busy sound. There was a jauntiness to her step which for some reason made him feel an obscure pity for her, as though someone had already made a withering or sardonic remark.

He opened the passenger door of the car and she got in, arranging herself, turning to give Donny a smile. "So handsome, sitting there," she said.

"Thank you," said Donny with a faint supercilious nod of his head.

"I think he's a sourpuss," Tilson said, and gave his son a

warning look. Without waiting for a reaction, he closed the door and walked around the back of the car, thinking of the silence between them, while they waited for him. His mother had pulled the rear-view mirror around to check the line of her lipstick. She adjusted the mirror as he got in, but it was crooked, showing him not the road behind them but Donny's pouting face. The boy was staring glumly out the window. Tilson readjusted the mirror, then started the car.

"Ah," his mother said. "I love to be heading out on a trip. Let's see if we can hold off breakfast until the train gets up to its turnaround point. We can eat there, up in the mountains."

"That'll be close to eleven, won't it? I know Donny says he's not hungry, but I think he should eat something before then."

"I already had a bowl of cereal," Donny said, "before anybody got up."

"You see?" said Constance. "And you and I can hold out."

Tilson looked back at his son. "Thanks, pal. That does make it easier."

"Don't call me pal," he muttered.

Tilson chose to ignore this, and they were quiet for a time.

"Gammie, how come you're staying with us?" Donny asked suddenly.

Constance took a moment to answer. "It's just until Herb's boy can find a job. It's a bit crowded."

"I know," Donny said pointedly.

"Hey, boy," said Tilson, "you watch your tone."

His mother looked at him, but said nothing.

They crossed into Maryland, still heading north and west. The road wound upward, into the mountains, around bluffs of rock, through the shade of overhanging oaks and sycamores. Along a wide crown of grass and flowers, they passed a sign advertising the scenic train. Constance turned in the seat to address her grandson. "This train goes seventeen miles right up through the Cumberland Gap."

Tilson now wished he could see Donny's face in the rear-view mirror; the boy's silence was awkward. "Son?"

"He's enjoying the scenery out the window," Constance said.

"Donny."

"What."

"Did you hear what Gammie said to you?"

"I was watching the trees," Donny said with an edge of petulance.

"They get occupied," said Constance. "You used to daydream like that, and no one could get through to you."

He remembered once pretending to concentrate on the dull text of a history book rather than responding to her forced cheerfulness. When had that been? His father was still alive. A long drive to New York for some business with the Airline Pilots Association. His father had been unscrolling, mile upon mile, the epic proportions of his unhappiness, sniping at her, being scornful and caustic, and Tilson could not stand that she took it from him. He had seen the white oval of her face turned toward his father, heard the small vivacious insistence of her voice, the straining for brightness, and a part of him had hated her for it. Recalling this now, something shook through his chest. "Donny," he said. "Gammie spoke to you."

"Don't," Constance said. "Really."

"I'm not going to tolerate it," Tilson told his mother. "Unhappiness is not an excuse for rudeness. Donny."

"Okay," Donny said.

"Apologize right now."

"I'm sorry," the boy muttered.

They were quiet again. The road curved and climbed through the mountains, and spilled out into a clear vision of Cumberland, with its white houses scattered in the dips and hollows of the steep hills and its square-roofed, sign-painted, dark brick buildings ranked across from each other on Main Street. The old train depot was beyond an abandoned foundry and parking lot, and a crowd was already gathering there. Tilson pulled the car in and stopped.

"Good thing we left when we did," Constance said, her voice trembling only a little. She smiled, glancing back at her grandson, then opened her purse and peered into it, for her cigarettes, no doubt — though now her bony features betrayed her, be-coming faintly mournful, the watery, light blue eyes frowning with concentration, looking almost panic-stricken — and Tilson had a moment of feeling what it must be to have had her trou-bles, to have been through everything she had been through. For that instant he was weirdly separate from her, felt the arc of her life as if it were the life of a stranger, and it made him wince inwardly. He watched, almost awestruck, while she began pick-ing through the contents of the purse, as though somewhere at the bottom of it might be the one answer which would stop the progress of her bewilderment and her pain, and let her rest at last, relax at long last, those nerves with which she had, all those years, kept her brave smile turned upon the world.

"What an ugly building," Donny said.

Tilson reached back and took his son by the wrist. "Don't make up your mind before you know what you see. You're not old enough to know." He'd held the small wrist too tightly, and the boy began to cry.

"Arthur, for heaven's sake," his mother said, hurrying out of the car, throwing her purse over her shoulder and opening the back door. "Come here, darling."

Donny scooted across the seat and into his grandmother's arms. "There," Constance said. "It most certainly is an ugly building." They walked off together across the parking lot.

Abandoned by them, Tilson locked the car, then followed, remaining a few steps behind. There was still the rest of the day to do, the rest of whatever the next few weeks would be. He had not meant to cause any ill feeling or upset; he had merely wanted his son to understand how wrong about simple things a person could be.

Off in the distance, the train whistle sounded, exactly as he remembered it. The wind blew. Leaves rattled in the sunlit corners of the lot. A few feet away, his pouting son turned slightly and gazed at him. Tilson waved, forcing the smile.

Rare &
Endangered
Species

Single

That morning, she was awake first. She lay in the pre-dawn and listened to him breathing, and after a time, being careful not to disturb him, she got her robe on and made her way downstairs. The kitchen was all deep shadows and gray light, the surfaces looking as though they'd been lined with silver. She put bacon in the skillet over a low flame, then made coffee. The room began to take on a definiteness, the shadows receding. For a while she sat in the window seat, sipping the coffee, breathing the warmth of it and feeling the chill of being awake early. The view out this window was of fog and dripping trees. You couldn't see much of the wide field which surrounded the house, and the mountains beyond were completely obscured. She remembered that when James and Maizie were small and required her to be up so often at first light, she had liked watching the fog burn off the soft green slopes, like an enormous ice floe melting away. The fog was thick this morning, and the light was a watery color.

It had rained most of the night.

The smell of the frying bacon filled the small kitchen. She knew it was traveling through the house. And now she heard him stirring upstairs.

Though for years he had struggled with insomnia, rising several times each night, restless and angry with himself, often unable to fall asleep until the small hours of the morning, he was usually up with the sun. Force of habit, he would say. Creature of habit. He padded into the kitchen wearing his robe and slippers. "Hey," he said, "you're up early." He cleared his throat, scratched the back of his head and yawned, then tied the robe tighter. "That bacon smells awfully good."

"Turn it, will you?"

He stepped to the stove. "What got you up at this hour?"

"Dreams," she said.

"Nightmares?"

"Busy dreams. Things piling up, and me trying to organize them."

"I wish I could sleep deep enough to dream."

"I heard you snoring once."

"Not me," he said.

"I'm going to go look at some antiques today with Pauline Brill and Missy Johnson and maybe some others, if they can make it."

"I wouldn't be thrilled about having more stuff to move," he said.

"I'll keep that in mind." She sipped her coffee, then opened a book which lay in the window seat, one of his big coffee table books about aircraft, the history of flight.

"You want me to finish this?" he said.

"If you want to."

"I hadn't planned on it."

She closed the book and moved to where he stood. They had been married forty-two years, and there were certain codes of speech and gesture they had developed for the sake of peace. These polite exchanges masked acts of will and contention: he wanted his breakfast cooked for him, for instance. Or he wanted her to stay home. He was not in the mood to be by himself.

"Sit," she said to him.

"I'll help."

"You'll get in the way."

He shuffled over to the table and sat down, then rose again. "Think I'll have some coffee."

"Coffee?" she said. "You? You're having trouble sleeping."

"Want me not to have the coffee?" he said. "I won't have the coffee."

"You never drink it."

He sat down again. But he was waiting for her to speak.

"I'll pour you some if you want it," she said.

He didn't answer.

She poured the coffee and set it before him, and for a little space there was only the sound of bacon frying.

"How do you want your eggs?" she said.

"Think I'll just have the bacon with a couple slices of toast."

At the stove, she turned the bacon again, put four finished strips of it on a paper towel to drain. The rain increased at the window briefly, then sighed away in the wind.

"What do you have in mind to buy?" he said.

"Probably nothing much."

"I don't know where we're going to put everything," he said, looking around the room.

"Maizie said she and Leo could keep some of it for us. And the same goes for James and Helena."

"Yeah, but why? For what? We'll never have a place for it again."

"Well then, they'll have to keep it all. We'll look at it when we visit them."

"Including whatever you decide to buy this afternoon?" He said this with a crooked smile, which she acknowledged with a shrug.

"Maybe," she said.

"If you see something nice," he said.

"If I do, yes." She put two more strips of bacon on the paper towel.

"Maybe I'll have eggs after all."

"Will you or won't you?"

"You going to have some?"

"I might," she said.

He cleared his throat. "We should've had more children."

She ignored this. The bacon was done. She turned the gas lower and went to the refrigerator for the eggs. "Scrambled?" she said.

"Is that how you want them?"

"I don't care how I have them."

"That's not like you."

She shrugged. "Make up your mind, Harry."

"Scrambled."

She poured the bacon grease into an empty coffee can, then washed the skillet and set to work on the eggs. He watched her.

"You're not taking Maizie with you on this antiques run?"

"Maizie has a doctor's appointment."

"Seems like Maizie's always running to the doctor."

"It's a regular appointment, Harry."

"I remember how Buddy Wells was always running to the doctor."

She was silent.

"Didn't do him any good."

"Would you put a couple of slices of toast in?" she said.

"I hadn't thought I would." He stood, moved to the cabinet where they kept the bread. "It's strange to think of a person like Buddy Wells now. Being this much older than he got to be. I can't even imagine him in his fifties, you know? Any more than I can really imagine myself being sixty-seven."

"What made you think of Buddy Wells?" she said.

He shrugged. "Walking around sleepless, you think of a lot."

She was breaking up pieces of American cheese and dropping them into the scrambled eggs. Then she moved to the refrigerator, brought out a carton of milk, and poured some into the mixture, stirring.

"Speaking of not being able to imagine a thing, I can't imagine living somewhere else," he said. "Can you?"

She said nothing.

"I was standing here thinking about the bread. Silly? Where will we keep the bread?"

"I suppose there'll be a place," she said.

"Seems like too much to have to think about." He dropped two slices into the toaster, then put the loaf back in the cabinet and shut it. "It wakes me up at night, but then I can't think about it clear enough. Can't imagine it. So I walk around and try to get sleepy."

"Are you going to want more coffee?" she said.

He stared at her a moment. "I guess I better not."

"Why did you look at me that way?" she said.

"What way?" He smiled, then touched her arm above the elbow. "Funny thing to be thinking about bread."

"I guess so."

"You ever think about Buddy Wells?"

"Not for years," she said.

"No," he said. "Me, too. But I thought of him last night. We're twenty years older than he got to be. Think of that. It's like we left him there and went flying into our old age. I was going over all that last night, you know, doing the arithmetic. Who was how old when. He never even got as old as you were at the time."

"Please, Harry."

"No, really. Think of it. You were fifty and he was almost forty, and he died at — what was it — forty-six? forty-seven? I know he didn't get out of his forties."

"Yes?" she said, as though waiting for him to finish something.

He shrugged. "Seems odd to think about it now."

"There are things I could mention, Harry."

His gaze settled on her hands, and she paused. "I didn't mean it as a contest," he said. "Forgive me. I got to thinking of Buddy Wells."

She took his wrist. "I'm sorry."

When the toast came up, he buttered it. She had put the

plates out, the bowl of steaming eggs. The bacon. He poured orange juice and brought out a jar of strawberry jam for the toast, though it turned out that neither of them wanted any. They ate quietly, looking at the lawn and the field beyond it. The fog dissolved in the sun, which peeked through the clouds drifting over the mountains. It would be a bright, breezy day. Cool air came in the open window.

"I didn't think I could become accustomed to the idea of leaving this place," he said.

She said, "I guess you'll have to."

"You've gone past it somehow, haven't you?"

She didn't answer.

"I don't mean that to be a challenge, either, Andrea. But I wasn't speaking rhetorically."

"I didn't think you were."

"Well?"

She put her fork down and picked up her piece of toast, looked at it, then put it back on her plate. "I wouldn't know how to gauge such a thing."

"It's a simple concept. You were as desperate as I've ever seen you, and yet you seem to have made peace with it. You're not even angry with me about it, like James and Maizie are."

She merely returned his look.

"You seem almost settled about it now. I admire you for it."

She began eating again. "It's a house. I've loved it here. And it's over."

"Just like that."

"Harry, what do you want me to do?"

"No, I admire it," he said. "I'm still going through all the stages of grief. Walking around last night, I felt this pain in my chest. And it wasn't even quite physical, I could tell."

She went on eating.

"We don't tell each other much these days," he said.

"Yes we do. You were telling me you didn't know where we'd put the bread in the apartment. And you said you were broken-hearted about leaving."

"I am. If we could afford to stay, I'd stay. Besides, I think I was talking about something else, too."

"I understood that."

"You couldn't've really wondered why I mentioned Buddy Wells."

"Buddy Wells has been dead nine years, Harry. I don't understand you."

"You'd've been a widow all these years."

"I can't believe we're talking about this now."

"I sometimes wondered if you didn't wish you'd gone with him."

"No," she said.

"Not even a little?"

"It's absurd talking about something that didn't happen fifteen years ago. I didn't go with him. I stayed here."

"You never once wondered if maybe you shouldn't've left me? I could be such a son of a bitch in those days."

"Oh, Harry, I don't feel like this now. Really I don't. I know you're only woolgathering, but please."

"It's — well, I don't know. Leaving the place. You think about everything."

They finished the meal and started washing the dishes together. He remarked about the beauty of the day, and she agreed. And she let the quiet go on.

"What're you thinking about?" he said.

She smiled out of one side of her mouth. "Do you mean, a penny for my thoughts?"

"It was a question."

Again, they were quiet.

Presently he said, "James and Maizie still seem to think we'll walk into some miracle and be able to stay. The place is sold and they're still entertaining fantasies about it."

She was drying the dishes and putting them in the cabinet over the sink.

"I get the feeling James thinks it's our fault we're clearing out," he said. "I want to yell at him sometimes. It's their doing, really. They could've had it if they really wanted it. They could've gone in together and bought the place."

"You want them to pay for us to live here?"

"I thought we'd all live here."

"Well." She dried her hands and went into the next room, and he followed her. The light through the front window was too bright. She picked up a magazine from the rack and lay down on the couch.

He stood gazing at her.

"You're making me edgy, Harry."

"You know, you're still pretty," he said.

"Thank you. I like you, too."

"*Like?*"

She smiled at him.

"You never cease to amaze me."

She held the magazine up. "You know I could never stand compliments."

"Well," he said. "It's exactly true."

He was in the utility room when the time came for her to leave. She called to him from the living room door. "Goodbye, Harry."

"Oh," he said. "Okay. Bye."

She went through the house and in to him. He had started work repairing a purple martin birdhouse that had been damaged in a storm last month. She put her arms around his neck and held tight.

"Hey," he said. "Sure you don't want to stay?"

"No," she said to him. "Gotta go."

In the car, she turned the radio up loud. The news was about the fighting in Bosnia. She let this play for a time, not really hearing much of it, then looked for music and found something baroque-sounding. The sun shone brightly; it would be a humid day. The sky over the mountains was milky with haze, and the mountains themselves looked almost bleached. Pauline Brill had already arrived at the Cider Press Café on Mission Street, where they had agreed to meet. They would eat lunch and then browse in the antiques stores along the block.

"Anyone else coming?" Andrea asked, getting out of the car.

"Just Missy. And she can't stay long." Pauline's voice had been made raspy with years of cigarette smoke, though she had recently quit. "I swear, all it needs is for me to plan something and it falls apart under my hands."

They stood and watched the road for a few minutes. "I can't really stay very long myself," Andrea said.

"I've got all afternoon," said Pauline. "My summer classes are done. I was supposed to meet with these people about their dreadful child, but they canceled. Kid almost flunked summer school and I have him again this fall. Dreadful. Although *I* should talk about a dreadful child."

"I don't have all afternoon."

"Have you started packing yet?"

"No."

"Some companies will pack for you, you know."

"I haven't given it much thought."

Pauline lived in a mansion off Highway 15 North. Though her husband had left her with an enormous amount of money, she continued teaching school out of what she described as a need to be earning something on her own. The truth was that she had been through hard times before her marriage to wealth, and now that her husband was gone, she felt that living off investment income and a trust fund was tempting fate. Something bad would happen to a person living off the fat of the land. Work was a relief from the daily trouble of trying to keep a stepdaughter in line, and in fact she liked to teach; it had been something at which she was skillful enough. It provided a contrast, she would say, to the failures of life at home — the war in the palace, as she called it. The stepdaughter was now twenty-three and seemingly determined to find some way to destroy her reputation, if not herself, the two of them stalking through the rooms of that huge house in an ongoing battle, speaking, if they spoke at all, merely to taunt or chide or challenge each other.

The girl, whose name was Pamela, had the looks of a movie star and was inclined to the sort of recklessness that caused talk. Pauline felt guilty and confused about her all the time, and often sought Andrea's advice when she wasn't trying to see what Andrea might know, since Andrea's daughter Maizie had worked with the girl and had become friendly with her. "Does Maizie know if Pamela is on drugs, do you think?" Pauline asked one afternoon.

Andrea said she never talked to Maizie about things like that.

"But Maizie would know. They do still see each other socially."

"I suppose."

"Does Maizie take drugs?"

"Pauline, I honestly never asked her. I assume she doesn't."

"I'd ask Pamela," Pauline said, "but I'm terrified what the answer would be. She wouldn't tell me the truth. And anyway, there's nothing I can do about it. She's of age."

"I'm not sure Maizie would tell me the truth, either."

"Sure Maizie would. You and Maizie are so sweet together. Maizie would tell you."

"Maybe," Andrea told her.

"I think it's all to spite me," said Pauline. "Absolutely everything that girl does. As if I did anything to her at all except try to be there for her."

"Don't cry," Andrea said. "Please."

It was Andrea's natural reserve that had always calmed the other woman down. Pauline had said as much on more than one occasion. Now Pauline toed the gravel at their feet and asked if Maizie had visited on the weekend. Lately, Maizie hadn't had much time to spend with Pamela, and so the question was asked without any ulterior motive. Andrea said, "We talked on the phone."

"I think Pamela's been meaning to call her," Pauline Brill said.

Andrea looked at her and thought of the many strands of hurt pride, anger, and worry behind that ordinary statement. "I'm sure Maizie'll be glad to hear from her," she said.

"Of course," Pauline said with a small, pained laugh, "I'm just guessing."

Missy Johnson pulled into the gravel lot, turned her engine off, and stared at them through the windshield. "Why didn't you go on in and order something to drink?" she said, getting out.

"We just got here," Pauline said.

Missy wore a white blouse and slacks, showing off her slender shape and her long, lovely legs. Younger than the other two women by almost twenty-five years, she was nevertheless the one among them who was most anxious about her health and her appearance, as though all her good looks and happiness were about to be taken away from her. She was always imagining the disasters that might befall her, and Pauline had taken to calling her Ms. Little, after Chicken Little.

"I have to eat and run," Missy said. "My damn babysitter has an orthodontist's appointment."

They went into the café and were seated in a booth by the window. The waitress was a young woman with luminous blond hair. "If she didn't get that hair out of a bottle," Pauline said, "I'm buying lunch for us all."

"How will you find out?" Missy said.

"I'll just ask her."

When the waitress brought menus to them, Pauline said, "Honey, is that your natural color?"

The young woman stepped back and seemed embarrassed. Her hand went up to the small shimmering curl at her shoulder. "Yes, ma'am."

"It's very pretty," Andrea said.

"And this lady's buying lunch." Missy indicated Pauline with a nod. "Give the check to her."

"Yes ma'am."

After the waitress put glasses of water down, Pauline said, "I swear it's the same color Maizie's was when she dyed it in February."

"I think Maizie looks good blond," said Missy. "Don't you like it, Andrea?"

"Maizie likes it," Andrea said. "I guess I do, too. Sometimes I don't quite recognize her. It's like she's this — this woman I ought to know and can't quite place."

"That's the thing," Pauline said. "It's so much harder when it's your daughter. I mean, I have an idea of it. I never wanted my stepchildren to change anything, even hair color. Of course, I've got Pamela threatening to get a sex change operation."

"You're kidding," Missy said.

"She just does it to upset me, and I'm used to it now. I play along. But I know several young men who'd go into mourning."

"She is a knockout, isn't she," said Missy.

"She's dangerous, if you ask me. I don't know what she's into anymore."

"I didn't mind when Maizie dyed her hair," Andrea said. "She has a different life. It's not connected to me anymore."

The other two looked at her. "What're you thinking about, sitting there?" Missy wanted to know. "You've got a faraway look."

"She's thinking about the antiques she's going to buy," said Pauline.

"I don't know," Andrea said. "This morning Harry said he didn't know where we'd put anything if I did buy it. Pauline, I wonder — what do you think of Harry?"

Pauline waited an instant. "I think Harry's a sweetheart."

"No, that isn't really what I meant."

"I do, though."

"I don't think he's accepted what's happened," Andrea said. "I don't think he grasps it yet — that he's going to be living in that little apartment, and that strangers are moving into the house."

"Well, you both really ought to have started packing by now," said Pauline Brill.

Andrea sipped her water and looked out the window. The haze had disappeared from the sky. There wasn't a cloud anywhere, just the endless blue skies of August. A moment later, the blond waitress came to take their orders. Andrea said, "I'll just have the water."

"That's it?" Pauline said.

"I had a big breakfast with Harry."

The other two ordered sandwiches and then began a conversation about Pauline's student, the one who was causing problems. "He's a sweet boy, really. Only he just can't listen when he's told to do something. It's a stepfather situation and so I have a special — you know, but I think there's some trouble in the home. You should hear the way this woman's voice changes when she talks about her husband. She's carrying some grievance. Something he did, I'd bet — and that she's chosen to forgive him for. I'd give anything to know what it is."

"Sometimes," Andrea said, "being forgiven is worse than being thrown out."

Missy wondered if the boy was on drugs. "It's so easy to get them these days. But it's worse than drugs. When kids in the high schools can get guns, where are we? And what are we coming to?"

"It could be drugs with this boy," said Pauline. "You can never rule that out. I worry about that with Pamela. She has all that money to throw around. Sometimes I feel like she's doing it to me — to get at me — and then I wonder if maybe I'm imagining everything and it has nothing to do with me at all. Hell, there's times when she doesn't even seem to know I exist anymore."

Missy said, "I read somewhere that ninety percent of the population is walking around with drugs on them of one kind or another, including the over-the-counter stuff. Sleeping pills and tranquilizers and stomach pills and cold capsules, and every one of them does something to you that nature didn't intend."

"Excuse me," Andrea said, and went out to stand in the sunlight at the entrance of the café. The other two hurried to finish their sandwiches, and didn't take long to join her. "You're eager," Missy said.

"I'm sorry."

"Well, I wish I could shop with you."

"Oh, come on," Pauline said. "One store."

Andrea said, "One store is all I can do, too."

"Well, this is certainly a bust."

"I've got fifteen minutes," Missy said. "Then I've got to scoot." There were five stores, each in its own old house, ranged along this part of Mission Street, and they went into the first one. There, Andrea almost bought a soup tureen. Missy looked at a Tiffany lamp, and left a deposit on it. Pauline bought some turn-of-the-century postcards and photographs. One was of a large family ranged across the wide veranda of a big Victorian house. At the center of the photograph was an ancient woman, supporting herself on a cane and looking out at the world with a fierceness.

"I envisioned this for myself once," Pauline said.

Andrea looked at the picture. "Oh," she said. "Yes."

They went out to the parking lot, where Missy was waiting. "I don't know how you can be so interested in that sort of thing," she said. "Old scattered families. It's depressing."

"My family's all over the map," Pauline said. "The pictures console me somehow."

"I hope my kids never grow up," Missy said. "You and Andrea are lucky, really. You still have Pamela, no matter how much you fight with her, and Andrea has Maizie, and James is only an hour away. I'd love to be able to think my kids'll stay around."

Andrea was staring off at the line of mountains and sky. It had come to her that her friend Missy still had the unimaginable future to think about: her children growing up, her life achieving its shape, whatever that might be — its one history.

"Well," Pauline said, "I've got more stores to hit."

"All right," said Missy. "One more. For two minutes."

"Andrea, you coming?"

"I'd better get going," she told them.

"I just might get you that soup tureen, you know," Pauline said. "You might find yourself opening it for your birthday."

"That wouldn't be a surprise, then."

"We'll see."

"We have to go now, Pauline, or I can't do it," Missy said.

"Come on, then." They started off.

"Take care," Andrea told them.

She got into her car and drove east, past the old courthouse and the match factory, to the base of Hospital Hill and the Mountain

Lodge Motel. There were cars parked outside two of the rooms, and the Vacancy sign was blinking. She went into the office and stood at the desk, waiting for the young man there to notice her.

"Yes, ma'am," he said.

"I'd like a room, please."

"Single or double?"

"Single," she said.

He gave her a little card, and she wrote *Andrea Brewer. Witlow Creek Farm. Point Royal, Virginia.* She looked at what she had written.

The boy took it and looked at it, too, without really reading it. He put it in a card file and fished a key out of a drawer. "That's twenty dollars, ma'am."

She opened her purse and got out a pair of tens.

"Room seven," he told her. "You need help with luggage or anything?"

"No, thank you."

Outside, she looked at the highway, the cars going along next to the railroad bed. The smell of coal and tar drifted by on the air. At the gas station across the street, two black men were shouting good-naturedly at each other from a distance, and two others were laughing. A woman came out of one of the bathrooms and walked briskly around to give the key back to the attendant. The woman's car was open, and a man sat waiting for her. Beyond this, the hills rolled on toward the dark blue eastern sky. She drove the short distance to room seven, got out, and locked the car. Up the other way, in one of the yards behind a house on the other side of the fence there, dogs barked and complained. A breeze shook the leaves on the trees and lifted the flag in front of the hospital at the top of the hill, those low brick buildings where her children were born — only yesterday, it seemed.

She went to the door of the room and opened it. A small place with brown walls and dark brown furniture, smelling faintly of cigarette smoke and cleanser. The bed sagged in the middle. A Bible was on the nightstand. She closed and locked the door, but left the chain off. Then she went into the bathroom and got out of her clothes, standing before the mirror over the sink. She was sixty-five years old, but she looked younger. It was an objective thing one could look at in a mirror. She did not look sixty-five. Fifteen years ago, she had almost left her husband for a man ten years her junior. She had not done so, and Buddy Wells was dead now, eight years or nine years — nine years. And so it would only have been six years; that would have been all. And perhaps it would have been enough. But she had chosen to stay in the house with its view of the mountains, where she had raised her children.

How strange, that she should feel so far away from them now.

She took a shower, then dried off, wrapped the towel around herself, and poured a glass of water from the tap. She brought this to the nightstand, where she'd left her purse. Dropping the towel, she got into the bed and pulled the blankets to her middle, propping herself up on the pillows. The sheets were cool and clean-feeling. She breathed deeply, closed her eyes a moment, then reached in her purse and brought out the bottle of pills. She did not think anymore, nor did she hesitate. She swallowed the pills quickly, one after another, until the little bottle was empty. There was the noise of traffic, and it lulled her. When the pills were gone, she put the phone on the floor, then lay on her side with the blanket pulled high over her shoulder. The light over the bed was on, and she thought to turn it off. It was too bright. She could feel the heat of it on her face. She saw herself rise and reach for it, and was unhappy to find that it couldn't be reached. A while later, she was disturbed to see that it was still burning. I'll have to get up to do it, she thought. I'll just have to do that one more thing. It's keeping me awake. And oh, my children, I wanted to tell you what I mean. I wanted to say why. I meant to tell you somehow, only I couldn't get around to it, couldn't get to any of it, couldn't find the way, and there wasn't time. There was never enough time, and you would never have believed me anyway, that it could be so important. A simple view from a window, my children. That it could mean so much, that it could give me back all the time you were small. That it could come to mean more than anything else. Not even love, oh my darlings. Not even that. But listen. I can tell you now, I think. At last. Oh, finally. Listen, she heard herself say from somewhere far off. And we can stop.

Patiently

When they pulled onto Route 4, at the far end of the property, with its bright new Sold sign and its straw-strewn field, James Brewer saw several dark shapes pinwheeling in the gray sky at what looked like the base of the driveway in front of the house. It made a disturbing sight. His mother's suicide was a little less than a month ago.

"Are those vultures, for Christ's sake?"

"Crows," his wife said. "I think they're crows."

Before them, to the left, a wide field of grass went on to the line of trees which bordered the neighboring farm. Small white stakes with flags on them were placed intermittently across the length of the field. Beyond the trees there were more fields, more stands of trees, and the soft, worn-down crests of the Shenandoahs, with dark, threatening clouds trailing along the top edges. A blue sheet fanned out beneath the clouds and blurred the treetops, the deep green swells of the hills. It all looked wild, uninhabited. The owners of the houses that were going to be built here would have a good view of the mountains. It was lovely country, as Brewer's mother had so often said. Brewer had a moment of realizing how astonishingly, painfully beautiful the world was when you thought of never seeing any of it again. As he thought this, lightning forked out of the center of the huge escarpment of cloud, and a thunderclap followed. He counted the seconds. "That's only three miles away."

"I can see the rain from here," said his wife. "See it? I've been watching it come. It's kind of scary watching it build like that."

"Don't watch it, then."

"A simple solution," she said. "Like not talking to your wife about anything but weather and vultures."

"What did you want to talk about?" he said.

"Oh, anything you want to talk about." Her voice shook.

"For Christ's sake," he said, "I've been driving for an hour. Give me a break."

She touched his cheek. "I know I've said this, but it — this thing happened to me, too, you know."

He slowed and pulled into the driveway, past still another Sold sign. From here they could see the circling birds more clearly.

"Those *are* vultures," he said.

There were five or six of them, sailing and drifting with the motions of the wind above the creek bottom, perhaps two hundred yards away, where the property line was demarcated with barbed wire that ran along the overgrown creek bed.

"They look like crows to me."

"They're too big to be crows."

"Vultures are endangered, aren't they?"

"Why don't you stop being so goddam ameliorative," he said.

She sat back. "I don't even think I know what that means."

"I can stand the evidence of my own eyes, Helena. You might've noticed that I'm not shrinking from any of the realities."

"I'm lost. Would you like to catch me up on what this is you're telling me?"

"Those are vultures, all right? Not crows. Big, getting-ready-to-feast-on-dead-flesh vultures."

"Okay," she said crisply.

"Calling them crows won't change any of the facts."

"I thought they were crows," she said. "Jesus."

Next to the house there was a car he didn't recognize, parked beside his father's Ford and his brother-in-law's Trooper. "Somebody come here with Maizie and Leo? Who's this?"

She didn't answer.

"Now you're mad," he said. "We can't go in there mad at each other."

She said, "You mean we have to be ameliorative?"

"Okay," he said. "You want to be cute."

He turned the engine off and sat with his hands on the wheel, watching the shapes circle above the creek bed. She got out and started toward the house. The wind caught her blouse and made it flap at her middle like a flag. He waited a moment, then got out himself. "Hey," he said.

She stopped, turned into the wind to look at him.

"I'm sorry," he said. "I don't know what gets into me, Helena."

"We should go in," she said.

He walked up and peered in the window of the strange car. There were paperback books and fashion magazines on the back seat. It looked like a student's car. He left it and went on a little ways into the field. When he glanced back, he saw her standing at the edge of the asphalt.

"What're you going to do?" she said. "James, please."

His breath caught. The wind swirled at his back. Everything was vivid and, abruptly, quite terrible. Above him the birds wheeled and turned, dipped and seemed to ride suspended on invisible wires. One swooped low, no more than twenty yards from where he stood, the big wings beating the air heavily. He saw the ugly red wattle on the side of the head, and then it rose, heavy, veering off toward the creek bed.

"Come on, James. I'm getting chilly standing here."

"Be patient, can't you?"

"James, do you want to be alone awhile? Is that it?"

He turned. The sun had come through an opening in the clouds, and there were two wide sections of the field now, one in shade, one in sun. She stood in sun. A young woman trying to understand and to do what was needed. She held her handbag with both nervous hands, and the sun made her squint so that her distress was exaggerated. But she looked very pretty standing there. His mind hurt, gazing at her. For no discernible reason, he remembered that people had told him she would be one of those women who got better looking with the years, like his mother. At the funeral, people had talked of Andrea Brewer's vivaciousness and humor, her youthful appearance. Like Loretta Young, they'd said. The same definite features, the same lasting beauty. The same elegance, energy, and grace. A beautiful, vivacious, interested woman. And I can't imagine, they said. The phrase kept coming up. I can't imagine. Can't imagine. Nobody could imagine. It was all unthinkable, out of the pale of questions and answers.

He started toward his wife. "Vultures."

"Even if they were crows," she said, "it amounts to the same thing."

He had reached her, and he turned again to look at the black shapes circling. "Jesus, God. Look at them."

"You're turning everything under the same light," she told him. "Stop it."

He said, "Any other comments you want to make?"

She took his arm. "All right. But please."

"They're vultures," he said. "I could see their horrible little red wattles. I can't help what's true."

"Okay. I'm sorry I said anything. I swear, I can't say anything. What did I do, James? Will you please tell me what I did? I'd really like to know what it is that I did. I would like to know why I'm the one who takes your anger and sarcasm. Why is that? You never cut Maizie or Leo or your father or anyone else about it. Why is it me all the time?" She brought a handkerchief out of her handbag and dabbed at her eyes. "It hurts me, too, doesn't it? I loved your mother. Don't I have a right to feel it? I'm in this, too."

"Oh, look, don't cry," he said. "I'm sorry. Please — please stop."

"I'm trying," she sobbed.

"Honey," he said. "Here." He put his arms around her. "Come on. I'm sorry."

"It gets so I don't know which way to turn, which way you want me to turn. I didn't do anything. I see Maizie saying the same kind of things to you, and you don't snap at her. I don't understand."

He held her. The windows of the house reflected the folds of ashen cumulus in the moving sky. "We'd better go in," he said finally. The storm was rolling toward them, and the sun had dipped behind the biggest part of the cloudbank.

"I've streaked my mascara."

"No," he said. Then: "Here." He took the handkerchief and touched it to the corners of her eyes. "That's better," he said.

"I don't look like a raccoon?"

"You look beautiful," he said. And it was true.

Through the window of the front door, they could see his father sitting in the kitchen, beyond the far end of the hallway. On the table before him was a coffeepot and some cups.

Brewer opened the door and called, "Hey, Harry. You feel like company?" It was what he said every week.

His father nodded without speaking. Then Brewer saw that he was listening to someone else, and in that instant a dark-haired woman peered around the frame of the kitchen door. "Hello," she said. Brewer recognized her as one of the women his mother had been with the day she died. The woman's name was Pauline Brill.

"Hi," Helena said to her. The false cheer in her voice made Brewer ache, deep.

They entered the house and went along the shadowed hall. Brewer's father had put black cloth over the three large pictures here — they were all of Brewer's mother, in her days as a dancer and teacher of dance — and it was as though the cloth somehow took a degree of light out of the air. In the kitchen, the old man stood but remained where he was at the table, and in the brightness coming from the window, his face had a pallid look. Brewer walked in and took his hand.

"You're early," the old man said. Then he turned to Mrs. Brill. "You remember my son, his wife Helena."

Mrs. Brill offered her hand. Helena touched her fingers to the other woman's palm and then excused herself to go freshen up. Brewer thought of his mother working in her garden, the rough texture of the inside of her hands. This morning, getting ready to come here, Helena had sat on their bed painting her toenails, her hair bunched up in a towel, bath powder showing on her back and shoulders. For some reason, he had found it necessary to avert his eyes from her in this homey tableau, and now the image raked through his soul with the power of something taunting him.

"How was your week?" he managed to ask his father.

"It was okay. Maizie and Leo came by a few times. And Pauline, here. Friday was bad."

"What happened Friday?"

"Nobody came by. It was murder. Murder."

Brewer glanced at Pauline Brill again. He couldn't help the feeling that she was here out of morbid curiosity, to look at the ones Andrea Brewer had decided to leave. "I go by here on my way to school." She smiled. "Today I was on my way back from church, and thought I'd stop in and see how he was doing. He wasn't in church."

"No," Harry said. "I didn't give it a thought on this particular morning."

"We're fine," Brewer said to Mrs. Brill.

"Yeah, well you look sleepless," his father said to him.

Helena came back into the room, patting the sides of her head lightly. "This weather does it to my hair," she said.

"You look gorgeous," said the old man.

She kissed him on the cheek, patted his shoulder, and her eyes swam. Brewer thought of the mascara, without wanting to.

"I haven't done much around here, but I did box up some of your mother's things," Harry said. "You can look through them if you want, see if there's anything . . ." Then he seemed to drift, staring off. They watched him. "Forty-two years," he murmured with a disbelieving shake of his head.

Brewer said, "When did Maizie and Leo get here?"

The old man shrugged. "A few minutes ago. Sit down — you give me a crick in my neck."

Brewer and his wife sat down at the table. Pauline Brill remained standing. Outside, the storm clouds had blocked out much of the light. Everything was suffused in a silvery gray glow, like dusk.

"Anyway," the old man said, "I've been deciding maybe I won't mind leaving this place after all. It was your mother's, really." He shook his head.

James Brewer leaned toward him slightly, but could think of nothing to tell him.

"Are you sleeping any better?" Helena asked.

The old man looked at her. "I've been taking the pills they gave me — they knock me out. I sleep all right but it's not restful sleep. I feel like someone hit me over the head when I wake up."

There was a silence. Helena gave James a sorrowful look, which he could not bring himself to acknowledge. "Where's Maizie and Leo?" he asked.

"They're around somewhere. They went for a walk. Said they'd be back in a while."

"They're going to get caught in the rain," said Helena in a small voice.

Pauline Brill said, "I should be leaving. Just wanted to check on you, Harry."

"Pauline teaches school, too," Harry said to his son. He looked at Mrs. Brill. "James is a principal."

"Yes, I knew that."

They were all quiet a moment. Harry lifted his cup and drank from it. He swallowed loud, then cleared his throat. "My brain's like Swiss cheese. Can't remember from one damn day to the next. It's these drugs, I know. They eat away at your memory. I didn't even know it was Sunday today till Maizie and Leo showed up."

Brewer said, "Have you made any other preparations to leave? You said you'd call the moving companies and get estimates. And Maizie said over the phone that Leo's got the guest room in their place all ready for you."

The old man shook his head. "They've got a baby coming. I'm still not sure I shouldn't've gone ahead with the apartment idea."

"Do you want us to call the movers for you?"

He glowered. "Don't talk to me like I'm a kid, James. I'm not some kid in that school you run. I forget things, but I'm not completely incompetent."

"We're just worried about you," Helena said, glancing at Mrs. Brill.

Harry cradled his cup of coffee with his two big hands. "You don't need to be worrying about me. There's nothing to worry about."

"Well, of course not," Helena said.

"Helena, please," Brewer said, then touched her wrist to reassure her. He turned to his father. "Maizie and Leo went out?"

"Went for a walk, I told you."

"Did they go down toward the creek?"

"They didn't say where they were going, and I didn't watch them."

"Stay here," Brewer said to his wife.

"Who're you ordering around," the old man said. "If I ordered your mother around like that, she'd have knocked my block off."

"What about the storm, James?" Helena said. "It's a lightning storm."

"I'll be right back."

"You can never tell them anything," said the old man. "That's what their mother used to say, too. The both of them. I told Maizie the same thing. You think she'd listen? They don't listen, and they never have, either one of them."

Brewer walked away from this, back down the hall and out into the leaf-, rain-, and ozone-smelling wind. Some of the vultures must have settled to the ground for their meal, because there were fewer of them in the sky. He started across the field, and as he neared the creek he heard his brother-in-law's voice: "Get away from here, you goddam dreadful, ugly sons of bitches. You foul, coprophagous, carrion-eating grotesqueries!"

He saw Maizie first. She was standing, with her hands in the pockets of her slacks, on the near side of the creek. The gray light made her hair look darker. The roots were growing out of the blond dye she had used. "Hey," she said as he approached. Across the narrow creek and up toward the opposite field, Leo stood poised with a handful of stones. The big dark birds had risen at his shout, and had settled on the lowest branch of a bare tree perhaps fifty feet away.

"Bastards," Leo said. "Heartless unredeemable bags of death!"

"Leo," Maizie called, laughing with desperation. "They're just birds." She turned to James. "Listen to him. Where does he get that stuff?"

"Scat!" Leo yelled.

Lying on the ground near him, its back hoofs badly twisted in the barbed wire, was a calf, eyes bulging, tongue protruding and swollen. The eyes were frantic; there was a sort of staid terror in them, and no animation at all.

It had been James Brewer who went to the motel room and, with the proprietor, opened the door upon the lifeless shape of his mother in the bed.

"I keep telling him," Maizie said. "It can't live. Its leg is broken. We worked like crazy trying to get it loose, but most of its strength is gone. It was past help when we got here, really. Even if we could cut the wire."

"Oh, Jesus Christ," said Brewer. "Let's go back to the house."

"Leo," Brewer's sister called to her husband, "there's nothing you can do."

"You go on," Leo said, without looking back. He was climbing the fence. "I'm going to chase them away. The least they can do is wait till it dies, for Jesus' sake."

"This is a lightning storm, Leo. Please."

"I can't just leave it here. Maybe the storm'll drive them away."

"You're supposed to be helping me with Dad."

"I'll be up in a minute, Maizie. I'll just take a minute."

Brewer walked with her up to the crest of the field. The wind was now coming at them in heavy gusts, and from here they could see Leo running across the neighboring field, waving his arms and shouting, his voice almost failing to reach them because of the wind.

"Mr. Quixote," Maizie said. "It's getting embarrassing."

"Was Pauline Brill around when you guys got here?" Brewer asked his sister.

She had been thinking of something, and for a moment she didn't answer. Then she turned to him and said, "What? Oh, she came in a little after we did."

They watched as Leo roused the birds from their branch. The vultures beat the air with their big wings and settled in another tree, and he was starting toward them. Beyond this, they could see the darkest part of the cloudbank moving across the open space surrounding the neighboring farmhouse.

"I found out something," Maizie said. "Pauline Brill let it slip."

Brewer waited.

"The day Mother — the day it — she — she haggled with a man over a damn soup tureen. The day it happened, James. They went back and forth about a soup tureen. She wanted to buy it and the guy wanted more than she was willing to pay, and she tried to talk him down. You know how she could be about those things. She tried to talk him down."

Brewer saw again the image of his mother lying in the motel bed. It was always waiting under the stream of his thoughts. In the movies, people walked into rooms and spoke to the dead, and minutes went by; they had to touch the bodies to make sure. It always took them a stupid amount of time to figure it out.

"Do you believe it?" Maizie said.

"Jesus Christ," he said. "I can't think about it anymore. It's killing me trying to think about it. I'm sick of everything."

She made a sound almost like a laugh. "I just wish I could make any sense of it. What in the name of God she was thinking of. How could she do it to us? How could she be so cold about it? Didn't we mean anything to her at all? Didn't this baby I'm carrying mean anything to her? How could she just lock herself away from us forever, without even a hint or a word to us about it? She must've known what it would do to us."

"I can't feel anything with Helena anymore." He hadn't known he would say this. Maizie regarded him, seemed to be waiting for him to go on. When he tried to speak, his voice broke. He took a breath, swallowed, not looking at her. "The whole thing's done something to me inside, Maizie. I keep hectoring her all the time and I can feel myself doing it and I can't make myself stop. She's trying to love me and make me feel better, and everything she says, everything she says just irritates me more. The sound of her voice — I feel crowded all the time, and when I look at her I see only a — a body. Meat."

Maizie took his arm. "What?"

"I can't explain it," Brewer said.

"Don't be so morbid. Try not to be morbid, that's all."

"I'm — I don't feel anything."

"That'll pass," Maizie said. "I've felt that way before."

"No," Brewer said, "it's not that. I do feel something. I feel like I can't stand to have her around me."

"I'm telling you it's been the same with me."

They were watching Leo walk across the far field.

"I know I love him," Maizie said, "but I can't talk to him about this. There's a man at work. A nice, quiet, dignified guy, not even very good looking or flashy, you know, maybe forty-five. Funny and friendly and I — we got to be pretty close friends. I'd talk to him about Leo sometimes. And he'd tell me about his wife and his stepson. We were friendly and we made each other laugh. And not long ago there was a — this thing passed between us. We'd been such dear friends. And sometimes Leo's so — stiff and formal, like a kid trying to be grown up. Everything is so self-improvement-oriented with him. Do you know he spends an hour every night with a thesaurus? And when he talks sometimes I can feel him bending the conversation around so he can say another one of his words. It irritates me sometimes, and sometimes it endears him to me in a funny kind of way. Because he wants to be better for me. He's really doing it for me."

James watched her comb through her hair with her long fingers. The wind blew, and lifted it, and she pushed it back again.

"Anyway, I got to where I was thinking about this nice man at work. Do you see?"

In the field, her husband threw a handful of stones at the lifting dark shapes of the vultures. He whooped and shouted, running at them.

"Nothing really happened," she went on. "But it could've been pretty serious. And for a while there when it was going on, whenever I was with Leo I felt — I was restless, and even a little bored. It was as if I didn't want him there, and I worried about whether or not I loved him anymore. And now Mother. I don't know. I've been talking to the guy, the one — I've been talking to him about it all. It's like there isn't anything I can say to Leo about Mother. Nothing Leo doesn't know. And he was always so gaga about all of us. You know how he's been. But I've felt the need to talk about it, and so I talk to this, this friend. It's all perfectly innocent, and I still feel guilty sometimes but I'm not letting that bother me. I'm doing what I need to do for myself right now, to get through, and I'm not worrying about why or wherefore because I know that's all just — this. You know? This by itself — Mother checking out on us. And with me five months pregnant. Just this and not anything else."

"I hate this dead feeling," Brewer said. "I feel dead."

"Maybe that's Mother's part in us. Did you ever think that? An element of her that made her do it is in us, too. And isn't that a sweet thought. Look, you just have to wait for it to pass, go about life a certain way until it passes, that's all. Wait it out and try to be as kind and gentle as possible until it goes away. And then you — you're sort of in the habit of being kind."

"And you feel that way with Leo now? I mean we always told each other everything, Maizie, and you can tell me, can't you? Do you feel like having Leo near you might drive you out of your mind?"

She shrugged. The wind lifted her hair again. The expression on her face was that of a person steeling herself against something. "At times. Haven't you been listening to me, James?"

"You feel it now?"

"Come on," she said. "You're fine."

"I'm afraid I'm losing my mind," he said.

Now she did give forth a bitter deprecating laugh. "That's apparently a thing we know for sure now. It runs in the family."

"I'm serious," Brewer said, wrapping his arms tight around himself.

"You're not losing your mind," said Maizie. "Look what we've been through. Look what *you've* been through."

"I don't know anything anymore," he said. "God. I love her. I mean I think I love her. But I keep seeing Mom in that awful little motel room, and then Helena talks to me and I can't stand the sound of her voice."

Leo had started back down to the creek. Behind him, the birds sat in their tree, all uncomprehending patience. To them, Leo was like the weather gathering and staggering toward them on the wind. He was something to be waited out. Down in the creek bottom, he bent over the trapped calf, and then he started up to where Maizie and her brother were. "I guess I look pretty silly," he said when he had reached them. He was a tall, nervous, sometimes awkwardly friendly man with a way of looking aside when he spoke, and an air of perpetual surprise about him. It was in his eyes, a way he had of staring with raised brows. As with most other people, Brewer liked him without being particularly able to describe his qualities. For the past two weeks or so Leo had been using most of his spare time to fix up a room for the old man in his and Maizie's house. He worked for the county government as an office manager, a job at which he excelled, but he knew carpentry and some masonry, having come from people who believed in the healthy practice of finding work to do with one's hands, no matter what one did to put food on the table. In fact, he knew enough and had the skills to build his own house, a thing he and Maizie were planning to do one day.

"I guess I didn't do much but make a lot of noise," he said now.

"A man railing against nature," Maizie said, and squeezed her brother's arm.

"Too much," said Leo, looking back toward the creek. "I hate the way the world works sometimes."

"Oh, shut up," Maizie said. "You're not helping anything." But she kissed him on the side of the face.

"Well, anyway, it's over. The heart's stopped finally."

"Oh, Christ," Maizie said. "Let's go inside." She took a step and seemed to falter.

"I'm sorry, honey."

She clung to him. Brewer stayed back and watched them as they walked toward the house, and then he followed. For a while they didn't speak. Brewer could feel the lining of his own stomach. Lightning flashed somewhere behind them, and Maizie said, "Good Lord," picking up the pace. They reached the driveway as the first drops of rain hit, and abruptly Brewer found that he couldn't go back inside, couldn't face the others yet. "You guys, tell Helena I'm going to sit the storm out here. I want to watch it here." He stepped to his car and opened the door. The rain was coming hard, and his sister had stopped to speak to him. "What're you going to do?" The rain pelted them. "Do you want me to stay with you?"

"Go ahead. I need a little time alone."

"Are you okay?"

The question seemed almost aggressively beside the point. He said, "Go ahead. I'm fine."

"Come on, you guys," Leo called. "It's lightning."

"You're not going anywhere, are you?" Maizie said.

And Brewer thought about how for the two of them it would always be like this. Some element of their being together would always contain a watchfulness.

"Maizie, I'm just going to sit here a while."

"Suit yourself," said his sister in the tone of someone choosing to dismiss her own doubts. She went on, and when her husband took her arm, the two of them hurried to the entrance of the house and in. He saw them go past Helena, whose gestures showed first puzzlement and then embarrassment. Helena stood in the doorway, looking out through the wind-driven rain.

Brewer waved once, and after a moment she waved back. She was probably crying, worrying about him. He waved again, knowing this, and then she went back into the kitchen, where, he knew, she would try to put the best face on things, smiling and pretending that she wasn't suffering at his hands.

He simply needed the time to compose himself.

In the other direction, illuminated by a vein of lightning across the whole length of the sky, the ugly birds clung to their perch. He caught a glimpse of them, five black tears in the crooked branches. He was thinking about how they would soon enough be continuing with what they had begun down in the creek bed, because it was in their nature to do so and because choosing did not even enter into it and because they were always, always the same. Brewer watched them through the flashes of lightning. He shivered, holding his arms around himself, and the storm went on. He remembered his mother running across the lawn in a storm like this, with a winter coat held up over her head. She laughed and got in under the eaves of the porch, shaking the moisture from her hair and talking. That was not a woman who hated life. Brewer remembered that her hair made a damp place on the shoulders of the white blouse she wore, and oh, when was that? When was that? He could never have imagined it. And he could never believe or forgive it, either. The rain kept coming. The sky grew darker, but against the lightning the birds were still visible. The black hulking shapes sat unmoving in the branches of the tree.

Penance

Perhaps it wasn't much of a puzzle after all, if you really thought about it, why a person decides that enough is enough in this life, and then acts on it. So Gehringer thought, pulling into his own driveway, home from another strained day at work, discouraged, tired, thinking about a stranger's suicide. Before him, his house shone in the late evening sun; the sharp shade on the porch gave a luster to the white clapboards and the railing. He came to a slow stop and let the car idle a moment, gazing at the demarcations of shade and light. It was a pleasant, roomy old place, and he had always felt so much at home in it.

When his wife crossed the front window and glanced at him, he got out and made his way up the walk. Yesterday's storms had shaken some of the branches out of the trees and caused the creek to overflow, and now the fields beyond the lawn looked badly rumpled and unkempt. The grass stood up, showing the dark mud beneath. In one corner of the near pasture, in the shade of the big oak tree there, three cows stood chewing, staring at him. The sky was clear blue, and a crisp, cool breeze blew. It was all only itself. All futile, somehow.

And here he was, with these uncharacteristic thoughts. One person's refusal to go on living made others turn and look at their own lives.

He believed he understood it.

Everything in the house was discouragingly spotless. Abigail had spent another day going over the place, top to bottom, like someone trying to eradicate the vestiges of illness. Making his way through the polished, shining family room to the kitchen, he found her down on her knees, scrubbing the baseboards. "I'm home," he said, trying to take a normal tone.

She said, "I saw you pull in."

He put the car keys in their place on the hook above the sink. "The field looks like a hurricane went through." He watched her work. "Didn't you do that on Friday?"

She said, "Jason's flunking math, too, now."

He moved to the kitchen window and looked out. His stepson was shooting baskets. The ball swished through the net and dropped into a puddle of rainwater at the base of the pole. Jason picked the ball up, holding it away from himself, and dried it off with a terry cloth towel.

"Did you hear what I said?" she asked.

"I was wondering if you heard what *I* said."

"I heard you, Marty. This needs doing."

"No it doesn't," he said. "No it doesn't."

She worked on.

"Isn't math Jason's favorite subject?"

"If you were more involved, you'd know it was."

"I think I did know, Gail. I said, 'Isn't math his favorite subject?' I knew, see. And so I asked. The question was reflexive."

She said, "Math was his favorite subject."

He watched her moving along the floor, concentrating on the work. It was unnerving. "Can I help?" he said.

She didn't answer.

"I'll spell you, if you want," he said. "We could take turns. We'll eat off the floor when we finish, to celebrate having a house cleaner than a hospital. What do you say?"

"Cute."

He paused, thinking she might say more. There was the sound of the ball hitting the rim outside. "Well, what should we do? You want me to talk to him?"

"We can't do anything yet about the math," she said. "His teacher sent home a note that he'd be putting together a list of tutors for us to go through. I've set up a conference with Mrs. Brill about the English grade. We were supposed to have one with her a while back, you might remember, and it didn't work out. I want you to come with me."

He chose to ignore her tone. "Have you talked to Jason about it?"

"Yes."

"What's he say?"

"He says she has something against him."

"You believe that?"

His wife looked up at him, then went back to her scrubbing.

"Well, kids have been known to bend the truth about these things, Gail."

"Just come with me and we'll find out."

"I'd be glad to," he said. "When is it?"

"We have to leave in half an hour." She kept on working, moving along the kitchen floor.

"Gail," he said.

"What."

"Shouldn't you start getting ready?"

"I am. Just a minute."

"Everything's so clean," he said.

She said nothing.

"We ought to have people over so they can see it. Remember Celie — what the hell was her last name? — the one who was always redoing her walls. You used to make fun of her."

"I don't remember making fun of her."

"Oh, yes. You were wicked about it."

"I'm almost finished here," she said. "Are you ready to go?"

"I was asking you about Celie. Was her name Celie?"

"Yes."

"Wonder whatever happened to her. You used to have such a lot of fun laughing at how she was about her house."

"What are you telling me, Marty?"

"You don't really need it spelled out, do you?" he said.

"Look, are you coming with me or not?"

"I said I was. You're the one who needs to get ready to go."

"Won't take me a second," she said.

Outside, Jason bounced the basketball, playing an imaginary game. Gehringer saw the look of excitement and seriousness in the boy's face.

"I told him not to get dirty," Abigail said.

"He's just shooting baskets," said Gehringer.

She went on working.

"Gail," he said.

"What."

"Honey, look at me."

She did so. There was a kind of tolerance in her face.

"Nothing happened, understand? Nothing's changed. I know I keep saying that. But there's nothing going on at all."

"I don't want to think about it now," she said.

He let another moment pass. Then he went to the sink and got a dishcloth and began wiping the spotless counter. "Isn't this nice? We're cleaning together."

"I don't need your sarcasm, either," she said.

"I'm not being sarcastic. I'm saying isn't it nice, we're cleaning together, and in a little while we'll go to Jason's school together and we'll be just like a family."

"You don't have to go hold Maizie Brewer's hand?"

"Well, I thought you might not get around to saying it. And it's not Brewer. She's married, Gail. Remember? She's expecting a baby."

"Does she know whose?"

"That is a completely shitty thing to say. That's not fair, and you know it."

"I haven't had a lot of time to think about being fair, wouldn't you agree?"

"Nothing ever happened. Can you understand that nothing happened? And I swear to Christ you take us farther away from each other every day."

She went on scrubbing the baseboard.

"Stop that and listen to me."

She straightened. "You're spending time with her again when you said you'd avoid her."

"Nothing happened the first time and nothing's happening now. But I work with her, and she's going through some hell right now over the death of her mother. It's only the simple concern of a friend."

"And there's no one else she can turn to?"

The look of pain in his wife's face hurt him. "Everybody else turns to *her*. Please, honey. Don't do this. I'm telling you there's nothing going on."

She went back to her work. "I'm almost through," she said. "I won't take long."

"Gail," he said. "Really."

"These explanations," she said. "They hurt me. I don't want to hear anymore."

"No," he said. "I know. But honey, nothing's changed. Nothing ever changed."

"Please," she said.

"For Christ's sake," Gehringer told her. "You're doing this to yourself."

She shook her head.

"I have been a faithful husband," he said. "I may not have been as attentive as I ought to be, but I have been faithful."

"Will you please let me finish this?" she said.

He went upstairs to the master bedroom and got out of his suit. Then, thinking about the conference, he put it back on. The bed was made, the floor had been scrubbed and waxed, the furniture dusted and polished. The odor of the polish stung his nostrils and made him aware of his bronchial tubes. There wasn't a place to sit down and be comfortable, and anyway, he was still wearing the suit. Then it occurred to him that he might change suits. This one was rumpled from the day's work. He opened the closet door and chose a blue one, and another tie. He would keep the same shirt. As he was putting on the pants, his wife entered the room and took off her jeans and blouse. He said, "Is this okay?"

She looked at him. "Fine."

"As I recall, back in the early Pleistocene period when you were still happy with me, you liked me in this one."

"You look good in it," she said simply.

He smiled. "Thanks."

She went into the bathroom and closed the door. The shower ran. He finished dressing, then went downstairs, where he found his stepson making a peanut butter sandwich. The boy looked guilty for a second, then seemed to recover himself.

"Hey," Gehringer said.

Jason only smirked. His mother had said nothing to him, and yet he seemed to know there was trouble between his parents, and he was behaving rather badly about it.

"What's the story with math?"

He shrugged. "I don't know. I have to make up some tests."

"Tell me what Mrs. Brill has against you in English."

"If I knew that, I could handle it myself," the boy said.

"Well, how does she show it?"

Again, he shrugged. "I don't know."

"Oh, come on," Gehringer said. "There must be something."

"I don't know."

"Well, son, you can't make an accusation and then just let it stand without anything to back it up. What is it that she does that tells you she has something against you?"

"I don't *know*," Jason said. He seemed irritated.

Gehringer walked away from him, into the living room, with its freshly laundered curtains and its ironed and starched doilies, its look of a place waiting for close inspection, a display rather than a room where people might be comfortable. There were newly cut rose blossoms in a glass vase in the middle of the coffee table, and the fireplace looked as though it hadn't ever been used. Sun poured in the windows onto the oriental rug. He sat on the couch and then, worried about wrinkling the suit, stood again.

"She makes me wait to go to the lavatory," Jason said from the entrance to the room.

Gehringer stared at him.

"She knows I have to go, and she makes me wait."

"Anything else?"

"There's other things," the boy said.

"Well, like what?"

"I don't know."

"You ever hear of the Salem witch trials?" Gehringer asked.

"No."

"Interesting situation. They hanged some people as witches. And a lot of it was just these — these kids making loose accusations. Standing around saying things. Without anything to back it up."

"I guess they listened to them back then."

"Oh, yeah — they hanged several innocent people as witches," Gehringer said through his teeth.

"Well," the boy said. "I'm not making loose accusations."

"I didn't say you were, particularly, did I?"

"I'm not stupid," the boy said with certainty, moving out of the doorway. Apparently he felt vindicated, and believed the conversation had been a success.

Gehringer let him go. There was no use pursuing a discussion with him in his victorious mood. He heard the front door open and close, and then the house was quiet. Stepping to the window again, he looked out at what he could see of the mountains and the surrounding fields. Part of the highway was visible through a cut in the trees at the end of the property. Over there was town, the Mountain Lodge Motel. A woman who could so systematically do away with herself had to be thinking about it for a long, long time.

He and Maizie had been friends at work, allies. They had laughed together about the foibles and vanities of others in the office, and they had enjoyed the times when work brought them into proximity with each other. Somehow the laughs had led to a feeling of heightened expectation. Without having to decide upon it or think about it, they had entered a zone of mutual concern that made for exchanged glances and a thrill whenever she spoke his name. Or he said hers: Maizie. Maizie. The whole thing was absurd, of course, since she was devoted to her husband, and since she also happened to be fifteen years younger than Gehringer. But the result of the few moments of awkwardness between them had been a strange unease, a nervousness, almost as though lines *had* been crossed.

Abigail, coming to pick him up one afternoon, noticed the difference.

Understandably enough, given her nature, she assumed the worst. And for all his efforts to explain the whole thing away, in her mind something had been acceded to in his heart. Abigail had once described herself as the sort of person who found it difficult to believe anyone could remain interested in her. Her confidence was too easily undermined. In consequence of this, he had sworn that he would have nothing else to do with Maizie, and he had been trying to make his way back from it when

Maizie's mother committed suicide. And if he was certain that it was only the solace of an old friend that Maizie sought now, the new situation was still quite confusing and worrisome: for she was indeed beautiful in her grief, and Abigail grew daily more difficult to live with, clenched as she was on the suspicions she still held about him.

Each day felt more discouraging than the last. Abigail's face had taken on a new harsh, pinched look — the look of bitter religious anger. There had been times over the last few days when he couldn't bear to look at her.

"Ready?" she said from the kitchen. Her heels sounded on the tile floor. He went through the hall to the front entrance and she started toward him, pausing to put an earring on.

"You look nice," he said.

She frowned.

"You do," he told her, resisting the urge to look away.

"I don't feel nice."

"Isn't Jason coming?"

"He's waiting outside."

"I asked him about it," Gehringer said. "He's pretty vague."

She went past him, out onto the porch. Jason had started the car and was sitting in the middle of the front seat.

"Maybe we ought not to go into this with an attitude," Gehringer said.

"Nobody has an attitude."

"It's just possible that this teacher is right, you know. She doesn't have anything to gain from lying about it, and Jason does."

They had come to the edge of the porch. Gehringer was troubled to find that his wife was trying to hold back tears. "Are you going to take this tack when we get there?" she said.

"Well, good God," he said. "What tack are *you* going to take? Don't you think we ought to go into this without having our minds made up? For Jason's sake."

"I'm going to try and do what is best for my son. And that means I'm going to try trusting him."

"Just blindly?" Gehringer said. "No matter what you learn about it or what anyone says?"

She stared at him. Her expression was almost satisfied.

"No," he said. "I'm not accepting that look, either. Don't give me that look. I have not violated your trust. In no way have I violated your trust."

"This is not the place to discuss it," she said, going on.

"Jesus Christ," said Gehringer. "Unbelievable."

She stopped. "Are you finished?" Again, she seemed near crying.

"Do you know how ridiculous all this is?" he said. "I love you."

"You use that like a club," she told him. "It's a weapon when you say it."

"Just trying to be heard above the roar of condemnations," he said. "Christ."

She went on to the car, and she was irritable with Jason, telling him to quit sitting there staring and to get himself in the back seat and buckled.

The high school was built out of the side of a hill, surrounded by fields of grass and dark wooden fences. A stream ran along the front — clear water running over stones — and you crossed a small walking bridge to get to the entrance. Basketball courts flanked the building, and beyond these, the metal bleachers of the football field reflected the sun. Jason led the way inside and along the hallway to his English classroom. Mrs. Brill was not there. He sat at one of the desks in the front of the room, and his parents stood by the door. They had not exchanged a word since driving away from the house.

"What do we do now?" Jason said.

"Be quiet," said his mother.

"Well, she said she'd be here."

The three of them waited. From somewhere else in the building, the sound of a brass band came to them. It seemed to originate in the walls.

"Straighten your tie," Gehringer's wife said.

Gehringer walked to the window and did so, peering at the faint reflection of himself. Then he turned and faced her. After a moment, he said, "Maybe we got the wrong day."

"It's today."

Perhaps ten minutes went by. Gehringer watched school buses roll out of the lot across the way, and there were boys in the farm field on the other side of the highway, playing a game of touch football. He watched and grew interested. Then, remembering himself, he turned from the window. No one spoke. Jason leaned back in his seat, biting the cuticles of his fingers, his feet stretched out into the middle of the aisle. Abigail stood just inside the door, like someone afraid to be thought snooping. She looked tired and beset. Gehringer took his eyes from her.

And now the music in the walls gave way to something else: an agitation, a shuffling mixed with female laughter. The music started again, seemed to punctuate the laughter, which was coming closer. Gehringer's wife turned to face the door as a young woman appeared there, a dark-haired girl of heart-stopping beauty, bracing herself in the door frame. She'd been running and had just been caught. She looked at Gehringer, at Jason. "Oh," she said, laughing. A young man was behind her, and his hands were around her middle. Gehringer saw that their eyes shone with an unnatural light.

"Come on," the young man said. Then, peering in at Gehringer, "Oh, forgive me, folks. We were just leaving."

"Stop it, Ridley. This is the room."

"But there's nobody here — she's not here. Come on. Let's go find her."

"Ridley." She held on to the frame of the door, looking behind her at the young man, then she wrenched free and stood unsteadily in the doorway, her hands going through her astonishingly soft hair. With forced dignity, she said to Gehringer, "Excuse me, I'm looking for Mrs. Brill."

"Nobody here," the young man was saying. "Anybody can see that."

"My mother-figure," the young woman said. She laughed, turning. "Well, I guess I can't introduce you, Ridley."

"Come on," he was saying. "Please. Les' go the office. Huh?"

"Shhhh," she said, laughing again. "Drunk in the middle the afternoon."

They went out into the hallway, and for a few minutes their voices carried back into the room. "Should've known not to bring you here —"

"I do have hon'rable intentions —"

"— won't want to see me for that matter —"

"— marry you and —"

"— won't like you anyway —"

"You unnerstan'? I'm in love — all truthful hon'rable up an' up."

When it was quiet again, with only the faint sound of the brass band in some far room, Gehringer said, "Poor Mrs. Brill."

His wife went to the doorway and looked up and down the hall. "Gone," she said.

They waited.

Finally Gehringer said, "I don't think Mrs. Brill is coming."

"Maybe she forgot," said Jason.

Again, they were quiet. The sound of the band stopped. Gehringer stood at the window and watched the slow progress of the light trailing toward the horizon. The undersides of clouds looked like guttering coals. It came to him that these two people waiting here with him were the ones he had sworn his life to, and that in the moments they had all stood under the baldly sardonic leer of the beautiful drunken girl he had felt this acutely, like a jagged pain in his abdomen. He turned and looked at them — Abigail with her frown of concern and her nervous hands, folding and unfolding a handkerchief, and Jason staring at his own knotted fingers on the desk. Abruptly he wanted to reassure them. "Let's go somewhere tonight," he said.

They looked at him blankly.

"No matter what happens," he said, meaning it with all his heart. "Just us."

"If you want to," his wife said.

"Sure," said Jason in a tone that barely missed sullenness.

"It's settled, then," Gehringer said, understanding that nothing had been settled at all, but that he could muster the patience to wait for it. "I'm glad you asked me to come along to this conference."

"Well, how could I know she wouldn't show up," Abigail said.

"No," he told her. "I *am* glad."

"The woman sets a time and says she'll be here and then doesn't show up."

"I said I meant it, Gail. I am glad."

"Well, I don't see why."

Now he was rankled. He paced across the room to look at some pictures along the back wall — eighteenth-century men, poets and novelists. Pope, was it? Swift. The names went through his mind, and he wondered if they belonged to the staid, staring faces. Behind him, Jason stirred, and then there were heels clicking on the hard floors of the hall. Gehringer turned in time to see Mrs. Brill enter the room and hurry to her desk, apologizing for the delay, talking about a meeting she hadn't been able to avoid.

"People have schedules," Abigail said.

"Yes, I am sorry."

Gehringer moved to stand with them. Mrs. Brill offered them desks, and in a moment they were seated before her like students. "Now," she said, rifling through pages on her desk. "Jason, Jason. Here we are."

"Do you want Jason here for this?" Abigail asked.

The other woman hesitated. "Yes, I think that's fine."

"I mean, if there's something you think we should hear, alone," Abigail said.

"Well, Jason knows he's not doing well," said Mrs. Brill.

Gehringer spoke up. "Jason says you don't like him personally."

Mrs. Brill stared at him. "He does."

"That's what he says. He says you make him wait to go to the bathroom."

Now she looked at Jason. "And how is it that I do that?"

"He says you know he has to go, and you make him wait."

"I see. And how do I know he has to go?" Mrs. Brill rested her left elbow on the desk and put her chin on the folded fist of that hand.

"Jason?" Gehringer said.

Jason shrugged.

"Son?"

"My son doesn't feel comfortable in the class," Abigail said. "I think that's the point."

"No one feels comfortable in the class," said Mrs. Brill, "because Jason keeps trying to disrupt it."

"Now wait a minute," Abigail said.

"Listen to her side of it," Gehringer said to his wife.

"You can just stay out of it," said Abigail.

"Let's all please calm down," Mrs. Brill said.

Jason sat staring at his hands.

"Would you like to say something, Jason?" said Mrs. Brill.

"Jason?" Abigail said.

Gehringer stood. "I think we're wasting time here. It's obvious, Mrs. Brill, that you're not ready to deal with my wife, who's been inclined to jump to conclusions —"

"I beg your pardon," said Mrs. Brill, having apparently jumped to some conclusions of her own. "I have been under some strain lately, yes. But I'm fully ready to talk about Jason."

Abigail stood. "Come on, Jason."

"Well," Gehringer said to Mrs. Brill, "you see? They just won't listen." He could hear the anger rising in his voice, moving in his chest. "They take it into themselves and decide, and that's the end of that."

"Mr. Gehringer, I have documentation," Mrs. Brill said. "Please sit down and we'll discuss this calmly. Mrs. Gehringer, will you please come back and sit down."

Abigail had moved to the door.

"Can we please discuss this in an adult fashion," Mrs. Brill said.

"You don't understand," Gehringer shouted. "I'm agreeing with you. I'm telling you, you can't win. No matter what you say, no matter what you do, you can't win. They've stacked the cards on you, and that's the end of that."

Now they were all staring at him. Abigail held a handkerchief to her face. Jason had come to his feet.

"Perhaps if you would all like to be alone for a few minutes," Mrs. Brill said, rising.

"No," Abigail said, moving to her chair again.

"Aw, Christ," Gehringer said. "I didn't mean for this — look. I'm sorry."

"Please tell me what my boy has done to disrupt your class."

Mrs. Brill cleared her throat, eyeing Gehringer. "Actually, I thought I'd have Jason tell you himself."

Abigail had begun to cry. She wiped her eyes with the handkerchief. Gehringer sat down, turned so that he could look from Jason to Mrs. Brill and back again.

"I'll pay attention better," Jason said, watching his own nervous fingers. "And I won't talk out of turn."

Mrs. Brill nodded, and she made a notation with her pencil on Jason's folder.

"There have been some tensions at home," Abigail said, sniffling.

"I understand," said Mrs. Brill.

Gehringer knew he was the subject of this exchange. "If I'm not needed anymore," he said, "I'll wait outside."

Mrs. Brill was writing on the folder, and Abigail was watching her.

"If you'll excuse me."

"Of course," Mrs. Brill said.

He went into the hallway and down to the end of it, where the doors were, and the brilliant late afternoon sun. Out in the parking lot, the drunken young woman lay across the shining hood of a red sports car, one leg up, showing thigh. She held some tiny object close to her face, as if to examine it for flaws, and on the curb across from her the young man sat, his arms resting on his knees. Apparently there were no flaws in the little object; whatever she held was just the thing. It was in the way she reached over and offered it to the young man, who looked at it with clear satisfaction, admiring it. Then he put it in his mouth and smiled at her. They were perfect, Gehringer thought, their belief in perfection was all over them. They were without a care in the whole wide world.

Desire

"Things are worsening by the minute," Ridley says, meaning his own climbing panic, but knowing they'll think he means the culture — the failures of education and the depredations of the politicians, the general mess all around, the sense that nothing counts for anything anymore, the powerless, disenfranchised feeling of the whole population. This is, after all, what they have been talking about. It is always the major subject of discussion whenever he spends time with the Masons, the old couple who live downstairs, his landlords. And he owes them two months back rent that so far nobody has mentioned. "A whole system of beliefs is disintegrating," he says, trying to keep them in focus. He wonders if his eyes are showing any signs of what he has ingested. He knows he's likely to talk a little faster, a little louder, and so he tries to keep it slow and as precise as possible. The Masons have been kindly, and they do not deserve this, any more than they deserve to go two months without rent. They have made meals for him. They've befriended him, and he knows they're wondering about the money he owes them.

"The history of everything," Mr. Mason says, "is a path downward. The study of all history is really the study of decline. And this is the decline of the West. Don't you think?"

"People get old and pass on, and so do cultures," says Mrs. Mason. "I think each individual life mirrors the life of a civilization, in a way. It's the natural course."

"Or perhaps it's the other way around, dear," Mr. Mason says.

Then he hesitates, like someone leading a student through a lesson. "The civilization mirrors the life of the individual." He nods at her. "Don't you agree?"

"Well," says his wife, "perhaps. I think I meant it as I said it, though."

The two of them read a lot, and they like to talk about it all. It's a way of keeping up, as Mr. Mason once put it, a way of keeping mentally fit. But they are drawn to the most negative prognosticators and philosophers. It's amazing. They've been married about sixty years, and cling to each other now, like children in a storm. Ridley thinks of them holding on in the winds of what they have been reading. There's plenty for them to worry about right here. Their savings are dwindling. The taxes on this small two-story house, which was paid for more than a decade ago, are more than three times what their mortgage payment was. They rented the upstairs room to Ridley because they needed the extra money. But Ridley lost his job, and got involved with Pamela Brill, and what money he had managed to save started going toward trying to keep up with her. Pamela is twenty-three, and because she's never been without money, she never thinks about it — often forgets to carry any. She lets others spend it, quite unselfconsciously.

Ridley's hopelessly in love with her.

"So," Mr. Mason says, putting his hands on his bony knees. "We're happy you came to see us. Is there anything we can do for you?"

Ridley can't remember why he's come down here. He says, "Just, ah, wanted to say hello."

"Nothing else?"

"Can't think," he says. "My brain, it's a sieve."

"Our young man is a little out of sorts," Mrs. Mason says.

"You've both been so nice to me," Ridley says.

"Would you like something to eat?" Mr. Mason asks him. "I think we can rustle up something."

"I'll help you, dear."

It's obvious that they want to go off and talk about him. He searches his mind for the reason he walked down here. He runs through it all — remembers making his unsteady way down the stairs at the side of the house, knocking on their door, looking at the sky gathering heavy clouds over the mountains, another storm system on its way, rolling over the hills. Remembers standing there on the porch waiting for them to answer, and feeling immediately the sense of guilt for what he owes them. The talk. The genuinely convivial company they make, always so eager to engage him in conversation. And they're really very interesting people.

He listens to them moving around in their kitchen. They murmur, but he can hear them. He thinks he can hear the little fibers moving in their throats; he's attuned to everything. They're not talking about him, after all. They're preparing sandwiches, cutting slices of Swiss cheese, opening jars. "Fetch me that, will you, dear?" says Mr. Mason.

"Yes, dear."

"Do we have any horseradish?"

"Should."

"Do you know where I put it?"

"Can't say I do," Mrs. Mason says.

"Why don't you pay more attention to where I leave things when I forget to put them away?"

"Guess I'm just falling down on the job."

"Now I can't find the mayo."

"It's on the bottom shelf."

"No it isn't."

"Then I don't know where it is."

Earlier this afternoon, outside the high school where her mother teaches English, Pamela Brill had offered him some small red pills in a vial. They'd already had some whiskey to drink. "Know what these are?" she said, licking the edges of her lips.

"Pills?" He hadn't meant it to sound like a question. His embarrassment was extreme. It was way out of proportion. He forced a smile and tried to seem casual. He cleared his throat and said the word again, hoping the smile was sardonic. "Pills."

She lay across the hood of her Mazda. All languid grace, and that amazing skin. They were out in the sunlight, in the school parking lot. In front of the whole world. He was half drunk. He would never do anything like this sober.

"Okay," she said with a smirk. "But guess what kind of pill."

"I don't know," he said. "A non-pharmacy kind."

She offered it to him. "Very good guess."

He was horrified. "Really?" he said.

"It makes America beautiful."

"You're beautiful," he said.

"Oh, shut up. I hate that shit. Stop it. Come on, you know what I mean. It makes everything gorgeous."

"Well," he said, "I think that depends, doesn't it?"

She seemed perplexed, considered this a moment with her astoundingly perfect features scrunched up. She was a person who could get a man to commit murder. "Do you mean like, they say an unhappy person doesn't have a positive near-death experience?"

"Who says that?" Ridley asked.

"Like if your attitude is wrong when it happens, you know, they say you suffer the pangs of hell."

"Not me," he said. "I don't believe in hell." He thought he could remember her saying that at some point.

"Is your attitude wrong, Ridley?"

"My attitude's right. I said I don't believe in hell."

"That's nice," she said.

"You don't, either," he said. "Right?" He tried to smile.

"I've never given it much thought." Again, she considered. He wanted to kiss the corner of her lips, and thought of touching her hair. Just touching it. It looked like it might burn your hand.

"Where'd you get this stuff?" he asked.

"Never mind. Let's try some. Want to?"

"I'm a bit drunk," he managed.

"You look a little pale."

"No," he said.

"That's what I like about you." She laughed. "You're such a nervous cat."

"I only seem nervous," he said, swallowing suddenly.

"You get so formal with me. It's nice," she said. "Here." She handed him the pill.

"Thank you," he said, resisting, just in time, the urge to bow. He hadn't slept well in weeks. He hadn't been able to rest at all.

"Ready?" she said. Then she swallowed hers. "Now you."

"Don't have anything to drink with it," he said.

"It's small. Melts in your mouth."

"Okay," he said.

She was right. It went down to nothing almost as fast as it touched his tongue. And then he was waiting for it to do whatever it would do. At first there wasn't much sensation at all. But then he began to wonder if things weren't changing for him in a big way. He decided that he was becoming extremely aware of time. It seemed that time broke down into slow, discrete seconds which stretched themselves out. She had stepped down off the car and was talking about driving away. He wanted to drive, and she said she wanted to ride in back with her legs over the seat. They got themselves into the front, and he saw that someone was standing in the doorway of the school. They had been seen.

"Someone saw us," he said.

She didn't answer.

"Pamela?"

"I guess we'll go to jail, then. Have you ever been to jail, Ridley?"

"Of course not."

"I spent a night in jail when I was away at school. Drunk and disorderly. I was close to death."

He drove carefully to the Masons' old house. Home. The idea that he lived there seemed too strange for words. "Jeez," he said.

They sat there breathing.

"I think we should do some more," she said. "I've got it — let's swallow some of it with orange juice. That'll be like in the best tradition. Do you have any orange juice?"

"Orange juice."

"Right. You know, the orange stuff in the little frozen cans."

"No," he said. "Orange juice hurts my stomach."

"Poor baby. What do you have to drink?"

"I can get some orange juice," he said.

"What else do you have?"

"Beer?"

"Ugh," she said.

"I've got V-8 juice."

She looked at him. "Why?"

He had been using it to make up for the fact that he never ate any vegetables, and for the one gram of fiber in it. Ridley's main concern, when he wasn't thinking about Pamela Brill, was his digestive system and his health generally. This was not something he felt he could tell her, so he said nothing at all.

"Well?" she said. It was a challenge.

"I like it," he told her. "I make — I make bloody marys with it."

"Oh, okay. There you go, bloody marys. Let's have that."

They made their way inside. She was actually coming into his apartment. He stood in the doorway and thought about how it would look to her. He had become almost fastidious, living alone. As usual, he had made the bed this morning and hung up his bathrobe; his slippers were next to each other under the bed.

"It's so neat," she said, sounding disappointed. "I'm such a slob."

"Lady downstairs," he told her. "Real philosopher type. She cleans it. Comes in every day no matter what. I'm a slob, too, usually."

"I keep myself clean, though," she said.

"No," he said. "Right. Me too. It's best to stay clean if you can help it."

"I don't mean I'm anal or anything. You know, I don't mind a little dust. That's just living in a place. But mold and mildew and things like that. Things that grow. I'm pretty careful about it." She exhaled a satisfied sigh. "So the lady who cleans for you is a philosopher."

"Not officially," he said. "She does a lot of reading."

"That makes two of us. Except that nothing I've read has anything in it really about how I'm supposed to get through the days."

"Sure it does," Ridley said.

"I finished college, Ridley. I learned how to look at stuff, you know, and identify it. I learned the names of some places and some people and some wars. But nothing I read in the whole four years told me anything about how to get from one day to the next. Not really."

He searched his mind for some response. "That's not quite what it's ever supposed to do, is it?" he said.

"Then what good is it?"

"I think it's just supposed to be itself."

But she was on to something else, looking around the room. "Where's our bloody marys, anyway?"

He was fairly sure he didn't have the makings for bloody marys, since he wasn't sure what went into them in the first place. He had no gin or vodka. "I don't really feel like a bloody mary," he said.

She sat on the edge of his bed and leaned back on her hands. "I've never had one."

"It's a nighttime drink," he said.

Frowning, she said, "I thought it was morning."

"It's not a lunch drink."

"Brunch. And I haven't eaten."

"Oh," Ridley said. "I never have a bloody mary for lunch. I'm already crocked."

"Actually," Pamela Brill said, "I need a pick-me-up. That's what a bloody mary is, isn't it? A pick-me-up."

"No," said Ridley, "not for me. I take one, you know, before I go to sleep. Like a sleeping pill. I go right out. Bango."

She sat forward. "Don't mention that to me. Sleeping pills. Don't say that."

"I'm sorry." He didn't know why he was apologizing.

"Sleeping pills. God. This friend of my stepmother's — didn't you see it in the paper? And my stepmother was with her, too — had lunch with her — the day she did it."

Ridley watched her run her hands through her hair. Every cell of her was absolutely perfect. His chest hurt. He couldn't exhale all the way.

"You didn't read about it?" she said.

"I don't think so."

"This friend of my stepmother's. Went antiques shopping with my stepmother and another woman, then drove to a motel and swallowed a bottle of sleeping pills and went to sleep for good." She lay back. "It must be terrible to be old."

He moved to the bed and sat down at her hips. She was inches away. "Pamela," he said. "I love you. I want to marry you."

"Imagine checking into a motel room knowing it's where you're going to *die*."

"Maybe it was an impulse," he said. He was looking at the fine down on her legs, the smooth thighs, the way her shorts bunched up at the top of them and revealed the tan line. Oh God, he thought. Or perhaps he had spoken this.

"What," she said.

He *had* spoken. "Nothing."

"It makes you think, doesn't it?"

"What," he said.

"Dying like that. All alone in a cheap motel. My mother thinks she did it because she was having to give up her nice farm and everything."

"She didn't leave a note?"

"Nothing. Not a single thing. Isn't that eerie?"

He touched her knee.

"Don't."

He took his hand away as though it had been bitten.

A moment later, she said, "Do you ever think of suicide, Ridley?"

Oh, yes.

"Well, do you?"

"I have," he said.

She sat forward, so that they were side by side. "Me too."

"You?" he said.

She nodded simply. "Sure."

"Recently?" he said.

"I guess."

"Why?"

"I don't know. I think it's a kind of sickness with me. Sometimes I just don't want to be bored anymore, and I think of doing it. I actually think of it like it might be something to do. It's that sick. I've been unhappy, too. It's kind of scary that it's there, like a place you go to. Suicide. It's like there are times when I think it's waiting for me. Like I'm this little animal and everything's going extinct."

"If I was you," he said, "I wouldn't be unhappy. Ever."

"Oh, really?" Her smile was beautifully sardonic.

He was thinking of saying that if he had the luxury of living in that body, he would spend all his time in bed with someone. But then the someone he saw her in bed with, in this version of his imagined self, was her. She stared at him, and it was as though she were reading his thoughts.

"You know how to say 'Kiss my ass' in Spanish?" she said.

He shook his head.

"Hey, seenyore, come and keess my asss."

"Oh," he said, laughing. "Oh, right — I get it."

"Hey, seenyore," she said. "Come and keess my asss."

"That's good," he said.

"So, are you going to fix us these bloody marys?"

"I've got whiskey," he said.

"Okay." She shrugged. "Whiskey."

Neither of them moved.

"Well?" she said.

He leaned toward her, and she kept her eyes on him, watching him. He put his mouth on hers, seeing her eyes still open. He pulled back.

"What," she said.

He tried again. Her tongue was heavy; it moved with a languid, harrowing softness in his mouth. He felt his heart beating
at the top of his head. His hands were on her arms, pushing her
back onto the bed.

"Hey," she said, turning her head away. "Wait a minute,
lover."

He could feel his weight on her.

"Get up, will you?"

"Jesus," Ridley said. "Oh, man." He got to his feet. She
propped herself on one elbow and regarded him. "I'm sorry," he
said.

"Hey, seenyore," she said. "You just want to keess my asss."

For a moment, he could say or do nothing at all.

She reached into the pocket of her shorts and brought out
the vial of pills. "Let's ride on a cloud when we do it. I'm not
high enough."

"I'll get the whiskey," he said, out of breath. In the small
cabinet over the refrigerator was a flask of Old Grand Dad. He
brought it down, his hands trembling. The neck of the flask
ticked against the lip of his glass. He spilled some.

"I'm thirsty," she said behind him.

"Coming up." His voice caught. The word *up* had come out
in a falsetto. She laughed softly, lazily; she reveled in her effect
on people.

They each took another pill and sipped the whiskey, and for
a time everything seemed calm enough. They sat on the bed and
waited, and she talked about her stepmother's friend, who had
abandoned her family and hadn't even left a note. "I know her
daughter," she said. "Her name is Maizie." She laughed softly.
"I worked with her and we got to be friends. That's not exactly
the truth. Since she got pregnant, I haven't seen much of her at
all. And I haven't even talked to her about her mother. Actually,
I wouldn't even know where to begin. Maizie used to talk me
out of suicide, you know? Jesus — I wouldn't know where to
begin."

"Pamela," he said. "I can't stop thinking about you." He had decided that he should tell her now, before the drug took over. "I'm in love with you, and I want us to stop all this and settle down together."

She shrugged, not looking at him. It seemed as if she might even yawn. "Everybody says that. That's movie talk."

"It's true. I'm speaking the absolute truth as I know it."

"You watch too many movies," she said.

He was ready to swear off ever seeing another movie again in his life. "I know, but listen to me," he said. "I want to marry you and start a family." The words sounded oddly foolish on his lips. "I love you," he said. "No matter what else is true."

She laughed. "Stop it." Then: "Feel anything yet?"

"I feel that I love you," he said.

"Stop it."

"I do. I honestly do, Pamela."

"Here." She gave him another pill. He had begun to experience sharp pains in his left side. Shooting pains. He put the glass down with the whiskey in it, and tried to kiss her again. "Wait," she said. "Jesus."

"I love you," he said.

"Oh," she said. "Oh, wait. Feel that? Jesus. Tell me how it feels, come on. You must feel something by now."

He had experienced the pains, and now he noticed a strange tunneling of his vision; all the edges were beginning to blur and dissolve. He felt as though his eyes were bulging. He couldn't believe she would not react, his eyes bugging out of his head. "God," he said.

"Whoa," she said, opening her mouth. Her expression was that of someone flying down the steepest turn on a roller coaster, though she kept watching him, too. "Whoa," she said. "Jeee-sus. Feel that?"

He swallowed the rest of the whiskey, and the room grew liquid. She was sitting on the bed with her legs crossed, and he did not remember when she had arranged herself like that. He lay face down, arms dangling over the edge, head lolling, tongue out. He moved it, licked something — her knee. He had turned and was licking her knee.

"Okay," she said, lying back. "Ohhhh-kay."

He got to his knees on the bed, and then he was pulling at her shorts, the flimsy pink panties underneath. "Stop it," she said. "Tell me what it's doing to you."

Her hand pushed his away. Everything wavered and went up in waves of air. He lay down at her side, and his hands wouldn't work. He was tossing in a boat, riding an ocean, and she was murmuring in his ear, moving her tongue at his ear.

"Okay, lover," she said.

He couldn't raise himself up. He reached for her, felt the weight of her, and heard the laugh. They lay in a tangle of clothes. She was trying to unbutton his shirt. "I love you," he said. And then he was crying.

"Jeee-sus. What're you crying about?"

"I can't stop."

She pulled away and stood. "Where's the bathroom?"

"Pamela."

But she had stumbled away. He heard her in there, coughing. "Ridley," she said. "I have to be alone for a few minutes. That goddam whiskey."

"I'm in love with you," he said, still crying. Everything seemed so hopeless for a moment. He gathered himself, tried to clear his mind.

"Get out of here, Ridley."

"I'll be downstairs," he told her.

"Just get."

So he came unsteadily down the shaky wooden stairway, realizing that he had reached this level of intimacy with her; he had been in bed with her and she had called him lover. He knocked on the Masons' door. The world was suffused in a yellow glow, and he felt completely immutable and clean. The hopelessness had dissipated like a cloud. He was solid as a piece of marble inside. He thought of the curves of rock under his skin.

The Masons let him in, offered him a glass of water for the parched sound of his voice (he hadn't noticed the parched sound of his voice, but he took them at their word), and quickly enough after they brought him his glass of ice water, he began to feel everything shift toward fright.

He's ashamed, and he understands that lately whatever he's feeling seems somehow beside the point. Even so, he keeps finding in himself this little tremor of well-being, like a secret nerve discharging at the synapse. In those moments, it's almost as if, at the core of himself, he were a man standing on a boulder amidst a fast-flowing river. It convinces him, each time it happens, that things might soon take a turn for the better.

He's looking for that feeling as Mr. Mason comes back into the room.

"Well," Mr. Mason says, setting down a plate of crackers and cheese. "I myself always believed in discipline."

"Yes." Ridley looks straight at him, focusing. "And it's gone. Nobody even thinks about it." He remembers that this is the subject. And then he hopes it is.

Mrs. Mason says, "Civilizations are like arrows in flight. They arc and then fall to earth."

On occasion, Ridley thinks of her conversation as a series of captions for the pictures her husband paints. The old man has described himself as a history buff. Everybody, according to Mr. Mason, is a buff of this or a buff of that. There are computer buffs and movie buffs and radio buffs and song buffs. Ridley is a medicine buff, though it has been some time since he dropped out of college. He told Mr. Mason that he was a pre-med student when he quit. All this means is that he took one biology and one chemistry course. He failed them both, but this makes no difference to Mr. Mason. "Young Ridley here," Mr. Mason will say to visitors, "is a medicine buff." To Ridley's friends, Mr. Mason says, "Are you medicine buffs like Ridley?"

"Entropy is in God's plan," he says now. "As is our struggle with it."

Mr. Mason's views are all informed by his religious feeling. He's nondenominational, he says, with Catholic leanings. Ridley has privately described him to friends as a God buff, since all his talk leads inexorably back to God. Having read the works of Thomas Aquinas, and having once almost decided to attend the seminary, Ridley can talk the talk. Even now, with panic roiling in his heart. "When was the last time anybody asked for sacrifice?" he says. "Even the word sounds strange, doesn't it?"

"Never sounded strange to me," says Mr. Mason.

Ridley is always unnerved when something he has said that is a lie, and that he has thought would be picked up by someone and agreed with, is turned back in disagreement. It's always as though he's been caught out, the falsehood showing on his face somehow. For a second, he can't say anything else. The two people sit on their couch, their faces pleasant and empty. He feels them begin to slide out of solidness, feels the beginning of hallucination, and tries to talk again. "It's a great world," he says. He had meant to say *word.* Sacrifice is a great *word.* The old people simply stare back at him. "My eyes feel funny," he says. "I've got allergies to certain kinds of things in the air. And I hate war. I hate all different kinds of war. Guerrilla war and holy war and — and wars of liberation. Did you know that the albumen in eggs is full of strontium 90 from practicing for the war we didn't get around to fighting?"

They stare at him.

"Sometimes I think wars are like God's forest fire for people, you know?" This seems perfectly clear to him, but he can see the doubt in their faces. "My eyes sting," he says. "It's really something."

"Pollution," Mrs. Mason says, smiling to encourage him. She seems to think there's more. Out the window, behind her almost too bright bluish-gray hair, trees wave in the wind. There's a storm coming. The sky on the other side of the trees is black.

"I think suffering really comes from people realizing they're not doing what's right for their spiritual development," Ridley says. He's almost certain he got it out clearly, but the two of them look worried and nervous. "Really," he goes on. "Don't you think so? People have — they could have everything. Beautiful — you know. And they — they throw it away on nothing, a lot of empty shit like drugs and alcohol and running around like there's no tomorrow and talking about suicide that way, like it's a thing you flirt with, for Christ's sake. When a person would swear to love them forever in a minute and work to stop every bad habit just for the chance — you know. I mean if you love someone, I mean isn't that what we're all supposed to be doing?"

"Pardon me," Mr. Mason says, rising. He walks into the next room. Ridley hears the windows closing there.

"Rain," Ridley says to Mrs. Mason. "I didn't think it was supposed to." His voice shakes, as if someone has punched him. The sentence has come out all wrong. He thinks he must've said it wrong, because she's giving him a troubled look. "Rain is nice, isn't it?" he says.

She says something he doesn't quite catch, about her garden. During the summer, before things started running out of control, he helped her put the garden in. He worked all day for three days, bare back cooking in the sun, clean and pleasurably thirsty, so that water tasted better than anything, and at night he slept deep. He had not met Pamela Brill yet. He had flunked out of college and been disowned by his father for the failure, and he was unable to decide what he should do in the way of work, a career. The whole idea of a career made his stomach hurt and filled him with the dread of death.

He remembers digging in Mrs. Mason's garden, thinking about the cool water in the tin ladle from the well.

"It's terrible now," he hears, and realizes he has spoken aloud.

"Yes," Mrs. Mason says, agreeing.

"Pardon me," he says to her. "I lost my train of thought."

She smiles, staring.

"Did you hear me?" he says.

"Yes," she says in that agreeable way. When her husband isn't there, she becomes quite vague, Ridley has noticed.

"Do you remember what I said?" Ridley asks her.

"Discipline," she says, making a fist. She's watching him carefully. She's wary. "It started because we were talking about why a woman with a nice family and a husband and a lot of nice things would lock herself up in a motel room and do away with herself."

"Who?" Ridley says, more confused all the time.

"The woman. That person they found in the motel room down the street."

"Oh, my God," he says. He can't remember. He thinks of Pamela. He was talking to Pamela about this. Did they bring this up? "Did you bring this up?" he says.

"We were talking about her. She took a bottle of pills."

"We only took four apiece," Ridley almost shouts. "It just gets worse."

"Pardon?" she says.

He says, "Everything's coming apart at the seams."

"Are you all right?"

He nods, sees Mrs. Mason's features shrink. Is she frowning? She's leaned forward slightly to look at him.

"Are you sure you're all right, young man?"

"Oh," he says, "I'm just fine."

The rain hits the window with an insistence, as if it wants in now, and Mr. Mason comes back into the room carrying the box of crackers. "These are all I could find," he says. "I'm afraid the cupboard's bare."

This is a hint, and Ridley knows it. He can't put the words together in his head. "I've got a job interview," he says. But they don't seem to have heard him.

"All this makes me very nervous," Mrs. Mason says.

"She's never liked storms," her husband says. "That one yesterday really frightened us both for the lightning."

"I've never seen it so bad," she says.

"Well, I shouldn't've mentioned it," says Mr. Mason. "I can see it also upsets our young tenant here."

"Such an awe-inspiring thing," says Mrs. Mason.

"You mean the — that — the woman that — the suicide," Ridley gets out. It's as if he's solved a puzzle they've given him. "Her. I know about that."

They stare at him.

"I was talking about the lightning."

"It's a disgrace these days to tell a girl you want to get married and have a family. It's a fucking joke."

Mr. Mason draws a breath. It's clear that he's overcoming some resistance in himself.

"Excuse me," Ridley says.

"You're upset," says Mrs. Mason.

There's more talk, but Ridley can't quite follow it. Then he can.

Mr. Mason says, "I heard that she was lying in the bed with the covers pulled up, like someone lying down to sleep, you know."

"Right," says Ridley. "No note."

"A note?"

He waits. The next thing they say will give him something to latch on to.

"Poor woman," Mrs. Mason says.

Ridley realizes that his hands are gripping his knees. He tries to look calm. The Masons are changing before his eyes, drifting out of their own shapes. He almost leaps at them. "Hey," he says, too loud, and they sit forward. They have recomposed themselves. Their color is odd in the light.

"Yes?" says Mr. Mason with a faintly suspicious tilting of his head.

"Where were we?"

"There's no knowing what a person goes through," Mrs. Mason says. "We should talk about something else."

"No one can ever really know another person," says her husband.

It thunders. The sound seems to move across the sky, like a heavy ball rolling on a table, and then everything is still again. The rain comes down. Ridley has a moment of believing he can hear it splattering against the leaves of the farthest tree, and then he sees that on the branches of that tree there are two large black hulking birds. The sound now seems to rise from those shapes, and it comes at him through the small opening at the bottom of the window. He can almost see the air tremble with it. His heart shakes; he breathes the odor of wet wood and ozone, and thinks of outer space. Everything makes too much noise.

"Without discipline and sacrifice," Mr. Mason is saying, "I think some people learn to start expecting perfection. And when they don't get it" — he shrugs — "why, they jump out of the boat. That's the only explanation I've ever had for it."

"Maybe it's because they think life won't change," Mrs. Mason says, emphasizing the last word. "Or else they're too afraid it *will* change."

"I would like to know," Ridley says suddenly, "what the hell we're talking about." It's as if he has barked at them. Then, softly: "It's getting dark."

They wait. There's a greenish light at the windows. Ridley is floating loose inside, anchorless, guilty, while the Masons sit regarding him. His vision is clouding over. The wavering light changes and appears to flare up, and it seems to him that a ball of flame rolls out of the fireplace and licks across the carpet to the television set, where it flashes and makes a bright shower of sparks. It's like the Fourth of July. He sees flames climb the wall, crackling, bending and fanning out at the ceiling. It's a hallucination, the worst thing, and he grips himself, trying to smile at the Masons, who are huddled together, their faces calm as facts. He tries to think what he has said, tries to recover everything that led up to the moment, and the fierce heat on his face makes him fear that the fire is real, that he has not imagined it. The Masons are still huddled on the couch, apparently waiting to die. Their faces are blank.

"Come on," he says to them. "Jesus. I took something." He stands, reaches for them. "Get up," he says. "Jesus, it's real."

Mr. Mason tries to cover his wife's face. They do not move. Ridley pulls at the old man's arm, then bends down and puts his arms around him, lifting.

"What are you doing?" Mr. Mason says.

Mrs. Mason has flopped over on her side and is shouting for help.

"Here," Ridley says. "Lift her." But he can't get either of them to move. The air is burning his lungs. He can't see.

"Don't hurt us," Mr. Mason is shouting. "Please. Help. Help."

Every movement Ridley makes is doubled in his own perception, and finally, somehow, he finds himself on the stairs, tumbling down onto the lawn, with the Masons shouting at him from the stairs.

"— call the police," Mr. Mason is saying. "If you come near us again —"

Ridley moves off from the house into the rain, and lightning shudders nearby. When he turns, he falls, ends up lying on his back, arms spread, the black sky moving over him. The house is plainly not lightning-struck, and there's no fire. "Excuse me," he says. "I'm sorry." Then he tries to yell to them. "I thought it was a fire. I'm absolutely sick with love."

"Crazy," Mr. Mason shouts. "I won't have it."

Mrs. Mason says something he can't hear. Ridley lifts his head in the rain and there they are, holding on to each other, looking troubled and afraid, and above them, on her own part of the stairs, is Pamela Brill. He has a moment of brilliant clarity, remembering himself. She looks at him with a terrifyingly cold curiosity. "Oh, God," he says. "I want you. I don't have anything else. I don't want another thing in the world."

She says nothing, steps into his doorway out of the rain, still giving him that chilly, evaluative look. When the Masons begin shouting at him, she joins them, screams at him, the perfect teeth lining the red mouth. "It wasn't what you think," she says. "You with your stupid imagination. You're drunk, and that's about all you are, too. Plain old drunk." It's clear that she's enjoying this — that for her, it's all part of the same fun. For an instant they are all contending with one another and the storm, trying to be heard, saying words he can't distinguish for the anger and the shouting and the thunder. He lies back. It's as though the pure force of their displeasure has leveled him.

Except that, as the rain washes over him and lightning flashes in the sky, he feels an unexpected peace. It comes to him that his love makes him good, and for this one wordless instant he can believe it. Out of everything else, this true thing shines forth, perfectly clear. And he is reasonably certain that it's not coming from any drug. His love has elevated him. His wishes for honorable actions and faith have made him excellent, even in this disaster. Through the relative brightness of these intimations, he sees the others still shouting, still gesturing, and in his strangely exalted state, it's as though they are calling to him from a distant shoreline, long-lost friends, dear friends, loved ones, urging him on, cheering him, happy for him as he sets sail in search of his unimaginable future.

Goodbyes

Maizie, my darling, I'm sitting here trying to find something to say to you, and all I can think about is how it was when I was a kid and ran through the rooms of an empty house, the echoes bouncing around. I'm feeling pretty blue tonight. And the echoes are bouncing around here, of course. Every move I make gets repeated in the walls. It's so strange to have this house empty again, and maybe it's a good thing that your mother isn't here to see it like this. I remember you and James running through these rooms when we were first here, before the furniture got moved in, both of you yelling so loud I had to get after you. Tonight I feel like a little kid, and the way my voice echoes in the walls is at least partly what's doing it to me. It makes me more certain than ever that I shouldn't move in with you and Leo, and I'm sorry for all his hard work on the room. But you'll find some use for it, I'm sure.

You were so anxious to buttonhole me when we moved your mother's things out of here, and I guess I wasn't very helpful. I know I wasn't. I'm not the best man for getting things said that need saying, and there's a lot I miss, I know. James told me he was joking when he said that about how I miss so many close calls I ought to be an umpire, but I know he was serious enough, too. You both think I'm pretty dense, no doubt. And even so, you think I'm keeping something back, that I'm lying when I say I really don't have a very definite idea why your mother did what she did. You think there's something hidden, some secret we kept from you, and there just isn't. For instance, you both knew about it when she had her trouble about Buddy Wells. You both knew how close we were to separating.

I just don't have any clear ideas about it, and I wish that weren't so. I wish I could say I knew for certain what she was thinking about, or that I'd seen anything in her behavior or heard something in her voice.

To be exactly truthful, I thought she was happy.

I thought she was handling the move far better than I was. After all, she was the one who took charge, who went through all the papers with the real estate people, and showed the house and grounds. It was your mother who took us through each stage of the sale of the property and all the settlements. She wouldn't let me have anything to do with it. I had been having my usual trouble sleeping, and of course my stomach was giving me fits. The whole thing had me rattled pretty bad. But she seemed to have warmed to the idea and got comfortable with it — I remember, I even questioned her about it on that last day — at no time did she seem unfocused or despondent or indifferent.

Anyway, I refuse to believe that she could've done it just because we were leaving the house. That's a hardship, maybe, but nothing to kill yourself over.

There were, after all, things to look forward to. Being a grandparent, for instance. And having some time and money to travel a little. She always wanted to go to Rome and look at the Sistine Chapel in person. And there were all those Donatelli statues. The tombs Michelangelo did. You know me, Maizie. I don't know much about Art, but we were saving up for the trip. I'd love to have been able to give it to her. I would've let her teach me like she always said she wanted to. We'd go on one of those posh two-week deals, maybe. Or a combination cruise. Something really elegant. We actually planned it. I put extra dollars away for years, and I don't have any idea how much she saved on her own. But somehow school and work and the farm — things got in the way. She held the purse strings, of course, and she started dipping into the Italy money so she could get for you kids the things she wanted you to have. She didn't mind, either. Neither of us had any regrets on that score.

But I want to try and give you everything you want to know, Maizie. And so I've decided to tell you a story about your mother and me, and it starts with the night she told me about Buddy Wells. I knew Wells a little, enough to see that whatever else he was, he wasn't the sort of man who could've been much use to your mother. I think I also sensed that he was a little enamored of her. Wells was the sort of man who couldn't keep his own emotions out of his face, there wasn't a single subtlety anywhere in him. They began with a friendship, like a lot of people — he was bringing his daughter to your mother's dance classes, and they'd got to talking. The daughter charmed her especially. She invited him and the daughter to a party or two that we had, back when we were entertaining a lot. One day, out of the blue, Buddy made a declaration of love to her. It shocked her, apparently, though I can't imagine why. She didn't know what to do with it at first. For a few weeks she kept the whole thing to herself. She even sought ways to keep from ever being alone with him. But then she found that she was thinking about him in the nights, and wondering what he might be doing during the days. She decided she felt something for him, and on an evening toward the beginning of summer, she decided to tell me this.

"Buddy Wells has fallen in love with me," she said.

It was a Thursday evening after her spring recitals, and I had made my own dinner and settled into my chair with the crossword puzzle. I said, "Anyone could've told you that."

"You don't understand," she said.

I said, "Sure I do."

There was such a look of alarm on her face, Maizie.

I said, "What is it?"

"I feel the same way," she said.

I didn't say anything for a few seconds. It hadn't quite sunk in yet.

"I've fallen in love with him," she said.

I said, "You've —" but nothing would come.

"He wants me to move in with him."

I said, "You're joking."

"I don't know how to put this any other way," she said. "I know it sounds silly." That was what she said. Those were her words.

"You can't be serious," I said.

She stammered like a little girl in a school lesson, but couldn't get anything out.

I waited.

"Oh, for God's sake, Harry, you know what I'm going to say."

"No," I said. "I don't have the slightest idea."

"I'm moving in with him. He's in love — we're — we —"

"You mean this?" I said to her. "This is serious."

"I don't know," she said.

"Well, is it or isn't it?"

"I'm not making it up, Harry."

I didn't say anything.

"I'm not making it up," she said again.

I said, "Let me get this straight —"

She said, "Please, I told you. Don't make me go through it again."

"All right, Andrea," I said. "Suppose you tell me what you want me to say."

"I don't know," she said.

"You think you do, though," I said.

And she nodded. It was as if she were relenting somehow, as if I'd forced the answer out of her.

"Why don't you tell me instead of making me say it for you?"
I said.

She began to cry.

"Have you slept with him?" I said.

Maizie, it was as if I'd thrown something at her. But a husband has the right to ask certain things. She said, "Not — not yet."

"But you're going to," I said.

"I don't know." This was said with a good deal of frustration, and again it was as if I'd been badgering her about it.

"You came in here to tell me something. Is that all of it? I don't see why I should be put into the position of a goddam inquisitor about it, since you are my wife."

"I don't know," she said again. "I know I love him."

"Well, for Christ's sake," I said, "let me know when you know the rest of it." She had her purse in her hands and was standing over by the door. I was sitting more or less right where I'm presently sitting. She'd come through from the bedroom, where she'd been most of the evening. It'd been a normal evening. There hadn't been anything that would have led me to suspect a situation like this. I said, "Where are you going now?"

She said, "I don't know."

I said, "This is an appalling case of ignorance on your part."

"Please, Harry," she said.

I said, "If only you knew how silly you look, mooning over that open-faced kid. You're funny, you know it? A laughing-stock. No, you're ridiculous. I can't believe that you, with your goddam reserve and your refinement and your book and garden clubs and study groups and Arts Leagues, could be willing to make such a public fool of yourself this way, being sluttish like this with a kid ten, twelve years younger than you are."

She started to cry.

"Really, Andrea. I think you've gone off the deep end. Look at you. This kid's in his thirties, for Christ's sake. You were nursing James when Buddy Wells was in elementary school. It's so silly. Silly and sordid. What do you think?"

She stood there crying, not looking at me. And I felt suddenly almost sorry for her. Part of me sensed that she had blundered into the whole thing, and that she was perfectly and painfully aware of how ridiculous she had become.

I sensed, too, as any husband would, that it all had to do with me. But there were other reasons for me to feel that way, as you'll see soon enough. And it was what put me over the edge. When she started toward the bedroom, I followed her. I said worse things. I was getting carried away now, and even my sorrow for her couldn't stop me. I told her just what I'd do if she left — how the talk would go among the people we knew, and what I'd make sure you and James and the rest of the family understood about it, how she had carried on with Wells behind my back and betrayed everything we stood for. And I said that if I had any say at all, she would spend the rest of her life in Buddy Wells's circle, alone, without anyone to turn to when things went sour, as they certainly would, with somebody like Buddy Wells. I reminded her of her age, and of you and James — especially I reminded her of you, and what it would mean to you, starting into your womanhood. I was shouting, letting her have all of it, things I hadn't ever said to her, and wanted to say to her. Because what I never said to you or James or to anyone was that all my married life I'd carried the feeling with me that the woman with whom I was spending my days lived her real life separate from me. Somehow, Maizie, in a way I couldn't ever understand or appreciate, I wasn't the husband she apparently needed.

I stood there watching her cry, and I had said everything there was to say, and then I almost touched her shoulder. I knew I had gone under her pride and wounded her, and even as I was proud that I'd struck some of the wind out of her sails, I felt sorry.

I felt sorry, Maizie, but as you know it didn't stop me from calling you and James and getting both of you into the fight to keep her. I believed, and I still believe, it would have been a terrible thing for her to have gone with Buddy Wells. But then, given my disappointment and my anger, I thought for a time that maybe we should separate. I have always believed that loving involves an act of will — or, really, many acts of will. In my mind, she had decided against me, and as the days went by I found that I cared less and less about keeping her. I felt that I had been right about her. I had not imagined that she always withheld something. I watched you and James fight with her, and just couldn't bring myself to do or say much of anything.

One afternoon, as she was dressing to go to her studio, I said, "Have you talked about your little love affair with any of your friends?"

"They don't know anything."

"What about his friends?"

"No," she said.

"You can trust that?" I said.

"I can trust it."

"You have my permission to go with the son of a bitch," I said. "I won't fight you."

She looked at me. She had been pulling one shoe on. "What?"

"You heard me," I said. "I'm not going to try and stop you anymore. I'll even help you put the best face on it. Just get it over with quick."

She waited a few seconds. "I don't guess I deserve you being kind," she said.

"No," I said. "I'm being practical."

"Well, maybe so," she said.

"You're free," I told her. "And that's that."

"Thank you," she said.

And I thought that *was* that.

When she told me she was staying, it was as simple as saying the time of day. I was in the kitchen late the next morning, and she came home from the studio and walked up the back steps.

"Harry," she said. "I'm home."

I had been eating a bowl of cereal. I barely looked up.

"I'm not going to go away, either." She said this peering at me through the screen in the door.

I said, "Go or stay. It's up to you."

We didn't exchange another word that day, but in the morning we had coffee together and talked about the leaves changing on the side of the mountain, how they were always the first to change every year. She wondered about you, struggling with your classes. And about James. It was very ordinary and maybe a little hollow, but it was friendly, too. It was even conciliatory, I think. And we just went on from there. It wasn't long before we'd got far enough past it that we could talk about it. And then we could forget it, too. I believe, Maizie, that we were a fairly happy couple. There are pictures. You can see it in her face. She kept herself far from me in a lot of ways over the years, but she was never devious or dishonest. It was not in her to be dishonest. And those pictures show her being happy. We did talk about Buddy Wells on that last day, but it was me who brought it up. We bantered about him, in fact. I said something about how much money she'd have if she were Buddy Wells's widow. It seemed to me that she was amused. And later I told her that she was still beautiful, and that I loved her. Because I did. I did love her, Maizie. All the time.

And I ask you to imagine how it can feel like starvation to be intimate with someone you can't really reach — the sort of person whose love is somehow only partly there, who holds back something essential that another man was freely given, almost at the cost of a long marriage and a family.

I don't think I'm excusing myself. I wasn't the best husband a woman could have — I don't suppose James was so far wrong with his joke — but I'm not to blame, and after all, I am the one who's still here. I admit that my first reaction to the news of what she'd done was wondering what *I'd* done to head her there. I blamed myself, more than you or James ever could, and I know that some part of both of you does blame me — for not seeing clearly enough, for not sensing that something was so wrong.

But I refuse to accept any blame now, harsh as that sounds. If it were possible to speak to the dead and be heard, I'd tell her the same thing. I'd say, "Andrea, listen to me. No pity, Andrea. None. No excuses, no regret for anything, and no sympathy, either, for what you've done to us." And I'd mean it.

But as I won't accept any blame, I won't place it, Maizie. She did what she felt she had to do, and I can't change it, no matter how much I wish I could, and I don't blame her for it. I accept it as a fact, what she decided to do with her life. You and your brother will have to decide how you feel about it. When I close the door on this old house, I'll walk away recalling how your young voices sounded in it, and it'll hurt me exactly as it's supposed to, and I guess it'll even make me wish I hadn't finally said no to the room in your house.

But I won't entertain one regret about anything. Not one.

It's midnight now, and I just said my name aloud, and listened to the echo. Like most people my age, it's terribly hard for me to accept the idea that my boyhood memory of being fascinated with the way rooms sound when they're empty means nothing, or that thinking of it now means nothing, and I'm afraid that's what your poor mother tried to say to us — that none of it has any meaning. But that was how *she* saw things. I don't know what else to say about her now, or how else to think about it. She finally said no to everything, like a kid throwing a tantrum in a public place.

And I still love her.

I wish she was in the next room. I wish she'd chosen some other way to deny us herself. I'd like to think of her being alive and happy, even if it had to be somewhere else. Even if it had to be with a man like Buddy Wells, and even if I hated her for it.

Love, Harry

Diurnal

When Maizie's mother wasn't the subject behind their talk, they found time to be easy with each other, and to be like other expectant couples. They had taken the Lamaze classes, and done the exercises at home, and they had discussed names, and made plans. He had dreamed up whole lives for this child, made of triumphs and love, and sometimes he felt as though he had cut through the carapace of sorrowing distrac-

tion and worry that encased his wife. On one occasion, lying in bed sleepless in dawn light, they had even teased and laughed about the names, trying absurd ones on each other. "How about Attila H. Kelleher?" Leo said. "No, I have it, how about Adolf H. Kelleher?"

"I think if it's a boy," Maizie told him, "we'll call him Leo, after his very strange father."

"Not Leo," he told her. "And not Carl, either. I knew a kid in school named Carl and he was a total jerk. How about Judas I. Kelleher?"

"Stop it," she said, laughing. "Please." A moment later, she said, "Benedict A. Kelleher," and they laughed together.

"Sirhan S. Kelleher," Leo said.

"John Wilkes Kelleher."

They laughed. "Genghis K. Kelleher," he managed.

For a moment, neither of them could speak, and it was all as lighthearted as it used to be between them.

He said, "Suppose it's a girl."

She was wiping her eyes. She frowned, took a breath. "Let's talk about it later."

"I can't think of any notorious bad women," he said.

"Lizzie B. Kelleher," said Maizie, "for Lizzie Borden."

"How about some multicultural names? Retributia Kelleher. Or no, Corona. Corona Cigar Kelleher. Or there's all the nouns, right? The hippie names. How about Peace? No, too obvious. Disharmony. There you go. Disharmony Kelleher. What do you think? No? War Kelleher. Psycho Kelleher. Communist Kelleher. Thoroughgoing Kelleher. Hungry Kelleher."

"I don't want to talk about it anymore," Maizie said.

"How about Maizie?" he said to her, kissing her cheek. "A little Maizie for me to spoil."

"No," his wife said. "I mean it now, Leo. I don't want to talk about it anymore."

"There's a fifty-fifty chance it'll be a girl," he said, wanting to save the mood somehow. But she had sunk into herself, and was thinking again about her mother. Gently, he said, "Honey, we could name her Andrea, if you wanted."

"Oh, for God's sake, Leo," she said, rising, moving away from him. "Sometimes I don't believe you."

He said, "I can't very well be expected to gauge your feelings if you never tell me what you feel."
She said, "I feel right now that I want to be alone."

Today, Maizie walked in from the back, kicking the doorjamb to knock the snow off her boots. The snow powdered her shoulders and glittered in her hair. She glanced at her husband, breathed "Hello," then smiled, looking away, her eyes wide with the exertion of having climbed the porch stairs. There was something almost childlike about her face in this light, her cheeks rouged with the chill. She glanced at him and looked away again. Lately, whenever she caught him gazing at her like this, she seemed flustered, as if he had intruded on her in a private moment.

"Is it slippery?" he asked.

"What? Oh, not really — not in the grass. I walked in the grass."

"How far'd you go?"

"Down to the end of the block." She removed her coat, shook the snow from it, and hung it on the peg next to the door. "I guess we'll see whether the old family lore has any truth to it. If things go according to the story, we'll be parents by morning." Her mother used to tell about how walking during a snowstorm had brought about the labor that produced Maizie, two weeks after she was due, twenty-nine years ago. "This doesn't look like much of a storm, though."

"It's not bad on the road?" Leo said.

"It's not sticking to anything but the grass. We'll have clear roads for the ride to the hospital. If this has worked."

"I was thinking about James and Helena, actually. Whether they'll have trouble getting here tonight."

She smiled. "You don't believe this baby will ever be born, do you?"

"I'll believe it when I see it," he said, smiling back.

She had braced herself in the doorway to the kitchen, pushing one boot off with the toe of the other. Then she stopped and leaned her back against the frame, resting her hands on the amazing roundness of her belly. Earlier, she'd joked about not being able to button her coat, and he'd caught himself thinking about a day, sometime in the future, when she would be completely herself again; she was getting some of her natural humor back. It was true, as he had wanted to say so many times, that life insists on itself. Now she massaged the place where her navel was, with a gingerly, tentative motion of her fingertips. "I'm sore," she said. "Right here. It feels stretched to the breaking point."

"Need help with the boots?"

"I'm fine." She pulled at the remaining boot. When it came off, she made a harrumphing sound, then dropped it and leaned against the frame again, breathing hard.

"Your father called."

She said nothing.

"About two minutes after you left."

She moved to the sink and put the tap on, filled a glass of water and drank.

"He said he just wanted to know how you are."

"Did you tell him I'm fat?" she said, pouring the rest of the water out.

"When you stand there like that with your back to me, it's impossible to see that you're pregnant."

"I'm shaped like a big pear." She wet a paper towel and dabbed her cheeks with it. "I feel feverish." She walked over to him. "Do I have a fever?"

He touched her forehead. "Cool as a cucumber."

"I feel like I have a fever."

"You've been out in the cold."

Straightening her back, she put one hand at the base of her spine. "I'm going to go see if I can take a nap. Do I have time?"

"James and Helena said they'd be here about eight," he said.

She sighed, looking at the clock above the stove. "I have a little while, then. Oh, will this baby ever come."

He watched her go on back into the bedroom, and then he took a package of turbot fillets out of the refrigerator and cut them into smaller pieces for frying. From the window over the kitchen sink, he could see that it was still snowing. Gusts of it swirled under the streetlamp, but the road surface was still visible.

She called to him from the bedroom. "Did Daddy want me to call him back?"

"Didn't say so."

"Did anyone else call?"

"A Mrs. Gehringer. Asking for you."

For a while there was no sound from the bedroom, and he supposed she had drifted off to sleep. But then she spoke to him from the end of the hallway. "Did Mrs. Gehringer say anything else?"

"Just asked for you. I told her you were out, and I didn't know when you'd be back, and she thanked me and hung up."

Maizie started back toward the bedroom.

He followed her. "Who's Mrs. Gehringer?"

"No one," Maizie said. "Marty's wife. Remember Marty from work?"

"The older guy, sure."

"If she calls again, I'm asleep. I'll call her back."

"When do you want me to wake you?"

"I probably won't sleep."

He hesitated a moment, thinking she might say more. Then: "I'll come in half an hour before they get here."

She lay down on her side, facing away from him. "Okay?"

"It's fine," she said. "I'm just really tired."

"Do you want me to call and see if I can catch them?"

She sighed. "No."

"It's no trouble, Maizie, if you don't feel like company."

"Please," she said. "Just let me be quiet a while."

He was aware of most of his shortcomings, and he feared that there were others. He had never been the sort of man who dealt in subtle shadings — whether they had to do with the ebb and flow of emotions during the course of an evening, or with, say, the source of light emanating from the painted sky of a Monet — and no matter how hard he tried, no matter how many books he read to improve himself, there was no getting around his clumsiness, his nervousness in groups, his old tendency to bungle things during conversation, to put his foot in his mouth, or fail to get the joke, or lose the train of thought in mid-sentence. He was not slow, nor at any disadvantage in terms of intelligence, though he often felt that way; the problem was that his nerves often made him go blank. There had been times when she teased him about these failures, but lately they only made her restless and impatient. And yet when she had snapped at him, or been abrupt with him, she seemed almost too contrite, as though there were something coming that she was sorry for. He had found it increasingly difficult to speak to her beyond the practical exchanges of a given day, such as whether or not she wanted him to call her brother and ask him not to come.

She had kept so much of the pain about her mother to herself. Nothing he had been able to say could draw it out of her. "I don't want to talk about my mother," she told him. "Please. I don't even want to think about her."

"I just wanted to say, you know, I'm — I'm here if you do want to talk."

"Please, Leo."

There was the pregnancy to worry about, and for a while there was the fact that her father was coming to live with them. He'd kept himself busy enough putting the spare room together for the old man, doing what he knew how to do best, and he took special pains with everything — even put chair railing in, and crown molding. It was a lovely room when he was finished, with its own private entrance from the outside and its own little kitchen and bathroom. All that work, and then the old man decided he didn't want it after all.

When it was first completed, Leo brought her in to look it over.

"It's beautiful," she said. "I hate it."

He felt something drop in his heart. "I'm pretty proud of it," he told her. "What do you hate?"

"I hate that it's here. That the farm is gone and that my mother — it's the place for my father to come spend the end of his days because of all that. Do you see?"

"It's a place for your father, yes. I worked like crazy on it, Maizie."

"I know you did. Can't you understand?" she said. "It's all part of this whole awful thing. The farm getting sold off and my mother checking into a motel room and taking a bottle of pills and every time I heard the hammer down here, every sound it made, it just — it's part of the same bad thing and I hate it and I'm sorry."

"Why didn't you say something?" he asked her. He was almost glad that she had said this much to him about it.

"I don't mean to hurt your feelings," she said. "Please."

"No," he said. "Listen. It's the first thing you've told me about what happened, how you feel. I would've gladly stopped —"

"It's a room for Dad," she said. "It's just that it's necessary at all."

She put her arms around him. They had been married almost six years, and her touch still thrilled him. He turned and bent down to kiss her.

"Baby," she said, "sweetheart," patting his chest with the ends of her fingers. But there was something perplexed and distant in her voice.

At seven-thirty, he walked back to where she lay sprawled on the bed, her arms over her face. Standing in the doorway, he whispered, "You awake?"

"Yes."

"They'll be here in a little while."

"I had a contraction just now." She moved her arms and looked at him, seemed to study his face. "What's wrong?"

"Nothing," he said.

"You keep watching me."

"I'm sorry. I don't mean to. I'm trying to be here for you in this."

"There'll be plenty of time when it starts," she said. "Babies don't usually come all that suddenly. You keep hovering over me like you think I might crack open or something, like an egg."

He'd meant her grief over her mother. He decided not to pursue it. When she sat up, slowly, accommodating the heaviness of her belly, he reached down and took hold of her elbow, to help her stand.

"Don't," she said.

He stood back.

"I'm sore all over."

"Are you having another contraction?"

"Yes." She sat down again, lightly massaging her abdomen, breathing deep. "It's passing."

He watched her.

"Easing off now."

A moment later, she began to cry.

"What," he said. "Tell me."

"Nothing, honey. Really."

"I'm sorry," he said.

"You don't need to worry about me," she told him. "I don't want you worrying about me."

He nodded. Then, because she wasn't looking at him, he said, "I know."

"Going through all this, and being pregnant on top of it."

Again, he nodded. Now the situation was reversed: he had thought she was talking about the baby.

"I have to brush my hair."

"Right," he said. He walked slowly with her into the living room and helped her get settled on the couch. She wanted music, so he put the stereo on, then went back into the kitchen. He got out the rest of what he would need to cook the dinner. They'd been seeing James and Helena more often since the old man had left for Tampa, and on most of these occasions Leo did the cooking. He liked it that way. It eased him inside, and when Maizie appreciated what he had done, even when the appreciation was automatic — spoken in the middle of thinking about something else — he felt happy. It was a respite from the continual feeling that he ought to be doing more to make their lives change for the better, more to help the healing process, without knowing what that thing might be. Because of her mother, because of the pregnancy, he couldn't seek an answer from her about himself — about her feelings for him — because he did not want to become only another element of her suffering.

And maybe he was that, anyway.

He hadn't been working very long when she came into the room and crossed to the window over the sink, looking out at the snow. "Still not sticking to the road," she said.

"I saw." He watched her. "Have there been any more contractions?"

"No. It's just Braxton-Hicks, I'm sure."

A moment later, she said, "They're late."

"Probably took it slow," he said. He thought she looked tired. "I'm sure James would understand if you wanted to cancel a thing like tonight."

"You know," she said, "I never thought you'd be so comfortable with members of my family. You and James seem to get along so well now. And you used to be so afraid they'd disapprove of you."

"I guess that's — been a fear of mine." He felt his throat tighten, and this surprised him. Lately, the slightest things moved him. "I want to keep us all together," he managed. "It's a family, after all."

His own family was long gone — dead, or scattered to the winds. He had a cousin somewhere in Oregon, another in New Orleans, still another somewhere in Illinois, one or two in New York. His father's brother lived in northern California, with a wife and three stepsons. He rarely heard from any of them. He had met Maizie at college, and when she brought him to these Virginia hills to meet her family, he found himself doing and saying absurd things in an effort to ingratiate himself. He loved them immediately. They were so intelligent and attractive, so fortunate, and they seemed to contain elements of the charm and elegance of the house they lived in, as though each of them had sprung naturally from its graceful arches and sun-lighted, tall-ceilinged rooms. He was admiringly jealous of their stories, their shared history, and their happy knowledge of one another, and he envied them even their irritations and chidings and petty quarrels — all those familiar little aggravations and gibes that seem to arise from nowhere and yet are a part of the daily assumption, the lived-in confidence, that the other person's feeling for you will always be the same. It seemed to him that in order to find their way through the anguish of the thing that had happened to them, they must try to concentrate on what was good about them, as a family. To do this with all their hearts, and to take no one and nothing for granted.

Maizie looked out the window over the sink again. "The road's getting a little covering now."

"I hope they're not stuck somewhere."

"An excuse for necking." She gave him a small, sardonic smile. Another of her mother's old stories was about driving back to Virginia from her family home in Michigan, in 1951 — how the car had got stuck in the snow, and how she and their father had kept warm through most of the night by necking in the back seat under a pile of blankets.

"Want to see if we can get to Michigan tonight?" Leo said.

"Don't," Maizie said. "Why do you keep calling it up?"

"Honey, you brought it up that time."

She had already begun to correct herself. "I'm sorry, you're right. Let's just leave it."

Lights pulled through the snow and into the driveway, then went out.

"Is this them?" Leo asked.

"It's a pickup truck," Maizie said. She went to the door and opened it, pushed the storm door out. Someone was coming along the walk, carefully, almost falling down in the slickness.

Leo moved to stand behind Maizie, who now held the door open and said, "Yes?"

It was Pauline Brill. She stepped up onto the porch and stamped her boots. "Hello," she said. "Sorry to bother you. You're not eating, are you?" She stamped the boots again.

"Come in," Maizie said. "Leo, you remember Mrs. Brill."

Leo said he did. They moved into the kitchen, and he offered her a cup of something hot. She demurred, with a grateful smile, and said there was no time. She had not come to stay. They spoke of the weather and of the fact that Maizie was overdue to have her baby, and though they joked and smiled and seemed relaxed, there was of course the one subject they couldn't speak of, and its stubborn presence behind their talk made everything else seem produced, somehow. Mrs. Brill did not take off her coat. Maizie sat at the table and Leo leaned against the sink, and when all the pleasantries were done with, there seemed nothing left to say.

"Well," said Mrs. Brill. "I'm actually here to see if I might enlist you both in an effort to get the school bond issue put on the ballot in the fall." She reached into the pocket of her coat and brought out some sheets of paper, folded and dog-eared, water-spotted. "This is not a good night for carrying a petition around, but it was the only night I could spare this week. You know Pamela is getting married."

"No, I didn't know that," Maizie said. "I haven't seen Pamela in a while."

"Yes." Mrs. Brill nodded. "This young man she met at a dance in town. Isn't that quaint? A perfectly nice boy, too. Though he hasn't got the best prospects. Flunked out of pre-med at the university and just got a job at the car wash, if you can believe it." She handed Maizie the folded papers. "But I've long since given up any pretensions about those kinds of things, if I ever had them. After all, I was a hairdresser when I met Edward all those centuries ago."

Maizie opened the pages. It was a group of signatures, some of which were slightly smeared.

"I have a pen," Mrs. Brill said.

Maizie smoothed the pages out on the table, and the other woman handed her the pen. Leo looked at his wife's hands, the amazing creamy suppleness of them under the light, and caught himself thinking of what Maizie's family must've said about him in those first days: this clumsy, well-meaning boy from Ohio (he could hear them) with no family to speak of, and no special talent at anything. Maizie had said once that she found him beautiful, that she had chosen him on sight. She used to joke about how she had gone to school to shop, and he was what she had brought home with her. And yet when, recently, she read him her father's strange letter, sitting up in bed with the piece of paper in her trembling hand as he lay on his side staring into her dark eyes, he had heard phrases that might have been applicable to his own situation. If she hadn't been so distressed by it, he might've told her so. He'd held it in. He'd gone out into the chilly dusk and spent an hour splitting logs for the woodstove, working in a kind of fury, thinking about his wife's father — the work that had gone into getting the room ready for him — and feeling himself locked in the trap of his wife's condition and circumstances.

"Thank you," Mrs. Brill said.

"Should I sign it?" Leo said.

"Oh, sure."

He leaned over the table, taking the pen from Maizie. As he signed, the telephone rang, and Maizie reached for it.

"Hello."

Leo handed the paper to Mrs. Brill.

"This is she. Yes, Mrs. Gehringer. I — yes. Yes." Maizie looked at him, and then at Mrs. Brill. "I'm sorry, I can't really talk right now."

"I know her," Mrs. Brill murmured to Leo. "If it's the same Gehringer. I teach her son."

"Mrs. Gehringer," Maizie said in a strange, brittle tone of voice. "I'm almost nine and a half months pregnant."

Pauline Brill put the papers in the pocket of her coat. She and Leo were both staring at Maizie now.

Maizie was sitting with the phone at her ear and one hand visored across her forehead, the elbow of that arm resting on the table. "I appreciate that," she said. "It was a friendship." Then she repeated this phrase.

"Well," said Pauline Brill, "I'd better get on."

There were other lights in the drive now. James and Helena arriving. There wasn't going to be an opportunity to talk about this phone call. Mrs. Brill patted Maizie on the shoulder and made her way out the door, along the walk. She greeted James and Helena, and for a moment they stood talking. Mrs. Brill was telling them about her stepdaughter's coming marriage. In the kitchen, Maizie sat listening to whatever Mrs. Gehringer was saying on the other end of the line. Finally she put the handset down on the table and let her face drop into her hands.

"Honey," Leo said. "What is it?"

She stood with some difficulty and put the handset back in its cradle, set the phone in its place on the counter.

"Maizie?"

"I've — I told Marty some things." She seemed at a loss.

"What things?"

James and Helena were coming in, brushing the snow from their shoulders. "I don't know, maybe we ought to turn right around and go back," James said. "It's getting bad out there."

"You can stay with us," Leo said, taking Helena's coat.

Maizie embraced her brother, then led them all into the living room. They arranged themselves around the coffee table, with its art books and stacks of magazines, and Leo went into the kitchen to make drinks for them. He heard them laughing about something Mrs. Brill had said out on the sidewalk. Maizie sounded like herself. He poured the drinks — whiskey over ice for James, white wine for Helena, sparkling water for Maizie and himself — and made his way back in to them with all of it on a tray. Helena was sitting on the arm of the sofa, above the level of her husband's shoulders, and she had one hand resting on his back. James sat forward to take his and Helena's drinks.

"So," Leo said, putting the tray down on the coffee table and sitting across from them. "What's the story?"

"Story?" Helena said.

They all seemed to hesitate.

"What've you all been talking about?" Leo said.

"Where were we?" said Helena.

"We were wondering when Maizie is going to have this baby," James said.

"I took a walk in the snow tonight," said Maizie. Then, to James: "You remember?"

"Do I remember what?"

"Mom's story, about the night she had me."

"I don't think so."

"Oh, you know it, James. She used to tell it to us when it snowed."

James's face was blank.

"You can't tell me you don't remember the story."

James said, "I've been thinking about that time when we were at the Fourth of July celebration out at Blue Ridge Park, summer of — what — 'eighty-two? We were all there, the whole family. I don't know why we went that year. Dad was always so reluctant to go anywhere on holidays. We all went, and there was a band playing in a gazebo — this rock band, of all things. Playing in a gazebo in the park. And Mom wandered off. Do you remember? It took us the longest time to find her. We spent the whole afternoon looking for her, and we didn't find her until the fireworks started."

"I found her," Helena said. "She was sitting down by the edge of the pond, watching the ducks."

"Do you remember, Maizie?"

"I guess so," Maizie said.

"I remember," Helena said. "It was getting dark. I couldn't even make her out from a distance. It was the hat — I saw that straw hat she wore, sitting next to her. So I walked up and said, 'Andrea?' I said it two or three times before she heard me. I said, 'Andrea, what're you doing? We've all been crazy looking for you.' And she said, 'I went for a walk.' Really, she said it so simply, I wondered what I'd been so upset about."

"She was always doing things like that," James said. "You'd

look up — at the parties they threw, all those people around. It happened more than once. You'd look up, and she'd be gone. She'd be off in another room of the house, or out walking. She'd just slip away."

"Let's talk about something else," Maizie said.

"We can talk about this," said James, "can't we?"

For a small space, no one said anything.

"She was my mother," James said, "and I don't feel like I ever really knew her."

"We've been going through this," said Helena. "We keep listing qualities — traits, you know. She liked elegance. She worked at it. She ran a dance studio for little girls. She had a way of looking right at you when she laughed. She was good at conversation."

"I woke up one time and she was standing by my bed, staring at me," James said. "I was about thirteen years old. She was standing there, perfectly still. I thought it was a ghost or something, and when I yelled, she moved and scared me even worse. It was like a statue coming to life. It took her a long time to calm me down that night."

"Remember how she used to be about Christmas?" Helena said. "When did that stop?"

"I keep getting these flashes of memory about her," said James. "When she and Dad were having problems, she'd leave some part of herself undone. There'd be a button loose, or a strand of hair. Or she'd forget to put both earrings on. Remember that, Maizie? It was a conscious thing she did, like a statement or something. I said, 'Mom, your eye liner's smeared a little,' and she gave me the strangest look and said, 'I know.' Just like that. Like there was nothing unusual or in need of correction. A perfectly natural thing, in a woman who was always so concerned about how people saw her."

"Please," Maizie said. "I don't want to talk about her anymore."

"Maizie, you can't tell me you're not thinking about all of this."

They were quiet again. They heard the wind in the eaves of the house.

"I keep thinking about how everything looked in the motel

room," James went on. "She'd hung her clothes up in the bathroom, for Christ's sake. They were on a hanger on the back of the door."

"I've been seeing that picture of her," Helena said. "Sitting by that pond in the twilight. It's like I could almost call to her. I've dreamed it. I used to watch her standing in front of the house waving at us as James and I drove away. She always stood there until we got out of sight. Rain or shine. She'd get so small in the distance, still waving."

"When I was a kid," Leo said, "my mother used to talk about getting out of earshot. She didn't like the feeling. I'd head off to school and she'd keep saying my name, saying goodbye. I lived a block and a half away from school, and she'd yell so loud I could still hear her as I climbed the front stairs of the school. It was like a game, and we laughed about it. But when she was serious, she'd say something about how it always hurt her — the fact that I'd be out of earshot, away from the sound of her voice."

The others looked at him.

"What you said," he said to Helena. "It made me think of it."

"No," she said. "I understand."

"Every year," James said, "for how many years, she had that party for those little kids in her dance studio. We had to help out. Remember, Maizie? Didn't she — remember she slipped out of a couple of those, too. Once I found her sitting in the office with the lights off. Sitting at her desk in the dark."

"I've done something like that," Helena said. "I used to sit in my closet when I was a kid. It made me feel safe."

They sipped their drinks.

James said, "I have this memory of her, running to get out of the rain. It haunts me. She was laughing — I can see it so clear. This young woman, this person I thought I knew, enjoying life."

"She had such lovely skin," Leo said.

"Remember how she used to get about the way we dressed?" James said to Maizie. "She gave me such a lot of grief about my hair. She was always worried about other people. It seemed to me that she never thought about herself at all."

"Oh, she thought about herself, all right," said Maizie.

Now they all looked at her.

James shook his head slowly. "I still can't —" He broke off.

"I'll be back," Helena said, rising. "I have to powder my nose."

"Jesus, Helena," James said. "Couldn't you come up with something more original than that?"

Helena bent down and showed him her nose. "I'm going to powder my nose," she said. Then she turned and made her way down the hall to the bathroom. Leo took a drink, watched for a while as Maizie tried explaining to her brother about their mother's walk-in-the-snow story, then excused himself — neither of them heard him — and went into the kitchen to start the dinner. He put rice on, and came back toward them to ask if they wanted coffee with the meal, and as he entered the space between the kitchen and the living room, he heard Maizie say, low, "I had a call from Marty Gehringer's wife today."

"Who?" James asked.

"Gehringer. The one I told you about in September."

"Okay."

"She's blown everything out of proportion, and now Gehringer's moved into an apartment in Point Royal. She blames me."

"Jesus."

"I don't know what to say to Leo."

There was a pause then, in which Leo felt as though they might have realized that he was near. From down the hall came the sound of water running in the bathroom. He braved a silent step backward, then froze again as Maizie began to speak.

"How is it now?"

"Better," her brother said.

"You gave her grief about powdering her nose."

"I was teasing."

"It's really better?"

"I've simply decided to wait until I recognize her again. She looks very beautiful tonight, don't you think?"

"I love Helena," Maizie said.

"I love Leo," said her brother.

Leo made his way to the kitchen and ran the tap — wanting some sound to place himself in another part of the house. After a moment, he turned the tap off and set the fire going under the skillet. He watched the oil corrugate with the heat. When he put the flour-coated fish in, it crackled and sent several needle-sized drops of oil onto his wrist. He turned the fire down, hearing his sister-in-law come back through from the hallway, and now the three of them were talking about a movie that Helena had seen, and liked. It came to him that the whole evening remained to get through. He looked out the window at the snow, the swirling flakes under the streetlamp. It was quite possible that James and Helena would stay the night. In the other room, someone had put music on.

He checked the fish, took the salad out of the refrigerator. After a few minutes his brother-in-law strolled in, sipping his whiskey. The women were talking animatedly in the other room. James went to the back door and looked out the window there.

"Bad," he said. "Bad, bad."

"You can spend the night," Leo said automatically. He couldn't look the other man in the face.

"Maizie had a contraction just now."

"Braxton-Hicks," Leo told him.

"What's that?"

"Contractions that don't mean the baby's being born."

James was quiet a moment. Then he seemed to come to himself. "Hate the winter," he said. "Makes me feel like things are closing all around me. You know, the early dark."

"Whatever," Leo said.

"Is something wrong?"

"Not a thing," Leo told him. "Everything's completely jake."

"Jake."

"It's an expression," Leo said.

"Okay, yeah, I remember." James sipped the whiskey. "Did I say something to piss you off?"

"I don't know what you're talking about," Leo said.

The other man shrugged, looked out the window again, and sighed. "Maizie said the old man called."

"He wanted to know how Maizie was. Is. And I really couldn't tell him much."

"I haven't heard from him," James said without much inflection. "How does he like Florida?"

"I forgot to ask. We didn't talk very long."

James was silent. In the other room, the women had also fallen silent.

"He sounded chipper enough, though," Leo said.

"Chipper."

"I mean he didn't seem to be —"

"No, I know," James said quickly.

"Maizie's still mad at him about the room. And the letter, of course."

"The letter shouldn't make her mad."

"The anger in it surprised her. She wasn't ready to have it said out like that."

"Hell, I'm angry," James said. "Isn't she angry? How can she not be angry?"

"I wouldn't know." Leo turned and concentrated on the frying fish.

"I'm mad as hell," James said. "Still."

There didn't seem anything else to say.

"Everybody's a victim," James went on. "Right? I'm so sick of that shit. And I'm *still* mad. And Dad's right. No pity. No fucking pity. A part of me hopes he's forgetting her. I hope he's got himself a girlfriend or something."

Helena entered the kitchen. "You hope who's got himself a girlfriend?"

"Who do you think?"

"Well," Helena said, "he's about to have himself a grandchild."

For a little space, no one said anything.

"Did you hear me?" Helena said. "It's started."

The trip to the hospital was smoother than they'd feared it might be. The roads were covered with the snow, but it was mostly slush. They drove through it as though it were rainwater. "Do you need us to go faster?" Helena asked, because Maizie had abruptly taken hold of her arm and begun to squeeze; she was having another contraction. "Can you go faster?" Helena asked Leo.

"He's going fast," said James. "You want us to crash?"

"It's fine," Maizie said.

"Can I do something?" Leo said. "Do you want me to count with you?"

"No," said Maizie. "Jesus."

A minute later, she said, "It's going." Then: "Oh, that was hard."

They turned onto Hospital Hill Road and drove past the Mountain Lodge Motel. Leo glanced at the several lighted windows and couldn't help wondering which was the one. He looked at James, who had turned and was attending to Maizie. For a few minutes, no one said anything. They pulled up the hill and around to the emergency room entrance. Maizie got out on her own, then seemed to cringe, leaning against the wet car in the still-swirling snow, holding on to herself. "Wait," she said. "Oh, God."

James had run into the building, and Leo and Helena began helping her move toward the doors. They were supporting her by her elbows.

"Wait," she said.

And now an orderly came out pushing a wheelchair, accompanied by a nurse. They got Maizie into the chair, and Leo walked alongside her, through the bright open space of the waiting room, past double doors into a corridor and other rooms. He'd lost track of James and Helena.

"Oh," Maizie said. "It's bad."

He put his hand on her shoulder and she took it, holding tight. She was panting, trying to do the breathing that they had worked to perfect.

"That's it," he said. And he tried to breathe with her.

"The baby's coming," Maizie said.

"We'll take care of everything," said the nurse.

In the labor room, in the confusion of his getting the hospital gown on, and the mask, Leo heard Maizie whimper, and he realized that they had been separated. Someone, another nurse, talking in a hurried but very calm voice, told him he had to go back out and sign some papers. "We did all that," he said. "We're pre-registered."

"Leo?" Maizie's voice.

He pushed past the nurse and stepped into the little room where Maizie lay, her hands gripping the metal sides of the bed. "Oh," she said. "Oh, help."

Leo took her hands. "What's the object," he said. "Fix on something."

"Hah," Maizie said. "Ah. Hah. Hah. Ohhhhh." She closed her eyes and seemed to be straining to get up. Then she lay back and looked at him. "I'm cold."

"It's going to be fine," he said to her.

A nurse or doctor had lifted the sheet over her and reached in. Then she stood back and snapped the rubber glove off her hand, smiling. "This your first?"

"Yes," Maizie said.

"You're doing wonderfully."

"The baby's coming," Maizie said. "I walked in the snow." She looked at Leo and began to cry. "I walked in the snow."

"You're not quite dilated yet," the nurse said. "So do your breathing. It'll be a while."

"I feel like it's coming," Maizie said.

"It is, honey. But it won't be right away." The nurse, whose hair was the color of sunlight on straw, nodded at Leo and stepped out of the room.

"I walked in the snow," Maizie said again, crying.

"I know," he said. "I know, my darling." He leaned down and put his arms around her. A contraction had started, and she was doing the breathing, trying to get it right. But then she was just gasping, and holding on. "Oh, please," she murmured. "Please, God — it hurts. Is it supposed to hurt this much?"

"Is it easing off?" Leo asked.

"There — oh, a little."

The door opened and a man looked in, a doctor — not Maizie's doctor. "Hello," he said. "I'm Dr. Moyer, and I'm on call this evening. Dr. Ransom is in surgery, an emergency. So I'll be doing the delivery." He stepped over to the side of the bed and touched Maizie's shoulder. "We doing all right?"

"It's hurting her bad," Leo said. "Can't you give her something?"

The doctor spoke to Maizie. "We're going to give you an epidural, but it'll take a little while. Can you hold on a bit?"

"I guess so," Maizie said. Tears streaked down her cheeks, and she wiped at them with the backs of her hands.

The doctor put a rubber glove on, then lifted the sheet and examined her. Then he, too, snapped off the rubber glove. "Everything's going just fine."

"Oh," Maizie said. "Oh, no."

"Try not to tense up," the doctor said.

"Oh, God," Maizie said. She held Leo's hand so tight it hurt. He leaned down close to her ear and tried to do the breathing. "Don't," Maizie told him. "You're cutting off my air."

"Remember the exercises," he said.

"I remember the fucking exercises," Maizie said through a groan. Then she lay her head back and breathed out, a long, sighing breath of relief.

The doctor was looking at Leo. "It's all right," he said. "It'll be all right." Then he tapped Maizie's knee. "Listen to your coach."

When he had gone out, she asked for a cold washrag on her lips. "They're so dry."

Leo accomplished this, using one of the rags they had brought with them. She was quiet, and he touched the damp cloth to her mouth, lightly, using his other hand to caress her forehead. When she opened her eyes to look at him, he had the sense that she didn't quite recognize him.

"Is it starting again?" he asked her.

"No."

They waited. Perhaps five minutes went by, and then five more. She asked for the wet rag again, lay back, and closed her eyes. A moment later, she opened them again.

"Anything?" Leo said.

"No."

Presently she said, "If this is false labor —"

"It's not false labor," he told her.

They were quiet a moment. "Leo," she said abruptly, "that phone call tonight —"

"You don't need to be worrying about that now."

"I *am* worried about it." Her tone was aggravated and tired.

He held her hand, and waited.

"I've been friendly with Marty Gehringer, but nothing happened. Do you understand me?"

"Maizie, for God's sake," he said.

"I could talk to him, and that was all it was."

Leo was silent.

"It had nothing to do with you."

Unable to help himself, he said, "Apparently."

"Oh, hell," she said.

"Look," he told her. "Can we concentrate on this? I'm sorry."

"It doesn't mean I don't love you," she said.

"Maizie, this is not the time."

She was silent. Another minute or so went by. He thought she might've drifted off to sleep. But then she opened her eyes and looked at him. "I have the feeling something awful is going to happen," she said.

"Stop it," he told her.

They were quiet again. Somewhere in another room, a woman shouted.

"I love the walls here," Maizie said. "I wouldn't want to miss anything."

He put the damp rag on her forehead.

"Thanks," she said.

Again, they heard the scream.

Maizie looked at him. "Oh, hell," she said, and seemed about to cry.

"Is it starting again?" he asked her.

"No."

He waited.

"Ohh," she said. "Now it is. It's — ohhh, a hard one. It's — mmmm."

Leo held her hand. Together they tried the breathing, and it went a little better this time. The contraction eased off.

And then the doctor and nurse were there. Leo saw that the doctor's hands were freckled, that his wedding band seemed to cut into the ruddy flesh of the ring finger. "Could you excuse us, please? Just while we administer the epidural."

He went out into the corridor, and along it to the waiting room. James and Helena were sitting side by side against the far wall, James reading a magazine, Helena watching a couple make their way out the door. She saw Leo first, and stood. "Already?"

"No," Leo said, and remembered, with a little unbidden rush of elation, that he was going to be a father. "They're giving her an epidural."

"But everything's all right?"

It struck him that he had always liked Helena so much. He embraced her. "She's in a lot of pain. But the doctor says everything's fine."

"The epidural will help," James said. His face looked ashen, and perhaps it was the light. When he put the magazine back in its place on the small table at his side, Leo saw that his hands shook. James ran his thin fingers through his hair, then seemed to let down.

Helena said, "Are you all right, James?"

"I'm not having the baby," James said irritably.

"You look like you're about to collapse. And don't talk to me in that tone of voice."

"I'm fine," James said. "Really."

"I've got to get back," Leo said, letting go of her.

"We'll be here," Helena said. Then she sat down and put her arm over her husband's shoulder. "You'd think James was the father."

In the labor room, Maizie lay propped on pillows. The pillows were from the bag that she had packed weeks ago in preparation for this — and now, after the rehearsals and practice sessions, someone else had put the pillows under her, and Leo felt guilty.

"Sorry," he said. "I told James and Helena they didn't have to stay. But they're staying anyway."

"Leo, it hurts me. I've had two really bad ones close together. And these people left me. They just left me alone."

"I'm here now," he said, and felt the blood rise to his cheeks. "Do you want me to get you something?"

"No."

"Do you want the rag again?"

"I'm being such a coward, Leo. But I can't help it."

"Is the epidural —"

"Nothing helps. It's going to come again and I'm so scared."

He held her hands, and when it started, he worked with her to do the breathing, but at the height of it, she yelled. It was a sound he would not have believed; it terrified him. Then she was trying to breathe again, trying to count. "Ohhhh, God," she said when it had subsided.

The room seemed to be growing smaller, all the colors in it growing sharper, more defined and more lurid. The light hurt his eyes. Somewhere off in another room, another woman moaned and then screamed.

"What is this," Maizie said. "This is where they take you."

He wet the rag again and put it to her lips.

"Thank you," she said.

"Do you want it on your forehead?"

"Yes." She gasped. "Oh, God." Then she was trying to sit up, her face contorted.

"Is it starting?" he said.

"Ohhhhh, Jesus Christ God." Her nails cut into the skin of his palm, and she was trying to do the breathing again, and failing. "Ohh, stop it. Please, make it stop."

"Where is everybody?" Leo said. "Jesus."

The pain eased, and now Maizie was crying. "I can't do it." Leo held her. "Again?"

She shook her head. "I can't do it, Leo. I can't do it."

"Let me see if I can get the doctor," he said, and was secretly ashamed for the sense of relief he felt himself moving toward — to be out in the hall, to be heading freely away from this little room, with its instruments and its electronic sounds and its dry white light. "Do you want me to go look for the doctor?"

"No," she said. "Please don't leave me." The words were spent in a breath, and she was gasping again, trying to pant, holding his hand and looking into his eyes. "Ohhh, please. Help it — oh nooo. No." She lay back, and for an instant he thought she might've passed out. But then she had come forward again, and her hand relaxed. She rested her head on his shoulder. "I think the epidural is taking effect."

"I want to know where the hell the doctor is," Leo said.

"They said we'd be here alone for a while. I'm only five centimeters."

"I think a doctor should be here."

"I want *you* here," she said.

He kissed the top of her head. "Want the washrag again?"

"I'm dying of thirst," she said.

He wet the rag, and she put her head back. And the nurse came in. The nurse raised the sheet, paused, then moved back to the door. "Everything okay?" she asked.

"We're in a lot of pain," Leo told her.

The nurse walked over and took Maizie's other wrist, looked into her eyes. She checked the monitors and then smiled. "It's all normal. On schedule. When you get to ten centimeters, we'll move you into delivery."

"When will that be?" Leo said.

"Just a while longer," said the nurse.

"I'm having the baby," Maizie said.

The nurse smiled. "Is the epidural working?"

"Nothing's working."

"I know it feels that way."

"Ohhh no, I can't. Leo, please."

Leo held her while she cried and groaned, and when he looked again, the nurse had gone. Beside the bed, the console with the monitor on it made a soft beeping sound. He couldn't decide if he had heard it before. Maizie panted, sweating, then slowly relaxed. "I can't do it, Leo, please."

"It'll be okay, baby," he said.

"If it would only stop."

He wet the washrag again, but she didn't want it.

"I can't breathe as it is."

The doctor came in and examined her. "Progressing nicely," he said.

"She's in a lot of pain," Leo said.

The doctor nodded and gave a small, cryptic smile. "It'll be fine." Then he touched Maizie's shoulder. "Maizie, you've got a bit of a wait. The epidural should help. Soon you'll be able to push, and that'll make you feel better. Can you make it?"

Maizie nodded, glaring.

When the doctor had left the room again, she looked at Leo. "I hate this," she said.

"They're so blithe about it," Leo said.

A few minutes later, the nurse came in again. "How're we doing?"

"Drugs," Leo said. "My wife is suffering." He was almost crying.

"Oh, God, the baby is coming," said Maizie. "Now."

"I know it's hard," said the nurse. She moved to the foot of the bed and lifted the sheet. "Good Lord," she said. "I'll be right back."

"Ohhh," said Maizie. "Leo!" She threw her head back and raised her knees with an involuntary jerking motion. Leo moved to her side, and her hands tugged at the sheet over her abdomen. For a second, she seemed to be squirming toward the head of the bed, but then the sheet was pulled back and Leo saw the baby's head push out of his wife — it had come with a slippery ease that startled him — and now it was face down in a pool of streaked blood. "Ohhhh," Maizie said with a deep, exhausted sigh. She was trying to see, lifting her head.

Leo reached down and touched the wet surface of the head,

the shining, blood-soaked hair, wanting to turn the face up out of the blood but worrying about the neck. "Oh, Jesus," he said. "Jesus, help us."

"Leo," said Maizie. "Leo — please. Ohhh, ohhh."

He turned the head a little, looked at the small wrinkled mouth, the deeply shut eyes, and he couldn't move, couldn't get the face completely turned out of the blood.

"Leo!"

The baby's head had slid out of his tentative grasp and was face down in the blood again. He was watching his own baby drown, and the only choice seemed to be to pull it up, and risk breaking the neck. He reached down and took the head in his hand, and couldn't bring himself to move. In the next instant, the doctor burst in, and with tremendous urgency grabbed the baby by the head, his fingers digging deep under the tiny jaw, pulling. It was a struggle. The baby didn't want to come. At some point during all this, Maizie had got hold of Leo's hospital gown, and when a nurse looked at Leo and said "You, out," Maizie gripped the gown even tighter, so that while the bodies closed in around the bed where the baby and Maizie were being worked on, Leo was prevented from moving out of the way. "You must leave," another nurse said.

"No," came Maizie's voice, stronger than it had been in all the time they had spent in this room. "I want him here!"

Through the tangle of arms and moving shapes surrounding the bed, Leo saw his wife's face. Maizie was looking down at where they were working to free the baby from her, and she was crying, saying a word he couldn't make out. Finally she gave forth a long, sighing shout, and a nurse said, "It's a . . . girl."

"Oh, baby," Maizie said. "Little baby. Let me see her." She had let go of Leo's hospital gown, and the backs parted. The hands of these others — Leo didn't even know how many there were — guided him into the circle around the bed and toward Maizie, with the child on her belly. Leo's new daughter was gasping, the eyes so tightly shut that he could not imagine them ever being strong enough to open. But then they did open.

They opened, and seemed to see, and the nurse with the straw-colored hair picked her up and took her to the clear glass bassinet on the other side of the room, to bathe her. He watched them stick some suction thing in the little slack mouth, and it seemed to him that they were handling her too roughly. But it was all just expert speed, and then Maizie spoke, still crying. He didn't hear her. He moved to her side and leaned down to kiss her soaked forehead. The doctor was gently pushing on her stomach. For a few minutes, there seemed nothing at all to do except stand still and try not to get in the way. When the nurses were helping Maizie move onto another gurney, she looked at him and said, "Leo, it's a girl."

"Beautiful," he said.

And Maizie kept crying.

"It's over," Leo told her. "It's okay. You did great, honey."

"Leo," she said. "I wish she was here. Why isn't she here?"

He put his hand at the side of her head and pulled her to his chest. "I know," he told her. "I know."

"Oh, why did she do it, Leo? Why isn't she here for this? Why couldn't she fight through it and be here? How could she do it to us?"

"Don't," he said.

The baby let out a small, fierce sound, almost of anger.

"Listen to that," he tried to say.

"I wish she'd told me something. I would've helped her through."

He kissed her cheek, and she turned and kissed him back.

A moment later, he said, "You know how it was that day when you were all looking for her, that Fourth of July?"

She leaned against his chest. "What."

"Whenever there's a big gathering like that," he said, "music, dancing, and all that, I always think about how there are all these personal lives gathered together in the sound — like the sound holds them together. I'm not explaining this very well. It's like there's all these people living their own lives, with their own secrets and worries and desires, and the music connects them.

It's all part of their time with each other. And — but sometimes there are people who wander out of hearing, away from the others. The music can't reach them, and when you call their names they can't hear. Like the way *my* mother was, calling goodbye to me all the way to my school, just to keep the connection. And well, honey, maybe it's like your mother just — got out of earshot."

Maizie said nothing.

"I'm sorry," Leo told her. "I'm sure I don't make any sense."

"I've been so mad at her for it," Maizie said.

The others in the room seemed not to be there, and then they were. They spoke quietly about levels, and procedure, and already the business of the hospital was moving on, a woman moaning down the hall, the doctor talking to a nurse about what dosage of some drug to give still another patient, elsewhere. Several others were working on the baby.

"Is everything okay?" Maizie said to no one in particular.

"Everything's fine," Leo reassured her, although he wasn't certain of this himself.

Maizie said, "I want us to start over — go back to the way we were. I don't want to feel this anger anymore."

The doctor moved to the foot of the bed. "She's pinking up real nicely," he said. "You did fine. Both of you." Then he nodded at Leo. "All three of you."

They brought the baby over, wrapped in a hospital blanket — a dark pink, ancient-looking thing, with a head of black hair and small dark tufts on the lobes of her ears. The eyes opened, and they were a deep, deep shade of blue. The fingers of one tiny hand were jutting from the folds of the blanket, and they moved, closed over the edge of the cloth, and then opened again.

"Hello," Maizie said. "Oh, welcome my little baby."

"She's beautiful," Leo said. "Isn't she?"

Maizie looked at him, soft eyes, all his, giving him everything of herself; it was in the look. "Beautiful," she murmured. Then she opened her gown and put the baby to her breast. "Oh, see, honey? She's taking right to it."

"I see," he said, and felt time open outward. It was the strangest sensation, as though he were already decades older. He reached down and touched his daughter's leathery hand, the amazing fingers, perfectly formed, almost frightening for their softness.

The doctor was still standing there. Leo felt an abrupt surge of affection for him, as if they would go on from this moment to become the greatest of friends.

"Tell me," the doctor said, "this little girl's name."

August 1990–November 1993
Broad Run, Virginia